'A story of daring to dream, daring to love and daring to embrace the changes that can transform us in unexpected ways. Pim Wangtechawat is an exciting new voice from Thailand whose stories I will always look forward to reading.'

Nguyễn Phan Quế Mai,
bestselling author of *The Mountains Sing*

'*I Dreamed of You* is a touching and tender exploration of love, hope, family and the significance of dreams. Sunny and Dao are beautifully complex characters who pluck at the heartstrings of recognition due to how relatable they are. With this book, Pim has expertly laid bare the intricacies of yearning, of relationships in various forms and what it means to really want. A gorgeous work I'll return to again and again.'

Onyi Nwabineli, author of *Someday, Maybe*

'*I Dreamed of You* is a gorgeous, soft-hearted ode to love and friendship. It's every bit as magical as it is anchored in the messy realities of first love and heartbreak. Pim's writing continues to enchant!'

Elvin James Mensah, author of *Small Joys*

'A totally fresh voice.'
Jennifer Saint, bestselling author of *Elektra*

Also by Pim Wangtechawat

The Moon Represents My Heart

I Dreamed of You

PIM WANGTECHAWAT

MAGPIE
BOOKS

A Magpie Book

First published in the United Kingdom, Republic of Ireland,
India and South Africa by Magpie Books, an imprint
of Oneworld Publications Ltd, 2026

Copyright © Pimsupa Wangtechawat, 2026

The moral right of Pimsupa Wangtechawat to be identified as
the Author of this work has been asserted by her in accordance
with the Copyright, Designs, and Patents Act 1988

ISBN 978-1-83643-137-4
eISBN 978-1-83643-138-1

Printed and bound in Great Britain by Clays Ltd, Elcograf S.p.A

This book is a work of fiction. Names, characters, businesses,
organisations, places and events are either the product of the author's
imagination or are used fictitiously. Any resemblance to actual persons,
living or dead, events or locales is entirely coincidental.

The authorised representative in the EEA is eucomply OÜ,
Pärnu mnt 139b–14, 11317 Tallinn, Estonia
(email: hello@eucompliancepartner.com / phone: +33757690241)

Oneworld Publications Ltd
10 Bloomsbury Street
London WC1B 3SR
England

Stay up to date with the latest books,
special offers, and exclusive content from
Oneworld with our newsletter

Sign up on our website
oneworld-publications.com

MIX
Paper | Supporting
responsible forestry
FSC® C018072

To my Thai sisters and brothers.
To the dreams we paint ourselves
in our search for something more.

this love journey
is surely the hardest and
most twisted road i have taken
i began the journey but my heart
is still dragging behind
wrapped around your feet
                                        Rumi

PROLOGUE
Bangkok, Thailand

Approximately twenty-one days before Dao and Sunny meet and begin to fall in love, both of them dream a similar dream.

Both their dreams appear in soft, warm colours, with the sky brilliantly blue and the air sweet. For her, there is green everywhere she looks: plains and fields, forests and mountains. For him, endless water.

A person, standing in the distance.

A quiet melody playing in the background, just sweet nothings. The rich and easy sound of laughter, shared between two people who know each other so well that comfort has become second nature.

In the dreams, their eyes find each other's. Strangers. Yet there is understanding in that gaze.

The kiss, when it happens – and it's bound to happen – is what they've always imagined a spring breeze would feel like, so different from the intense humidity of Bangkok. The kind of thrilling, joyful sensation that makes your heart lift in your chest. Like oh, oh, you can breathe again. Properly. Alive.

//

Dao, ever the believer, consults a fortune teller the very next morning, after typing down every detail of the dream in her phone so she will not forget. Her parents would strongly disapprove if they knew, but at this point, she is past caring.

The fortune teller is nearly twenty years older than Dao – thick curled eyelashes, dark red lips, long acrylic nails that flash sparkles whenever she moves. She listens to Dao's dream in silence at first, then begins shuffling her deck of tarot cards before spreading them out in a half circle on a knitted mat.

"Pick a card," she tells Dao.

//

Sunny tells his mother about his dream while she oversees his packing. A large suitcase lies at the foot of his bed, already half-filled with the winter clothes he'd bought from the nearby shopping mall.

He knows what she'll say, and that he will end up disliking it, before he even finishes. But he can't help himself. As is so often the case in the presence of his mother, he is without defence. Or he has always held a fool's hope in wanting to share in her beliefs.

He doesn't mention the kiss, but he tells her of the dream in which he met the stranger. I'm standing by the shore, he tells his mother. A lake, an ocean, I'm not quite sure, but I'm not alone. Someone is holding my hand. I can't see her face, but I'm overwhelmed by her presence. I wake up, and it feels like I've been running up a hill.

His mother is quiet for a moment. She smooths out one of his T-shirts and begins folding it. Then says: "We can ask my friend Auntie Dee about it. She can tell us exactly what it means, she never misses."

"You know I don't believe in all that," says Sunny. "Dreams are just dreams."

There had been a time when Sunny would have said that this wasn't entirely true, a time when he would have lent some credence to this faith shared by so many people around him that there are indeed signs from the universe pointing to one's fate – karma, past lives, a bigger picture to make all of this worthwhile. But he had been a child then, and after everything that's happened, he likes to think that he knows better now.

His mother, however, smiles to herself. "You know that that's not what I believe though," she says. "If you're telling *me* about your dream, then a part of you must want to know what I think."

//

"You will be travelling," the fortune teller says, her eyes fixed on the first card that Dao has chosen. "Somewhere new you've never been before."

Dao's breath hitches. "That is true," she says. "I'll be moving countries soon." She can sense her best friend Teoy, who's sitting next to her, trying not to roll her eyes.

The fortune teller flips over the second card. There are three in total. "Here," she tells Dao. "The sun, like in your dream. Happiness. Joy. A time of celebration after hardship."

"And the man I saw?" Dao asks. "Who is he? Is he someone I already know?"

The fortune teller flips over the last card. "He is your pair."

//

"Go on, then," says Sunny, indulging his mother despite himself. "Tell me what my dream means."

Another shirt goes into the suitcase. A pair of socks. A second-hand jumper. But his mother doesn't smile. "You always take these things too lightly," she says, rebuking him.

"And you always take them too much to heart," he replies, a note of resentment creeping into his voice.

"You and your sister are here because I believed in the dreams I had. Your father and I—"

"Ma, just say what you want to say."

"It's obvious," she says, shrugging. "You're going to meet someone. A girl. The location of where you'll meet her will not be here. From what you describe, it doesn't sound like Thailand."

Sunny inclines his head towards his suitcase. "That's a bit too convenient, don't you think?"

"Well, *you* asked."

"And the girl?"

His mother looks thoughtful. "That's a bit more difficult. I don't know who she is. But I think when you meet her…you will."

Sunny laughs and shakes his head, but the laugh sounds forced, even to his own ears. His mother turns away to tuck a folded shirt into his suitcase. A gloom descends on him almost immediately.

Asking his mother had been a mistake, he thinks. She was right: a small part of him had wanted to know her interpretation – a part he wishes he could ignore.

//

Soon, Dao is on a plane, sipping on a glass of champagne. The alcohol brings colour to her cheeks and makes her eyes shine even more brightly. She looks out her window to the country sprawling below her. So much green and grey, contrasted against the deep blue of the ocean, and clouds floating in a sea of white. There, in the corner of her eye: the tip of the airplane wing.

It has been five years since she last flew.

Dao thinks of what the fortune teller had said, as she has done countless times before, ever since the visit: "You're leaving at the most opportune time. Your life is now diverting onto a different path. You will not return home the same woman."

Those words had sent a chill down her spine. But afterwards, her friend Teoy had scoffed. "You're moving abroad to do a degree, *of course* your life is going down a different path! *Of course* you're going to change as a person. What a load of nonsense!"

But Dao was quiet. She wanted to tell her friend that she didn't know what it felt like to wake up with the weight of that dream pressing down on her chest. The intensity – of both the joy and the terrifying thrill of the unknown – settling into her mind and body until it solidified into a certainty.

//

Sunny, too, is on a plane.

It has been eleven years since he last flew, and this is the first time he's ever travelled out of Thailand.

He is squeezed into a window seat beside a middle-aged woman who keeps drifting off to sleep; he's had to politely nudge her awake every time he's left his seat to use the bathroom. Next to her is a young, tattooed white man with blond highlights who gives the impression of someone who' just backpacked his way across Thailand for five months. The three of them have spent the whole flight in silence.

As the plane begins to descend, Sunny puts his earphones on and cranks up the volume. The song is by one of his favourite Thai bands, the Musketeers – he's never been one for English music. Like most Thai songs, the lyrics are incredibly intense and dramatic, pining about the distance between the mountains and the ocean, the length separating the moon from the sun. Longing measured in kilometres.

From his window, Sunny's first glimpse of Scotland is obstructed mostly by the wing of the plane. He catches sight of a strip of land: dark green and brown, shielded by clouds. Then just skies. The cold, however, seeps through the glass into the cabin. Not even the plane blanket and the jumper he's wearing can keep him warm. When he puts his hand to the window, he nearly recoils from the chill.

His dream with the beautiful girl had been lovely and warm. His mother was adamant: "When you meet her, this girl you dreamed about, she will bring light."

Sunny pulls the blanket up to his chin, trying futilely to ward away the cold. Dreams and signs and women and wishful thinking. He'd been down this road before.

What the hell am I doing here?

//

When the pilot makes an announcement that they are about to land in Edinburgh Airport, Dao eagerly adjusts her seat to its upright position. She folds her blanket, gathers up the pillows and toiletry bag, and puts them all on the ground in the empty space next to her chair. Lastly, she changes out of the comfortable slippers the airline has given her and into her trusty pair of trainers, then fastens her seatbelt.

She keeps her eyes fixed on the view outside her window for nearly the entire landing. Sunlight is peeking through the clouds. The city comes slowly into focus, like a friend she hasn't seen in a long time, getting closer and closer, until she can see every detail of their face.

She takes her camera out of her bag. As always, the weight of it in her hands feels like coming home. A smile grazes her lips. She lines up the shot. Takes it. The memory

of her dream – along with all its wonderful implications –
is warm inside her chest.

She has survived several lifetimes to be here. But it
makes no difference, she thinks.

You are on your way.

PART ONE

The Meeting

Edinburgh, Scotland

On an island halfway around the world from Bangkok, twenty-one days after their dreams, Dao and Sunny meet for the first time.

It's late September, and the first stirrings of autumn are beginning to make themselves known in Edinburgh.

He's homesick; she's alone. There's an instant recognition the moment their eyes land on each other. An 'Oh, there you are' kind of moment. There you are. Someone like me.

It starts with the simplest of actions: the tinkling of the bell above the shop door as Dao lets herself inside. Her footsteps resounding softly, announcing her arrival as the only customer at this time of day.

Her head swivels around to survey her surroundings. She's in a modestly sized Thai supermarket, with ten or so rows of Thai products – condiments, snacks, sauces and seasonings, packs of noodles, bags of rice, so on and so forth. There are two freezers at the back for meat, a fridge full of drinks they can't find at Sainsbury's or Tesco. Eggs and fresh vegetables occupy the space by the window. A quiet comfort, hovering in the air. And for a split second, despite the chilly weather and her warm ensemble, Dao is transported back to a mundane, ordinary day in Bangkok: she and her mother, strolling through the aisles at the gourmet market in a shopping mall.

Sunny looks up from behind the counter, where he is scrolling through his phone to pass the time.

"Hi," he says in Thai. He can't help it: a grin spreads across his face.

"Hi," she says. A smile, too. Relief.

He points, saying, "You can use that basket over there."

"Thank you," she says. "Do you have any of those Lobo packets? I'm trying to cook, you see, and I'm not very good."

"Oh, I'm rubbish too," he replies easily, picking up the conversation as though they've already known each other for ages. "But Lobo makes it a little bit easier. It doesn't taste like it does at home, though." He points to one of the rows. "They're over there. What are you thinking of cooking?"

"The panang curry," she replies, strolling to where he'd pointed as though following a choreographed routine. "And, yeah, you're right, it never tastes like it does at home. I also never know how much coconut milk I'm supposed to put in. Or how much water. I'm terrible at measurements."

"Did you just move here?" he asks. His phone is now put away. He leans over the counter, eager for conversation.

"Not even a week ago," she says, crouching down to examine the rows of ready-prepared seasonings. "Master's degree. You?"

"Two weeks," he says. "Working and studying English. My aunt and uncle own this store."

"That's convenient," she says. "Should I just get the panang? Or should I get something else too?"

It feels so good to talk without having to think beforehand, she thinks to herself. Words have been pent up inside of her for days, just waiting for a vessel to be poured into.

"The fried garlic looks easy to make," she tells him. "I'd just have to stir fry. The green curry is a little harder, but if I manage to make it properly, I might be able to impress my new dorm mates."

"You know what I think?" he asks, his eyes beginning to sparkle.

She can't help but smile back. "What?"

"You should go wild."

She laughs. "What does that mean?"

"Go wild." He spreads his hands open, shrugging. A playfulness that softens his angular features and makes him look almost like a teenager. "Get the panang, the green curry, the fried garlic, the hung lay. Hell, even the larb! Cook a whole feast!"

"No way! I just told you I'm a terrible cook!"

"But it's Thai food! You must miss it so much, you're probably going insane!"

"I've only been here a week, I can't be cracking that badly!"

"Oh, I cracked on the second day." Sunny nods towards the door that leads to the back of the shop. "I'm lucky my aunt knows how to cook. I just feel sorry for you, that's all."

"You feel sorry for me, is that it?" She laughs. Their eyes meet – a rush. "You would feel even sorrier if you could taste my cooking!"

"I have faith," he insists jokingly. "Come on, it can't be that bad!"

"Yes, it is *that* bad. I struggle to even fry an omelette! I always fail at the part when you have to flip it. My flipping skills are atrocious!"

He shakes his head with mock concern. "Can't measure, can't cook, can't flip an omelette... How are you going to survive living abroad all by yourself?"

"OnlyFans," she replies, deadpan. "I'm here to diversify the market."

He doubles over, laughing, and realises it's the heartiest, most genuine laugh he's had since he landed in Scotland.

They continue to talk and tease each other like this while she browses the store and tips things into her basket. They exchange names, ages: she twenty-five and he twenty-six. They talk about where they're from: Bangkok, around a forty-minute drive from one another. They discuss what she's here to study: photography. Where she's staying: student accommodation, a short walk from the supermarket. Even her maddening obsession with Instagram aesthetics and his distrust of drinking water straight from the tap. Little bits of themselves traded excitedly, but with an undercurrent of cautiousness. It feels marvellously, frighteningly easy.

He keeps putting his hands in and out of the pockets of his hoodie, smiling so widely she thinks he must be putting it on.

She frowns at him, not understanding. "You must be very lonely," she says matter-of-factly as she puts her basket on the counter. "You're acting like you haven't met another human being in months!"

He ignores her comment and instead scrutinises the contents of her basket. "Wow, so many snacks! Are you sure this is healthy?"

"A taste of home," she says.

"I see you've decided to go wild." He picks out numerous Lobo packets. "I'm proud of you."

"Thank you. But let's save that compliment until I've tried to cook the panang."

"Send me a picture when you do?"

"Oh, sure," she says, a little *too* casually. She adjusts the long purple scarf twined around her neck while he begins scanning the Lobo. She tucks a strand of hair behind her ear. Waits.

"Well," he asks, without looking up from his task, "let me give you my number in that case."

After this meeting, she goes back to her flat and attempts to make the panang right away, an unfamiliar sense of giddiness spurring her on.

A little after seven, while Sunny is still on his shift behind the till, a message flashes across his phone screen. He opens it to see a picture of a decent-sized pan brimming with red curry.

Fairly successful, Dao had written. *I need a rice cooker, though. I can now put "cooking rice in a pot" on the list of things I'm not good at.*

He chuckles to himself, already typing a reply: *Don't worry. We can sort that out later.*

7

Sunlight fades from the sky soon after and the street-lamps flicker into life. The moon shines luminously in the blackness, thinly carved. Empty evening hours beckon, longing to be filled. And you realise it is a matter of trial and error, learning how to be alone. So it's rather nice, both of them conclude to themselves in this silence, to find a friend.

Dao

One of Dao's most prized possessions is her Leica film camera. As she settles into her new life in Edinburgh and starts her photography course at the university, she often walks the streets of the city with it hung around her neck.

It's her first time living away from Thailand, and she uses her camera to capture every marvel she sees that makes Edinburgh feel like a postcard come to life – the cobbled stone streets, winding staircases, cathedrals, old Tudor houses. She snaps multiple angles of the castle on the hill, high above the city centre, and of the Scotsmen in kilts playing the bagpipes along the Royal Mile.

There's an undeniable romance to Edinburgh, especially in the evenings. She loves the blend of modern and medieval, and enjoys walking everywhere, something she can't do in Bangkok because of the humidity.

It's like we're living in a movie, she tells Sunny via text. Ever since she met him at the supermarket, they've been texting consistently.

She tells him about her classes and the joy of being fully immersed in something she loves for the first time. She describes her lecturers, their work, her favourite course mates: a strikingly beautiful Scottish-Indian girl named Simone, with hair plaited down to the small of her back; Cady, a sweet, soft-spoken American girl whose expertise is in landscape photography; and Ella, an English girl whose boisterous laugh gives life to every room she walks into. The three of them had bonded instantly on orientation day after discovering that they all lived in the same dormitory.

I don't miss my friends in Bangkok as much as I thought I would, she texts Sunny late one night. *The girls I've met here have been great. I really feel at home. Isn't that strange?*

It's not strange, he texts back. *You're made for this.*

For what?

Living abroad in Europe.

Are you teasing me?

I mean… I know your type.

My type?

Yeah. Rich, high society girls.

She chuckles and types back: *Fair enough. I'd admit to being rich, but not to being hi-so.*

You just said you feel at home here in Edinburgh!

You don't have to be hi-so to feel at home here.

I disagree, he replies.

Don't you feel at home here?

Not like you do, he types back.

Sunny tells her of his father's hardware shop that's waiting for him back in Bangkok. The close bond he shares with his mother, how hard she works around the house. His younger sister, Fai, and how she tried to follow him everywhere when they were smaller. The garage not too

10

far from his house where he used to hang out with his friends as a teenager.

He writes of the aunt and uncle he's staying with in Edinburgh, how much they seem to enjoy each other's company, unlike his parents. But how little time they have to spend with him. He describes the English classes he has to take for his visa at a language school close to the Meadows, how tiresome they are, how boring. *The other students are nice enough*, he explains, *but most of them are older than me, so we don't really have much to talk about.*

So you think this city is beautiful, she types, *but you miss home?*

I don't know if I miss home, he replies, *but I understand home. Here, I don't understand much of anything.*

You don't give yourself enough credit, she says. *You understand more than you think. I haven't known you long, but you strike me as being pretty smart.*

Smart? Me? He sends her numerous number fives, which in Thai is pronounced as 'ha', the laughing sound. *I get by, that's all I'd say. I'm not the one studying to become a professional photographer.*

How do you know I'm any good?

Trust me, I know. Send me a picture you've taken.

Film, digital or phone camera?

Anything.

So she sends him a recent snap she took on her film camera. Just a shot of her new friends, Simone, Cady and Ella, hanging out at lunch, caught off guard. Simone had clocked Dao, so her eyes are shining mischievously at the camera while she pulls a silly face. Ella's head is thrown back in laughter. Cady too is laughing, one hand resting on Ella's shoulder.

See? Sunny types back. *This is good.*

Good how?

Do you have to respond to everything I say with a question?

Good how?

The colours are nice and warm. I like the angle, and the way you captured your friends. They look…I don't know…genuine.

They are genuine.

Well, I'm not very good at describing things like this. It's just good.

Well, thank you, she replies.

Any more?

She sends him a few more. Mostly shots from her phone of the streets of Edinburgh, and her friends hanging out at cafes or on walks in parks. *These are nice*, he tells her in response.

Just nice? she prompts, teasing, fishing for more compliments.

They're nice, he texts back. *It's good that you have things to do here, and that you have friends.*

You have friends here too, she replies.

Who?

Me.

A few seconds pass. *Yeah, true*, he texts back. *I do have you.* And she catches herself smiling.

//

Sunny might have only one close friend in Edinburgh, but Dao now has three new sisters.

The closer Dao gets to her course mates – Cady, Ella and Simone – the more late-night talks in their dormitory common room turn into a frequent occurrence.

Teoy is Dao's best friend back in Thailand, but she has never had a group of girls she's close to before. At least not like this. In secondary school, Teoy was the only one she trusted. In university in Bangkok, Dao's friendship group consisted mostly of girls who'd flocked around Teoy, wanting a bit of her shine. They were friendly enough to Dao, but she knew that they only indulged her company because she was regarded as Teoy's best friend.

To Cady, Ella and Simone, Dao exists as a whole person. They trade their lives, feelings, insecurities and dreams freely, and it doesn't matter that they came from four different countries, with varying upbringings. They have enough grace and understanding to bridge the divide, and enough support to hold each other up when needed.

It has taken all of them by surprise, this camaraderie that has bonded them all so quickly. But when something special like this happens, you simply have to embrace it.

Dao tells her new friends all about her life growing up in Bangkok, from the loneliness of her childhood to the years she was bullied in school – everything up until the time she came to Edinburgh. Even the dreams that have held special meaning for her, and how she has always believed that they offer a glimpse of what the future holds.

"So, according to your recent dream, you believe you're about to find love?" asks Simone bluntly in her Scottish accent. She says everything bluntly, and the effect is always as startling as her beauty.

"When you put it like that..." – Dao almost blushes – "...it sounds ridiculous. But, yes, I do." She turns to Cady, who is sitting on the same sofa as Dao. "Cady, do you ever believe in your dreams?"

"I believe that God has a hundred ways of speaking to us," Cady replies. Her faith is one of the things that Dao finds most inspiring about her friend. "So I wouldn't ever rule out that possibility."

"Cady's only saying that because she's the most accepting person who's ever walked this earth," says Simone, deadly serious. "Me, on the other hand...I understand that there are these superstitions in both our cultures, like my mother keeps begging me to go with her to her fortune teller so we can start looking for my soulmate." She rolls her dark round eyes. "But I'm sorry, Dao, I think we dream about the things we want to see, or the things we are afraid of seeing. And the things fortune tellers tell us are just things we want to hear."

"You know I'd disagree with that statement," says Ella. She flicks her long hair over her shoulders. "I keep offering to read your cards and you keep saying no."

"That's because I don't want to live my life according to your crystals!"

"I've already explained at *length* about why that's not the case," says Ella, with extreme poise. "The cards read your energy, they pick up on your emotions, your vibrations. *You* make your own choices."

"Tell that to Dao," says Simone, not unkindly. "She's already decided that love is on the horizon."

"I haven't *decided*," Dao protests. "I'm simply...open to the possibility!"

"You should join me and Ella and sign up to a dating app. How else are you going to meet someone?"

"I've never been on one before. Which one are you on?"

"All of them," Simone replies. "Tinder, Bumble, Hinge."

"I'm only on Hinge," Ella tells Dao, giving her a comforting smile. "Don't worry! If this is your first venture, you don't need to be on *all* of them."

Simone shrugs. "I thought I'd cast my net wide."

Dao laughs and turns to Cady. "What about you, Cady?"

Her friend's expression turns serious. "I'm not ready to date," Cady says matter-of-factly. "My self-esteem isn't strong enough yet."

The three of them can see that there's a story behind that statement, but Cady is the most reserved out of all of them: she will peel back her layers only when she wants to, and only at her own pace. Simone swoops in to rescue her from the pressure of elaborating further with a hilarious anecdote about a recent dating app match.

But Dao quietly wonders: *What about mine? Is my self-esteem strong enough?*

That night, Dao decides to download Tinder and set up a profile, choosing three pictures of herself that she doesn't hate. Most of them were taken by Teoy. There's one of her from behind at the beach; she's in a one-piece swimsuit and shorts, looking over her shoulder at the camera. Another of her at Teoy's graduation party, with her face fully made up. The last picture is the one she's been using as her Instagram profile picture for the past three years: a simple shot of her holding up her camera, her face obstructed.

Dao begins swiping through the men's profiles. Someone with his arm around a golden retriever. Another skydiving, the next holding up a pint of beer, then one with a pouty mirror selfie, his shirt pulled up halfway to reveal his chiselled torso. A man playing rugby. Playing football. Skiing on a snowy mountainside. A gym selfie. A second gym selfie. Yet *another* gym selfie.

Every *"IT'S A MATCH!"* comes as a surprise, sending a thrill rushing through her body, even after she's already received several of them.

The longer she swipes, the more the faces blur together. Yet it only makes her want to keep going.

Is this what she's been missing for years of her life? The knowledge that she is, in fact, *not* undesirable?

//

Later that night, Dao texts Sunny: *Are you almost asleep?*
He replies a few minutes later: *Almost. Why?*

Her fingers linger over the keys for a few seconds too long. She thinks of confiding in him about how she'd just spent a shameful amount of time on Tinder, swiping and answering messages from strangers. But something stops her.

She thinks of the dream she'd had before coming to

Edinburgh. Would the man in that dream – the one the fortune teller had predicted would be her pair – really be someone from an online dating app? The idea sounds ludicrous.

Dao thinks to herself for a moment then decides she has nothing to lose. She begins typing to Sunny: *Do you dream often?*

She sees him typing, but no message is sent. Then the typing stops. She tries to explain: *It's just, I was talking to my friends about superstitions and fate and destiny and all of that. Ella also reads tarot cards. So we were discussing whether our dreams can predict the future.*

A longer pause than usual from him. *Well, sometimes I find it hard to sleep through the night,* he types back. *But I don't think my dreams are anything out of the ordinary. Do you really think yours are?*

She tells him cautiously: *I've had my dreams interpreted by fortune tellers a few times, like most people do back home. But I'm still waiting to see if any of those things will come true. What about you?*

My mum believes in them. She doesn't make a decision unless she's dreamed about it beforehand or consulted a fortune teller first. Even my coming to Scotland – she consulted a fortune teller who said that the time was right.

Are you like your mum?

I don't think I am. I think it's mostly nonsense. We just hear what we want to hear, don't we?

Oh, she says. *You sound like Simone.*

What should she say next? She could tell him of the dream she'd had before coming here, and the card reading

17

with the fortune teller that followed. But wouldn't he think she was being ridiculous? His messages are already heavy with scepticism. She realises then and there that she wants his approval. The realisation both surprises and worries her.

A new message from Sunny comes through: *What are you up to tomorrow?*

Dao seizes on the change of subject with relief: *I'm going to the castle by myself to take some pictures from up there. You?*

I'll be at work, sadly.

Well, you know you can always message me if you're bored.

Thanks, he replies. *I just might.*

Sweet dreams.

Night. Sweet dreams.

//

The next day, Dao is by herself in front of Edinburgh Castle, looking down from the battlements with the wind whipping around her.

She's taken off her gloves, and her hands are trembling as she fixes her camera towards the view: rows and rows of houses, old buildings with spires and towers, the mountains and the sea in the distance, the sky filled with grey clouds, streaks of light breaking through.

Something she'd read long ago by a famous photographer whose name she can't recall suddenly springs to mind: *The eye should learn to listen before it looks.*

So she lowers her camera and closes her eyes for a

few seconds. What can she hear? The sound of the wind, of course. Footsteps and conversations around her. The sound of her own breathing: calm, steady.

Then, out of nowhere, her phone ringing.

She opens her eyes and snatches it from the bottom of her purse. "Hello?"

"Hey. It's me."

"Sunny?" She takes the phone from her ear, gazes down at her screen and sees unanswered messages from Tinder, from Simone and, of course, from Sunny himself. "Sorry, I didn't see your messages," she says. "I've been walking around."

"Yeah, I thought so." There's a smile in his voice.

She smiles too. "What's up?"

"You said to hit you up if I get bored today. And I'm *so* bored."

She laughs. "But it's the middle of the day!"

"Yes! Exactly! And I'm stuck inside and there are hardly *any* customers!"

"What can I possibly do to help?"

"Tell me about the castle. What does it look like? How's the view?"

She rolls her eyes and puts in her airpods. "So you're just going to come with me as I walk around the castle?" she asks.

"Why not? I have nothing better to do."

She shakes her head, smiling again. "Alright, I'll take pity on you and let you tag along, you sad, lonely man."

He stays on the phone with her for an hour as she takes pictures of Edinburgh from above and tours the castle.

Sometimes she describes the things she finds fascinating – ancient tapestries, cannons, old rooms where kings and queens were born. But other times, there is only comfortable silence on the line.

"I have to go," he eventually says. "My aunt will be here soon."

"Oh, okay," she says. Her tour of the castle is almost at an end now. "I'll…talk to you later?"

"Yes. Talk to you later."

He hangs up, and she is left to wonder.

It makes sense that we're getting close, she reasons to herself. We speak the same language. He's the only Thai person I know here. Who else would I be talking to? And we're just friends. That's what makes it so nice.

The dream she had before…of meeting someone – a nameless, faceless someone – who changes her whole world…that dream can't possibly mean Sunny, can it? That would be too easy.

Dao

Dao first started believing that her dreams were more than just dreams around the same time her father started his paint import and export company.

She must have been eight years old. A lonely yet quietly precocious and curious child who created a world for herself in novels, picture books and movies. Her father was a man desperate to make a name for himself – all hustle and bustle and righteous indignation. Her mother had always been a gentle woman, content in simple domestic and familial pleasures.

Dao's father and mother met when her mother was thirty-six years old and her father was twenty-eight. Mother had never had a serious boyfriend before Father. Having seen her older sister and the majority of her friends married and settled, Mother thought that kind of life had already passed her by. But one day, at the traditional Christian church she had been attending since she was a child, Dao's father walked through the doors.

Father and Mother went out for a year before getting married in that traditional church. Mother's wedding veil was so long it reached the ground, and she had white orchids in her hands when she walked down the aisle. Mother's side of the family took up the majority of the seats – an old Thai family dating back to the time of King Rama I. Dad's family, who were Chinese immigrants, occupied only two rows.

A year later, Dao herself arrived on a bright, blazing Bangkok morning at the historic Bangkok Christian hospital, a few weeks after one of Thailand's biggest political protests. She was then brought home to an old, two-storey wooden house, complete with a sizeable front yard, in the affluent Ekkamai area. It had been a gift from Dao's grandmother on her mother's side, along with a nanny named P' Pun.

Father always maintained that their love story was only possible because of God, a higher power arranging every single detail so that their paths could align. Someone like me, he liked to say, could never end up with someone like your mother, and we wouldn't have been able to stay together this long if we weren't meant to be. Mother agreed: love, she told Dao, would happen according to God's timing. From the day Dao was born, Mother and Father had already started praying for her future husband.

Newlywed and newly a mother, Mother quit her office job so she could throw herself headlong into parenthood. Father, on the other hand, took a job at the American embassy for a few years.

Dao's childhood memories of her father were mostly of a very temperamental man, who was constantly frowning and veering between angry outbursts and brooding. Very rarely, he'd smile, laugh, pick her up to spin her around and tell her stories. Those were the times she lived for, so she taught herself to endure his less than pleasing moods. A small price to pay, she told herself.

When Father decided that starting his own business was the way to go, those rare moments happened less and less.

Mother was supportive, but not particularly understanding. "I'd hate to see you go through all this trouble and stress," she said to her husband, "especially when we're all set when it comes to money."

Dao, trying very hard to disappear into her seat at the dinner table, heard her father respond: "We can't live on your family's money alone."

A few days later, Father made Dao a promise: "I'll be back for your birthday with a present. You wait and see."

He had a briefcase and a huge suitcase, and an umbrella tucked under his arm. "It's monsoon season in Hong Kong," he'd told her. "So I need to be prepared."

He crouched down so that their faces were at the same level and ruffled her hair affectionately, a playful glint in his eyes. He was in a good mood that day. "Wait for me," he said.

And so Dao waited. Every day she would cross off the days on the Hello Kitty calendar Mother had given her to put on her bedside table. A week till her birthday. Then four days, two days. She went to bed every night excitedly imagining what presents her father would bring her. In his phone calls, he hinted that it would be something fun. "Something you can build with your hands," he said.

One more day. One more sleep.

She slept. And dreamed.

In the dream, she sat in the open doorway of their house, gazing at the front gate, waiting for it to open. She waited until the sun shrank from the sky, until the moon began to rise, a little slice of a thing. Her mother came and tapped her on the shoulder. "It's time for dinner," Mother said. But Dao shrugged off her touch. She leaned her head against the door frame, tiredness taking hold of her. Yet she forced her eyes to stay open. He's supposed to be back, she thought to herself. He promised.

Storm clouds began to gather. The scent of rain grew thick in the air, the sounds of Bangkok traffic rumbling in the distance. Then the skies opened up to a chorus of roaring thunder. Bangkok never gets cold, but the wind that blew through the gate made Dao shiver.

Darkness was falling all around her...

And no one was coming...

Dao woke to find her mother sitting on the edge of her bed, a soft hand running through her hair. There was a tightness to her jaw, a harsh, irate look in her eyes.

"Happy birthday, my sweet," Mother said. "Your father called this morning."

"Has his plane landed?" Dao cried, bolting upright with excitement. Despite a peculiar feeling in the pit of her stomach, she thought that maybe the dream had simply been a nightmare. Her father would be home in a few hours with her birthday present, like he had promised.

Mother shook her head. "I'm sorry, my dear," she said. "But your father said something came up with work. He has to get a different flight."

"He's missing my birthday?"

"Unfortunately, he has to." Her mother kissed her on the forehead fiercely. "He wants me to tell you that he's very sorry and he hasn't forgotten your present. We can give him a call once you've had breakfast."

The crushing disappointment Dao was feeling was too much for a little girl to bear. Tears filled her eyes and rolled down her cheeks unrestrainedly. "No," Dao said, shaking her head. "I don't want to call him. He promised. He promised to be here for my birthday."

"Dao, sometimes things like this can happen—"

"No! He promised. My dream was right."

"What dream?"

But Dao refused to say.

Later, Dao went to sit in the doorway of their house, her eyes fixed on the front gate, exactly as she had in her dream the previous night. She willed the dream not to come true. Maybe it was just a trick, she thought, and he simply wanted to surprise her. He'd come home before her birthday was over, his umbrella and her present tucked under his arm, with one of his rare playful grins on his face.

Her mother came to tap her on the shoulder when evening arrived, casting blankets of gold over their driveway and the tall tamarind tree in the corner. "Dao, it's time for dinner," Mother said.

A part of Dao wanted to continue sitting there, waiting, but the memory of the dream cut deep. So she let Mother take her hand and lead her inside.

Father came back five days later with Dao's birthday present: a model castle made of paper that she could put together by herself. But she didn't run into his arms when he arrived home, nor did he greet her with that mischievous smile of his that was her favourite. Instead he kissed her on the cheek absentmindedly and said, "Happy birthday", as though he were simply commenting on the weather.

That night, Dao pulled her blanket over her head to build herself a little fort, warding off the rest of the world.

Please, she prayed, her eyes pressed shut against her clasped hands. Let me not dream again. Please.

Sunny

One of Sunny's most prized possessions is his acoustic guitar. He'd brought it along with him to Edinburgh and keeps it in a faux-leather case, resting against the wall at the foot of his bed.

He has never taken lessons; over the years, he picked up skills from playing with friends at the garage near his house when he was a teenager, and watching tutorials on the internet. He doesn't think he's any good, but ever since he moved to this strange country, he's been playing a lot more than he used to.

This is Sunny's first time living outside of Thailand, and he finds everything about this new country confounding and inaccessible. Even the beautiful old buildings and parks seem blurred to him, as though he were being spun around like a top. He misses hearing and speaking his mother tongue.

As promised, he calls his mother back in Bangkok every day. She is eager to hear about every little detail of his new life.

"What are your classes like? Have you made any new friends?" she asks.

He thinks back to his first lesson two days ago. He hadn't trusted himself to take the bus without a hitch, so had chosen to walk nearly an hour to the Meadows, near his English school. As part of his short-term student visa, he couldn't afford to miss any of the weekly lessons.

He'd spent the entire class lost, as the teacher – a thin Scottish man in his forties with the look of someone who didn't care for his job at all – tried to inspire the class to practise conversational English with each other.

The other students are mostly from Europe, and Sunny had found himself flailing in their presence.

"I made two, three friends at the school," he tells his mother. The truth is that he stumbled through the class as best he could, and left immediately when it ended, despite one of the students asking if he wanted to join the rest of them for drinks.

"Good," says his mother. "Have your aunt and uncle been showing you around?"

Aunt Oom, Mother's older sister, and her husband Uncle Chang had simply walked Sunny through all the basic information he'd need to work in their supermarket before showing him to his tiny box bedroom. The room had nothing else in it besides a single bed, a tiny closet and a small window. They kindly left Thai food overnight for him in the fridge, but the three of them haven't spent much time together.

"Oh yes, they've been really nice," Sunny tells his mother. And for effect, he decides to add a few embellishments just for the hell of it: "Aunt Oom is exactly like I'd

27

imagined her from your stories. She took me shopping for jumpers and a new coat."

"That's great. So you're wearing enough layers, are you?"

"Yes, Ma," he reassures her. "You don't have to worry, I'm not a little boy anymore."

"You're not a parent, you don't understand." He can hear the frown in her voice. "No matter how old you are, we'll always worry. We just want you to be happy."

Sunny has always bridled against the way his mother uses the word "we" to try to cover for his father's detachment. For as long as Sunny can remember, his mother has always been the family's sole source of warmth and affection. His father, who disapproves of his decision to come to Scotland, dominates with sheer force of personality and a tight fist.

"I *am* happy, Ma. Really. You were right to suggest that I come here. I'm already learning so much from working with Aunt Oom. I won't be surprised if I find another job here soon that'd pay better and help get me a working visa. Plus…" – he suppresses a sigh – "…I'm loving the city, it's as beautiful as I thought it'd be."

Of course, Sunny doesn't tell her that he detests all the hills and all the walking, that he feels isolated in the confines of his small bedroom. Most of all, though, he loathes the cold. There seems to always be a chill inside his bones. No matter what he does, he never really feels warm enough.

"I'm just bored," he tells Dao over the phone one night. "I don't know what to do."

He and Dao have been talking on the phone quite often lately. He finds himself wanting to call her whenever he has something on his mind, or whenever the hours seem to stretch on and on in a monotonous rhythm. Sometimes he doesn't even say anything. He simply enjoys being on the line with her, listening to her talk on and on about one thing or another.

He likes, and has grown used to, the sound of her voice. Unlike the greyness of Scotland, he finds it warm, gentle, full of colours and bursts of humour.

"How can you be bored?" Dao asks him. "You *have* things to do. You work all day and you go to school. How can you be bored?"

"Work is just work," he tries to explain. "As for school, I'm only going three times a week. I feel like I'm on auto-pilot most of the time. Nothing is exciting, nothing is fun."

"You're living in one of the most beautiful cities in the world!" Dao says. "Have you tried going out?"

"I don't know who to go with."

"You can always invite me if you want to go some-where," Dao suggests carefully. It's one of the things he finds most pleasing about her: her tenderness with him.

"Alright, I'll keep that in mind." He smiles to himself. "What about you? Don't you ever get bored?"

"Of course I do," she says, scoffing. "But whenever I get bored, I try to go out and find things to do. People to hang out with."

"When I've worked all day, I'm already tired," he explains. "Sometimes I just want to do nothing with people I'm comfortable with."

"But how is doing nothing *not* boring?"

He laughs. "You've got me there. I don't know." He stares up at the ceiling as he adjusts his earphones. His phone is lying on top of his chest, rising and falling in time with his breathing. "I suppose some people might call that boring."

"So are you actually bored? Or are you just lonely?"

She has a habit of asking questions that make him think too much, especially when he doesn't want to. As much as it annoys him sometimes, he grudgingly admits that it makes him respect her more. "I don't know," he replies.

He wishes he were better with words so he could adequately describe the feeling. How do you explain not knowing how to be with yourself? Not being able to sit in your own silence without feeling a void inside you, dragging you down? Whatever words he chooses, they all sound either hyperbolic or insufficient.

"So," Dao continues, "what songs can you play on this guitar of yours?"

"What do you want to hear?"

"Why don't you play something that you're listening to a lot right now?" Her voice becomes muffled, and he knows it's because she's pulling her duvet over her face, which she tends to do.

"You know," he says, "there's this one song..."

He puts the phone on the bed, picks up his guitar and begins strumming. His voice is a bit raspy and dry, and he's never been much of a singer, but the song is in his key and he manages to remember some of the lyrics. He begins to sing.

Of course the song is Thai, and it is about loving someone who's far away. *Try looking up at the sky*, the lyrics go, *you'll see your star shining up there. That star is like me, who won't ever leave you. Just by looking up at the sky, you'll see us.* It's a song that would normally make him cringe, but for some reason, he enjoys singing it for her.

"I don't know this song." Her voice is faint. "It's really nice, though."

He trips over some of the words, misses a couple of the high notes and laughs at his mistakes. He can distinctly hear her laughing along with him. He likes making her laugh.

After the song is over, he puts down his guitar and lies back down on his bed. "So?" he asks. "What do you think?"

"Not bad," she muses. "Not bad at all."

Although he can't see her, he knows she is smiling.

//

A week after meeting Dao, Sunny makes his second friend in Edinburgh.

Surprisingly, it's not one of the students at the English school but a Thai girl three years younger than him who comes in to work part-time at the supermarket.

Noon is the very definition of "petite". Sunny can tell right away that many before him have underestimated her because of her slim frame, pretty face, long acrylic nails and preference for pink clothing. But it's obvious right away that nothing about Noon is diminished by her small stature.

From their very first conversation, the younger girl has no qualms about cutting Sunny down to size. She asks right away why he's in Edinburgh. He tells her that he's the nephew of the owner of this supermarket, and that it was his mother's idea for him to come here to gain "experience and much needed direction".

"I see nepotism is alive and well then," Noon says in a clipped tone. "You mentioned that it's your mother's idea. What about your father?"

"That's a very personal question," Sunny remarks, amused. "I don't even know you."

"I'm asking these questions so that I can *get* to know you."

"I don't talk about personal family business with someone I just met."

"So you don't have a good relationship with your father then?"

"I didn't say that," Sunny counters. "I simply want to be my own man." Once he's said it out loud, he thinks it sounds ridiculous.

Noon appraises him for a few seconds. "Well…we'll see how that goes." She claims the stool behind the till, the only seat available, leaving him standing foolishly beside it.

He spends the next few shifts they share interrogating her in return, and finds out that she comes and goes between Bangkok and Edinburgh. Whenever she's in Scotland, she divides time between her own tiny flat and the house her Thai mother shares with her Scottish stepfather and her younger half-sister. "My mother knows Aunt Oom from the temple," Noon explains. "That's how I got the job here."

"What other jobs do you have?"

"Oh, in Bangkok I print T-shirts, I DJ, I sell skincare products, I do whatever I can get my hands on. You?"

"I only have this job." He gives her a sarcastic smile. "You already know this, you don't have to rub it in."

"I'm not rubbing it in, I wanted to be thorough." She swivels around on the high stool so she can fix him with a curious stare. "You're on your phone a lot, by the way," she tells him bluntly.

The observation catches him off guard. "I am?" He knows this, of course. But doesn't want to lose ground against her.

"Who are you always texting?"

"Oh, mostly friends back home."

"Do you have a girlfriend, P' Sunny?"

He laughs. "Are you always this nosey?"

She ignores his question. "Do you have anyone you're talking to? Or dating?"

"Why do you want to know?"

"Maybe I can set you up with someone. As your little sister."

"I already have a little sister," he counters.

"Another one doesn't hurt." She flips her hair. "So, do you have anyone?"

"No," he replies at once. "Relationships are..." – he frowns, trying to find the right words – "...they're exhausting. Many women enter my life without wanting anything from me. Yet they tend to leave demanding so much."

Noon gives him a sceptical look. "But what if you fall in love?"

"Falling in love takes time. It doesn't just happen overnight."

"I'm just saying – don't rule it out."

He scoffs. "Trust me, I know myself. I doubt that *that's* going to happen."

Yet that dream he'd had before moving to Edinburgh still lurks in the back of his mind. That dream about a significant encounter he's supposed to have with a stranger – this woman whose face he can't recall – and the conversation he'd had with his mother afterwards.

Dao had asked him one night about dreams, and whether he believes they can predict the future. For a moment, he was tempted to confide in her about his mother's superstitions and ask her questions about her own. But then, at the last minute, he chose to change the subject.

After all, how can he begin to explain that his entire existence came to be only because his mother believed she had dreamed it?

Sunny

For as long as Sunny could remember, his mother had always told him about her dreams that had foretold her meeting his father.

The stories would be told at Sunny's grandmother's house in Bang Na: an old two-storey townhouse with cracked windows and a temperamental piping system, crammed between other townhouses lining a busy market street, but with wooden floors and high ceilings that his mother loved so much. It was the house Ma grew up in, and even when he was a small child Sunny could tell it was the only place she ever felt comfortable and at peace.

In the comforts of her childhood home, Ma would sit with her legs carelessly stretched out, her long, beautiful hair tied up in an unruly bun, and talk in a loud ringing voice, with only Sunny, his little sister Fai and Grandma as company. Sunny's father would never accompany them on these visits.

Sunny's parents met when his mother had just turned twenty; his father was ten years older. Their first encounter came just four days after Ma had a dream that she would meet the love of her life.

The dream, Ma said, felt as real as you and me right now, sitting across from each other. According to Ma, Father had looked and sounded exactly like the man in her dream, even down to the tiniest details of the colour of his shirt and his haircut. A fortune teller – an old lady who used to live on the same street as Ma – had confirmed the fact: "This man is to be your husband," she'd told Ma.

Fai would listen with her eyes wide with fascination. Sunny's grandmother, however, stayed silent, as she usually did, her face a serene mask. Sunny never knew how his grandmother felt about his father, despite her daughter's fervent belief that their union was written in the stars.

Once, when Sunny was just six years old, he gathered up the courage to ask his father: "Did you see Ma in a dream before you met her too?"

Father looked at Sunny incredulously. "What the hell are you talking about?" he barked. Father had never been one for mincing his words in front of his children. Stumbling over his own, Sunny repeated the story his mother had told him so many times before.

After he was done, his father let out a scornful laugh. "Your mother's always had these fantasies." Father waved a hand, as if he were brushing away a fly. "I didn't marry her because I had a dream, or because some superstitious woman I didn't know saw her face in a deck of cards. I married your mother because she was pretty, had manners, and came from a good family, and it was time I took a wife to keep my house."

Sunny didn't repeat those words to his mother. He might have been young, but he wasn't foolish: he learned very early on that there were things in his family that should be kept secret. He never mentioned any of his mother's dreams to his father again, nor the quick visits to fortune tellers on their school runs.

The only thing that brought his father any joy seemed to be their family business: a shop selling locks, keys and chains that Father bought right after he and Ma got married. It was on the first floor of a four-storey townhouse, the upper three storeys serving as their family home. The red sign on the front of the building pronounced the shop's name in bold, embossed golden letters, with the Chinese translation below in a smaller size: Prosperous Keys.

It was when Sunny started helping his father around this shop that he learned the biggest secret he'd ever had to keep.

Sunny was ten years old, the age his father thought was perfect for apprenticeship. "You'll be taking on this business one day," Father told him. "You should learn how everything is run."

Many of the interactions between Sunny and his father involved the older man imparting wisdom in glacial tones. "You must work extremely hard if you want to get ahead in life," Father often said. "Be careful with your money. Make sure you're making smart investments." Or, "You have to be disciplined and tough with the people around you." Another one of his favourites was: "You can't accept mediocrity, because one day you'll wake up and find yourself cruising along in life without having anything to show for it."

It was around this time that Sunny woke one morning to find himself burning up with fever and his head throbbing in pain. He could hardly get himself out of bed, but he knew what his father would say. So he forced himself to shower, dress and come downstairs for breakfast.

His mother was serving congee with fried dumplings, egg yolks and minced pork. Father was already scribbling in his accounts book, his forehead creased with concentration and irritation.

Sunny sat down at the dining table and felt lightheaded just from the effort, his stomach roiling at the thought of eating.

"I don't feel well," Sunny began. "I don't think I can go to school today."

Ma came over to feel his brow and remarked that he was indeed feverish. "Do you have a headache?" she asked. "Does it hurt anywhere?"

He said, "Yes, a headache." Ma was about to send him back to bed when Father finally looked up. His eyes, boring into Sunny's, brooked no argument.

"You'll go to school today," his father said. "You shouldn't take days off so easily. If you're still sick tonight and tomorrow, only then can you stay home."

When Father spoke this way, there was no point trying to dissuade him.

Sunny spent the entire day at school in a daze. When Ma came to pick him up in the evening, she found his face pale and pinched, as though he were about to throw up.

"Should I cancel our visit to Grandma?" Ma asked, concerned. "If you're not feeling better tonight, I might have to take you to the hospital."

"No, Ma, I'm alright," Sunny replied. "But maybe you should drop me home first. I'll sleep it off."

Ma dropped him off in front of their shop and drove away with his little sister, bound for Grandma's home in Bang Na, but not before giving him strict instructions to take a paracetamol and go straight to bed.

To Sunny's relief, there were currently no customers in the shop and his father wasn't behind the till, so he was able to make his way upstairs without having to answer *any questions. He was so exhausted, and fell asleep almost immediately.*

He woke to the sound of rain. His eyes were bleary, his skin surprisingly cold.

He heard a car pulling into their driveway; it was too early for his mother and Fai to be home.

He went to the window and saw that the car wasn't one he recognised: a sleek, silver Citroën that made their truck and Dad's old blue Honda look cumbersome and cheap.

The Citroën door opened and an umbrella appeared, followed by a pair of legs clad in long, flowing blue cotton trousers. A woman. But Sunny couldn't see her face.

Sunny remained rooted to the spot as the woman closed the car door and his father appeared from within the shop. Small gestures that felt monumental to Sunny: Father's sentences, abrupt but impassioned; his hand on the crook of the woman's elbow; his eyes scanning left and right; his head bent close to hers.

Sunny saw Father drawing the visitor inside, away from the rain and the eyes of their neighbours. His mother was still not back.

Sunny didn't know how long he continued to stand there. But eventually the visitor emerged from the shop, got into the silver car and drove away. Only then did Sunny go back to sleep.

This time he woke to find both his parents looking over him. It was dark outside, the room lit dimly by the lamp on his bedside table.

"Have you been sleeping up here all this time?" was the first question his father asked.

Sunny nodded. His mother touched his forehead. "Your fever seems to be gone," she said. "Are you feeling better? Do you need to go to the doctor?"

"No," said Sunny. "I'm alright, I'm feeling much better now." But his eyes were on his father, who looked back at him, unflinching. Sunny could read nothing in that gaze. Yet his father allowed him to stay home from school the next day in order to recover.

His mother brought his meals to his room. She smiled at him like she used to when he was so small that she could hold him on her lap. He thought of the silver car and the woman beneath the umbrella. Then of his mother telling him of her dreams, and the look in her eyes when she'd thought her marriage had been fore-told by destiny – an epic romance weaved together throughout every life, past and present.

Sunny felt torn between crying and shouting – at his mother, his father, even at himself for half believing in the fairy tale. But all he did was keep quiet.

From that day on, Sunny told his father that he could no longer work in the shop after school. "My teachers want me to get into more extracurricular activities," was the excuse. "To help improve my grades and future university applications." He cited extra tutoring, sports, anything that he knew his father wouldn't be able to disregard.

Curiously, Father didn't even try to object. "You're still young, I understand why you'd want to try out other things," was all he told Sunny. "But remember. You'll have no choice but to return to this business one day. Your place is here."

Dao

Now that Dao has been getting matches on Tinder, she begins going on dates. The first few are nothing special, but she deems them good and much-needed practice, especially since she's had very limited experience in the romance department.

There's the nice Scottish guy with a ginger beard who takes her for a walk along the Union Canal. He tells her about his time living in Thailand – the Thai phrases he's memorised, the local dishes he used to order, how much he loved it there. "But my family is here, so I moved back," he explains. They will never meet again. Nothing bad happens on the date. But not enough good happens either.

Then there's the self-described "food and fitness influencer" who takes Dao to a hotel bar, in which all the food and drinks are given to him for free so he can post a review. He spends the entire time talking about himself and ends their date by asking: "Would you mind filming me from behind as I walk into the bar and panning out to see the view?"

Dao simply deadpans: "Sure, why not? I'm a photographer, after all."

The man looks surprised. "You are?" He hasn't bothered to ask her a single thing about herself.

Dao tries hard not to roll her eyes. "Let's try and get this done in one shot, shall we?"

They, too, will never meet again.

Then there's the rich international student who walks her around the Meadows and regales her with tales of his family's business empire. She finds him physically appealing; he finds her a challenge. They agree to meet again, but the plan never materialises.

After that, there is the PhD student who is so shy and nervous that the conversation is halting and awkward. But Dao is able to coax a few smiles and laughs out of him until he becomes more relaxed. At the end of the date, they sit and chat comfortably on a bench in Princes Street Gardens with ice creams they'd bought from a nearby truck. Again, there will be no second date, but they will stay friends online for a while until he eventually finds himself a nice, uncomplicated girlfriend, whose pictures Dao sometimes looks up on Instagram.

Still, Dao keeps swiping.

"It's like an addiction," she confides in Simone. They are going through each other's matches and debriefing in the common room. "I'm having a good time meeting new people and I'm *still* surprised that people want to meet *me*."

"I wish you saw yourself the way we see you," says Simone. "Any of these guys would be lucky to have you, and I'm not just saying that." Before Dao can express her gratitude, Simone thrusts a guy's profile into Dao's face. "What do you think?"

Dao squints to get a better look at Simone's screen. "Personally? I'd swipe right. He seems wholesome. And the dog in his second picture is so cute!"

"You're very generous," Simone remarks, and proceeds to swipe left. "This is hopeless! Last week I had a full-on two-hour phone call with a guy. We bared our *souls* to each other! This is *not* an exaggeration, the man opened up about his father's death, only for us to never speak again! He didn't text, I didn't text, it was like an emotional one night stand!"

Dao nods and agrees: it *is* hopeless. Just mindless distraction and a fun novelty.

But then Dao meets Jamie.

//

Jamie is definitely not a generous swipe.

In every picture in his profile – holding a cocktail on the beach, belting into a microphone at a karaoke bar, showing off a cute Christmas jumper beside a fireplace – he has a handsome, effervescent smile that makes his eyes crinkle up in the corners.

From the moment he and Dao start texting, he is charming, funny, friendly. He is a year younger than she is, from the north of England, but he had worked in finance in London before relocating to Edinburgh. They spark up an engaging conversation right away, discussing and making jokes about food, TV shows, even football. He asks her out two days after they start texting, and it feels amazingly carefree for her to just say yes with more excitement than usual.

They meet in a bar near the Grassmarket. She's decided to wear black leggings, a leather miniskirt and a sleek red turtleneck that accentuates her curves. He looks suave in an oversized coat, a navy suit and tie, with a grey, woollen scarf that comes down to his waist. He wears several large rings on his fingers, and his cologne is fragrant and mature, indicating a man with style and swag. He gets up from his seat to give her a huge hug, enveloping her entire frame in his significantly larger one.

Not long after they've sat down to exchange basic information about themselves, she already knows they'll get along. They're like old friends, she thinks, meeting for the first time after years apart.

They order a second round of drinks, laughing and bantering, showing each other recent pictures of their lives, and it all feels easier than any of the other dates Dao has been on. His smile really does brighten up the whole room.

By the time the bar is about to close, a switch has flicked inside her brain: *I have spent so many years of my life thinking I could never feel this way again, but here is this person. Someone new.* Oh, how it all makes sense now.

Jamie pays for all their drinks before they leave the bar. It's nearly midnight now, but neither of them wants to go home. He suggests Thai food: "I haven't had it since I was in Thailand two years ago." They had discussed his holiday trip back at the bar, and he'd shown her the tortoiseshell bracelet from Koh Tao that he still wears.

"Let's go for Thai food," Dao agrees. "We can see how good you are with spice."

They banter about this as he looks up a restaurant on his phone and helps navigate them there. They walk side by side down the cobblestone street, occasionally veering towards each other and then veering off again, like magnets that are fighting against their true nature. It's a beautiful night, the city lively with revellers weaving in and out of pubs and restaurants. Occasionally, there's the sound of laughter in the distance.

They eventually arrive at a Thai restaurant next to Usher Hall, its decor consisting of small Buddha statues, potted orchids and a picture of the Thai king hung over an altar. Dao does the ordering in Thai and they share three huge dishes: beef krapao (stir-fry with basil and chilli), a chicken green curry and fish cakes that come with the traditional vinegar sauce mixed with chopped cucumbers and red onions.

Jamie stays true to his boasting and shows her that he knows how to use chopsticks. They continue to laugh so much, she thinks if she could only bottle up the sound, she would never feel lonely again.

It is both a frightening and exhilarating thought: realising that a person can become someone you might fall in love with one day.

Afterwards, Dao insists that he takes the leftovers home. They part ways at the corner of Usher Hall, their embrace lasting longer than their first. She suddenly realises that this is the first time she's ever been held so closely – so intimately – by a man, and the feeling is so overwhelming that for one frightening second, she is afraid that she might just cling to him and not let go.

If he makes a move to kiss her, it will be her very first kiss. His hand lingers on the small of her back, and she hopes.

But a breath or two, a shuffling of feet, and he pulls away.

"I'll see you again," he tells her before going on his way, his eyes twinkling.

She walks home feeling alight with possibilities, with a whole new life ahead of her. This is her future, just as she'd seen in her dream. There can be no denying it. The man in her dream had been faceless, but looking at Jamie, that man could be him. He makes her feel just as warm and thrilling and whole. Her dream and her card reading really might be coming true.

Dao is lost in thought and smiling to herself as she lets herself into her dormitory. Her phone buzzes and Sunny's message flashes across her screen: *Hey! So how's the date?* She'd told him about it beforehand. Of course she had.

She lets out a sigh, closes the door behind her and sinks onto the bed. For a few seconds, she stares at her phone. Then, on impulse, she presses the call button.

"So," says Sunny, "what's the gossip?"

Her lips curl into a smile. "I had a really good time," she replies.

"Oh." He sounds...surprised? Or...she doesn't really want to finish the thought. "*Oh*. You did?"

"Yeah."

A few seconds of silence. Then he says: "Alright. Tell me about it."

She starts from the moment she and Jamie met near the Grassmarket, followed by the conversations they had over drinks, and the humour in his eyes, his smile. How warm and friendly he is. How luminous. "We have a similar energy," she tells Sunny. "How he is with people. I'm the same way."

"It's only the first date," says Sunny. "How can you know that much about him?"

"Well, there are certain things you just *know* about a person, even if you've only met them once." She curls into bed, pulling her knees up to her chin, pressing her phone closer to her ear.

"You sound like a hopeless romantic," Sunny says.

"Is that a bad thing?"

"I didn't say that." She hears him moving around and knows he must be getting into bed too. "So has this guy texted you yet? Are you going to see each other again?"

Dao takes the phone away from her ear and looks through her messages. "Yes, he texted saying it's nice to meet me, let's hang out again. So I think that's a yes?"

"Are you going to fall in love with him?" Sunny asks.

"Don't tease."

"Does it sound like I'm teasing you?"

"A little." She smiles. She puts her phone on speaker, charges it and rests it near her pillow. "So...what did *you* do today? Tell me everything."

They talk until it's nearly three in the morning. Until her eyes are drooping shut, her speech growing slower and slower. His voice is soothing to her ears, even though she can't quite decipher what he's saying.

"Dao? Dao?"

"Yes?" she mutters, her eyes closed.

"I'm falling asleep," he whispers.

"Me too," she whispers back.

"Can you end the call?"

"Sure," she mumbles.

"Hmm. Goodnight."

"Goodnight."

She doesn't remember dreaming. For the first time in a long time, her night is peaceful.

She stirs when she hears the sound of floorboards creaking. It's coming from her phone. Sunlight taps against her closed eyelids, and then she hears Sunny's voice: "I think my aunt is awake. That's probably her going downstairs to make breakfast."

"I didn't know you were still there," says Dao. She opens her eyes slowly and picks up her phone. They've been on the call for nearly eight hours.

"I told you to hang up," says Sunny, his voice groggy with sleep. "I was too tired to do it."

"I thought I did," she says. "I must have fallen asleep too."

Last night comes rushing back to her – the date with Jamie, their almost-kiss, the long conversation on the phone with Sunny afterwards. A warmth erupts inside her chest. "Well, good morning," she says.

"Good morning," Sunny replies. And she reckons she can hear a smile in his voice.

Dao

When Dao turned nine, she began to have trouble sleeping.

Mostly on Sunday nights, when the prospect of school the next day loomed ahead like a frightening shadow. She had just been moved into a new class, where all the kids were interested in nothing but their high grades and laughing at Dao behind her back.

The first time she raised her hand to answer a question in class, she heard whispers erupting all around her. At first, she didn't think they could've possibly been aimed at her – what was funny about her anyway? But after she'd lowered her hand and answered the question, those whispers reached her ears.

"Her hair looks so oily! Did she not wash it this morning?"

"Those glasses are ugly as hell!"

"Why did she have to raise her hand so quickly? What a show-off!"

"Shhh! She'll hear us!"

"Let her hear, who cares?"

Soon, Dao began to learn that everything about her was amusing to most of her classmates – her appearance, her awkwardness, her round reading glasses, even how she spoke English with the slight American inflections she'd picked up from watching Hollywood movies.

After that, it didn't take long for Dao to stop answering questions in class, and to quit trying to make new friends. She moved to the back of the room, to the table farthest from the blackboard. The person sitting next to her was another outcast: a tall, dark-skinned girl named Teoy who rarely talked to anyone and glowered if you dared look at her for too long. Unlike Dao, however, Teoy never seemed to care that she wasn't popular.

Those were also the years that Dao's father's business began to expand. At Mother's insistence, he was home for dinner every evening. But the time he spent on his phone to colleagues and business partners became longer and longer. His moods, too, did not improve; he was sullen and exhausted, as though he was simply gritting his teeth to get through the ordeal of being with his family. Then, after Dao's ah-gong passed away from cancer, Father moved his mother, Dao's ah-ma, into their guest bedroom downstairs.

The more Dao had trouble sleeping, the more she dreamed – fitful dreams that left her waking up feeling panicked and exhausted. People were chasing her – screeching, hooting, mocking her – trying to tackle her to the ground. In her dreams she could never see their faces, only their voices and the sounds of their footsteps. Sometimes she managed to outrun them. But there were times when she couldn't.

She never remembered what happened in the dreams after she was caught. But when she had to be in school the next day, she would feel like she was sitting in a glass cage, an animal at the zoo, naked and exposed, for people to come and gawk at.

These dreams, she felt, were like the dream she'd had about her father when she was younger: they were a warning, she was sure. They came true.

A dream she'd had when she was almost twelve years old helped to cement this belief even more.

It was during monsoon season. Cockroaches were crawling out of the drains, and a thick, heady humidity hung in the air as the sky darkened with thunderstorms.

In this new dream, Dao was being chased again. This time not by faceless assailants, but by a feeling she couldn't see: a terrible sense of doom and finality. The sound of a storm raging. She could feel her heart beating out of her chest, her sobs rising up inside her. She tripped and fell, pain piercing through her when she hit the ground.

Then, from far away, someone cried out her name in desperation. It was a voice she recognised, and it filled her with fear. She tried to fight through her pain and get to her feet; she must help, she must do something!

But that voice was fading quickly – too quickly for her to reach – and disappearing into darkness and grief.

Dao woke to rain lashing against the house and the sound of the branches of the tamarind tree whipping in the ferocious wind. Thunder continued to rumble in the distance.

When she looked outside her bedroom window, she saw water pouring in through their front gates and down their driveway. Her father stood knee-deep in the flood, with his trousers rolled up to his knees, as he struggled to block the tide from reaching the front door by putting down sacks of concrete and sand.

Dao came downstairs to find her mother standing in the doorway watching the rain with her brows knitted together, as though she disapproved of it the same way she disapproved of food being too salty.

"It's one of the problems with these old houses," Mother said quietly. "It's built low, so when it rains, this is what happens."

She looked at Dao distractedly. "Can you check on your ah-ma? She woke up early to help P' Pun with breakfast, but I haven't seen her since. She might be resting in her room. You can tell her not to come out. The flood might worry her."

Dao went to knock on her ah-ma's door, but there was no reply, so she pushed the door open lightly and stepped inside.

Ah-ma had left the window with the mosquito netting closed. But the glass one was open, so rain drifted into the room, wetting the wooden floor around her closet. Ah-ma lay in bed with her eyes closed and her hands tucked firmly at her sides. The fan spun on, rustling the pages of the Chinese newspaper on her bedside table.

Dao already knew that her ah-ma was gone before she reached out to touch the old woman's cold, lifeless arm.

Somehow, Dao felt, her dream had already told her.

//

Ah-ma's funeral meant Dao had to take a few days off school. When she came back, everyone in class seemed to know what had happened. The whisperings and the laughter lessened a little. But no one came to offer their condolences to Dao until a week later.

It was during lunch hour on a Tuesday. Dao's desk-mate, Teoy, sat down next to her in the cafeteria, along with a boy Dao didn't know.

Teoy wore her signature scowl as she addressed Dao directly for what felt like the first time: "My ah-ma passed away last year too. My parents told me she went to heaven, but I don't believe them. She was a horrible woman. I hope yours was better."

Dao was so shocked that she was being spoken to that all she could say was: "Thank you. I didn't know mine very well, but she lived with us for a while and she had always been kind to me."

"Well, it's sad that she died," said Teoy, and the boy next to her nodded in assent.

The boy was the same height as Teoy, but with none of her intimidating energy. Dao thought he had a handsome face, with round eyes that looked oddly sweet contrasted against his uncomfortable demeanour.

"This is Shane," said Teoy. "He's new, but our parents are friends so I'm supposed to be looking after him."

Dao caught Shane's eyes. "Hi," she said, smiling.

"Hi," he replied. He didn't smile back.

"I'm sorry about all the teasing," Teoy said, without any preamble. "I've known these kids since Grade One and they've always been like this. Just don't pay them any mind."

"I would if I could!" Dao said, aghast. She thought of an incident a few days before when she had to give a presentation in front of the whole class in English. The entire time she was talking, three girls in the middle row were whispering to each other and rolling their eyes, clearly making fun of her. When it was their turn to do their presentations, one of them made a point of starting theirs off by imitating Dao's accent, but heavily exaggerated. The stunt drew gales of laughter from nearly the whole class.

Dao had wanted to burst out crying. But she'd told herself: I must not embarrass myself any further. She curled her hands into fists, digging her nails into the palms, and stared down at them until the lesson was over.

She remembered that Teoy was one of the few who did not laugh.

"They're just miserable and nasty," Teoy was saying now. "And they're jealous because you're smarter than they are."

"I don't think that's true."

"You scored higher than them in our last English test and in the social studies test as well."

"I suppose so," Dao replied, not really believing her.

They slipped into a conversation about exams and homework. The boy, Shane, never spoke once. Dao didn't know what to say to him, nor could she find the courage to ask why Teoy had never spoken to her before today.

When the bell rang, Teoy announced that she had to go to the bathroom, then tore off with surprising speed. Dao got to her feet and began heading back to class, with Shane awkwardly accompanying her. He walked with his head down and didn't even give her a glance.

But when they reached the stairs that led up to their separate classrooms, he paused, cleared his throat and removed his hands from his pockets. "I'm sorry, too," he said. "About your ah-ma."

"Oh," said Dao, a little surprised and confused. "That's alright."

"If you need a friend," said Shane, "I can be your friend."

It felt both unexpected and simple. Dao was grateful. "Thank you," she told him. "And you, too. If you need a friend, that is."

"Do you like taking photographs?"

It was such a random thing for him to ask that she was taken aback. "I…well, I haven't thought much about it."

"I just started getting into it," said Shane, suddenly animated and chatty. "I found this old film camera of my dad's and I've been learning how to use it. Moving to a new school can be…

you know…" – he looked at her cautiously, scratching the back of his head – "…making new friends…" He trailed off.

Dao thought of the English presentations and felt her cheeks burn with embarrassment. "Yes," she said, "making new friends is not easy."

"Maybe the camera will help you feel better," Shane rushed on. "Like it did with me. If I brought my camera tomorrow, would you want to use it?"

Her smile mirrored his own. "Of course!"

The next day, Shane found her in the cafeteria after she had finished her lunch and was sipping on a Coke. Unlike the day before, he radiated excitement.

He gave her the film camera – silver and sleek, with a satisfying weight and size that seemed to belong in her hands.

"It's so beautiful," she gasped. "I don't want to break it, it feels so delicate."

"You're not going to break it," said Shane with confidence. "I'll teach you how to use it. Lift it up and look through here." He pointed at the viewfinder.

She did as he indicated. The world shrank, but the smallness of everything gave her a comforting feeling. "What do you want to take a picture of first?" he asked.

She thought of the dream she'd had during the flood, and her ah-ma's cold skin. But it was the warmth of Shane's smile that she remembered most.

"You," she replied without thinking.

She turned to fix the camera on him. And his handsome face – startled and a little flattered, but shining with contentment – became the first portrait she ever took.

Sunny

Late one afternoon, Dao comes unannounced into the supermarket while Sunny is on shift. She gives him a beaming smile as she breezes through the doors. "Helloooo! Surprise!"

Right away, Dao's vibrant energy catches him off guard. Despite talking on the phone often, it has been a while since Sunny last saw her in person. He's been working up the courage to ask her out for a walk or a meal, but for some reason, he keeps second-guessing himself.

"What are you doing here?" Sunny exclaims. "I thought you had class!"

He quickly puts away his phone. He'd been texting Noon, who's not on shift today, about her latest friend-group drama.

"That was this morning, silly," Dao replies. She picks a lollipop from one of the containers on the counter and twirls it around.

"Are you going to pay for that?" Sunny asks, laughing.

"No, I don't really like lollipops."

"Then why are you playing with things that are there for customers to buy?" He fixes her with a stern stare. But it is hard for him to be genuinely angry with her. "Are you just here to annoy me?"

"Nah, you're not *that* important." She drops the lollipop back into the container. "My date is a ten-minute walk from here. So I thought I'd stop by."

"A date? With that Jamie guy again?" He forces a smile. "Is this your second time meeting up?"

"Yes. He's taking me to dinner."

"Fancy!"

"Don't tease."

"I'm not." He shrugs. "It actually sounds nice."

"Oh. Okay." She picks up the end of her cherry-red scarf and begins winding it around her right hand.

He sighs. "Spill," he says. "Why are you really here?"

"I'm actually kind of nervous," she admits softly.

"Nervous?" He scoffs. "Why would you be nervous?"

"Like I told you, I've never really dated before. I had a really good time with this guy, and I can see myself really liking him. But…" – here she's not able to look Sunny in the eye – "…but what if he doesn't like *me*?"

"Nah, impossible."

"How would you know?"

"Well, I happen to think you're an amazing person."

"Oh, Sunny, stop it."

"No, I mean it." Sunny grins. "Despite your woeful attempts to annoy me, despite the fact that you never, ever shut up, I *still* think you're pretty awesome. This guy might be the coolest person ever to exist, but you should know that you have nothing to worry about. He's lucky to be dating you."

Sunny doesn't know if he's saying too much or too little. As with so many things between them, he's finding this situation hard to read. But he watches her face change: a softness melts into her expression and she gives a smile that makes him feel like it's just for him.

"Thank you," she mutters abashedly. "That's sweet of you." She comes over to claim the empty stool next to him behind the till, the one Noon usually sits on. He notices the look on her face, so he waits; sombre isn't an expression she wears often.

Eventually, Dao quietly reveals: "There is one more thing. It sounds stupid, but I can't get it out of my mind. I saw a fortune teller right before I came to Edinburgh. I had this dream, you see, and I thought it had a deeper meaning, so I wanted her to tell me what it meant."

Sunny thinks of his previous attempt to steer the conversation away from this very topic. His mind flickers to his own dream and his mother's interpretation – things he's been struggling to avoid ever since they'd occurred. He tries to keep his voice level: "What was your dream about?"

Dao shrugs, but keeps her eyes away from his as she speaks in a rush: "I had this dream that I was in a new country and that there was a stranger. A man. I couldn't see his face, but in the dream, we were close." She blushes and looks down. "It felt significant, so I went to this fortune teller, like I said, and she told me I was going to meet someone when I came to Scotland."

Sunny feels as though he's falling, scrambling for a foothold. It must be a coincidence, surely. It can't be the same dream as his own. For one quick moment, he nearly tells her all about it, including the ensuing conversation he'd had with his mother and all the other dreams that have defined their lives before this. But he finds that he can't speak.

Dao, still not looking at Sunny, fills the silence: "I know this sounds ridiculous." She grimaces. "But I think that man in my dream might be Jamie. That *he's* the one I'm supposed to meet. And now I'm afraid that I'm going to mess it all up somehow by doing something wrong."

She's looking at Sunny now, almost imploringly, and he searches for something clever or reassuring to say in response, but nothing comes. "Why didn't you tell me any of this before?" he asks.

"I didn't want to admit that I'm some sort of nutcase who believes that dreams can predict the future. You already told me you don't believe they do, so I didn't want to seem silly." She blushes again and looks away. "I didn't want you to think less of me."

His mother's face flashes through his mind, and an uneasy feeling takes hold of him, but he quickly shakes it away. This is Dao, not his mother, he reminds himself. And wasn't there a time when he, too, had been susceptible to such superstitions?

Dao is still not looking at him, but is focusing intently on a hair band that she is now rotating around her thumb. He feels a strong urge to reach out and tie it back around her wrist, where she always has it, but all he says is: "I don't think any less of you, Dao. Not at all."

Dao smiles at him, grateful, and the seriousness is broken. He keeps his tone light and a little teasing: "So according to your dream and this fortune teller, this Jamie guy is your future husband?"

"I don't know about *future husband*," Dao replies with a dignified flourish. "Marriage takes true commitment, and *commitment* is a choice. But love…for me I believe that love is all heart. You don't have a choice who your heart falls for."

The way she says it – with so much abandon and longing – gives Sunny pause. For the first time since they met, he realises how much braver – or more reckless – she is than him. For some reason, the knowledge disarms him.

He continues trying to tease her: "So has your heart fallen for this guy already? After one date and a week or two of texting? Is that all it takes?"

Thankfully, she lets out a laugh. "Are you saying I'm easy?"

"You? Easy? Oh, no! Never!"

Despite trying to prevent it, his thoughts will stray to that moment often for the rest of the day. How her expression shifts from seriousness to humour, like a rare glimpse of sun peeking through the grey Scottish clouds.

//

After Dao has left for her date, near closing time, Noon shows up at the supermarket.

The younger girl gives Sunny a short, clipped explanation: "I don't want to be alone this evening. Can we go grab a bite to eat?" So after she has helped him close the supermarket, the two of them end up at the nearby chippy.

Sunny notices that lately Noon has been texting him often, sharing details of her day and asking how he is. Occasionally, they go for a meal or a drink after work. He feels comfortable around her; they come from similar families and backgrounds. Unlike with Dao, he feels no underlying need to impress her or prove his worth.

Today, he and Noon share a huge pizza and a plate of chicken wings, while she sips on a Coke and he nurses a bottle of beer. She begins to tell him about how sad she's been feeling lately. She doesn't know why; perhaps she's lonely, though she's always busy and surrounded by people.

She tells him about her ex-boyfriend, who keeps texting and calling. "I loved him so much," she says, "but he had all these other women, I *had* to break up with him, you know? Out of principle. When someone treats you like shit, eventually you have to kick them to the kerb. But he won't go."

"One of these men you're talking to must be halfway decent," Sunny offers. "Are there guys back in Thailand? Or are they all people you've met here?"

"Mostly guys back home. A few I've met here through the apps. But I don't really like going out with *farangs*." She scrunches up her nose in derision with the use of the Thai slang word for "foreigners", which also means guava. "They make fun of my English and treat me like I'm stupid. And all they want to do is sleep with me."

He grimaces. "Well…"

"It's all part of the game, I know. Most of the time I have fun playing it." She shrugs. "But sometimes it can get…disheartening." A look passes across her face.

Sunny is about to ask if she's alright, but then she shakes it off and her usual playful smile slides back into place. "Don't worry, P' Sunny," she says, "you're still my favourite."

Then she quickly moves on to chatting about her half-sister's latest antics.

Still, when they step outside a little later into a light drizzle, Sunny can feel an awkward tension between them. He avoids looking at Noon by focusing on his phone instead. He notices her attempting to step closer to him, but then she changes her mind.

"I'm heading that way." Noon jerks her head in the opposite direction of the supermarket.

Relieved, Sunny glances up at her and nods. "Okay. I'll see you around."

She holds his gaze for a fraction too long. "Yeah," she says slowly. "See you around." Then she turns and crosses the road.

He heads for the supermarket, double-checking his messages as he walks. There are none from Dao. He wonders whether her date has ended yet, and he lets himself inside. He can hear the television from his aunt and uncle's living room one floor above. As he takes the stairs up to his bedroom, he calls his mother.

When she answers, the sound of her voice immediately soothes him. An anchor reminding him of the home he's left behind, and an illusion that, despite all the current unknowns in his life, despite Edinburgh feeling so unfamiliar, everything is still in his control.

But in the back of his mind, Dao's smile; her tremulous voice as she told him of her dream, her heart.

He thinks of telling his mother about everything that's happened. "She reminds me a little of you," he'd say. But he stops himself just in time.

He has learned his lesson: like their conversation about his dream before he came to Edinburgh, he already knows what his mother would say.

Sunny

Two years into secondary school, Sunny started to hang out with friends from school at a garage across the river from his house.

These friends sat in the last rows of seats in their classroom. They didn't care whether they were talking too loudly in class, and always spent their recesses smoking behind the school. Other boys at the garage were mechanics and older teenage boys from nearby trade schools who carried themselves with an air of what Sunny deemed ultimate coolness.

Before long, he started copying their patterns of speech, how they smoked and drank and played their guitars. He also imitated the way these boys talked to girls, and quickly realised that girls liked talking to him as well.

But most importantly, he learned how to have the other boys' backs as though they were his own flesh and blood. He'd never before had friends who felt like brothers.

He was fifteen when he had a dream that threatened to destroy this brotherhood.

Sunny had spent the majority of his life hearing stories of his mother's dreams that she believed were the foundation for their family. He indulged her tales of what these dreams meant – her trips to various fortune tellers who found meaning in the tiniest details to determine whether a day would be good or bad. Yet he didn't think his own dreams had any meaning at all. Not until this one.

Unlike his normal dreams, this one arrived with so much brightness, like Bangkok at the height of summer, when the city swelters beneath the sun's relentless glare.

In the dream, Sunny saw a girl untouched by shadows, whose face shone so clearly. There was a twinkle in her eyes and in her smile that sent a buzz through his whole body. Everything else around her seemed faded and colourless in comparison. She was a stranger, he was certain of it, yet he felt like he knew her.

The girl looked him straight in the eye, then called his name.

When Sunny awoke, he couldn't remember what else had happened in the dream, only how it made him feel: he was on top of the world, and there was finally meaning to every mundane, ordinary act that had so far amounted to the meagre contents of his life. He wondered if his mother had felt the same way after her dream about his father. It would explain why she'd believed in it so fervently.

Whoever the girl in the dream was, Sunny couldn't shake the feeling of wanting to be near her and have her light shine on him.

When he'd discovered his father's secret, he had shelved his childish fantasies that there might be something more for him on the horizon. But now, for the first time, his cynicism was tested. He couldn't shake the feeling that there was a story here. A story that was beyond his control.

//

Two days later, a Friday, Sunny lied to his parents that he would be home late because he was going to the outskirts of Bangkok for football practice with his friends. In reality, he went straight to the garage after school.

The place was even buzzier than usual, for it was one of his older brothers' birthdays. Crates of alcohol were brought in, someone had set up a speaker and a TV, and motorcycles came whizzing in through the gates every so often as more people continued to arrive.

Sunny was on his second glass of Regency brandy mixed with Coca-Cola when he first laid eyes on her. She was on the back of one of those motorcycles, her arms wrapped tightly around the birthday boy.

P' Bas was one of the boys Sunny most admired. At seventeen, he wore black rings in his ears, didn't care that his long hair went against school regulations, and always took the time to sit with Sunny while he drank and rambled on about things that he would forget about when morning came.

P' Bas slid off his motorcycle to cries of greeting. He gave a grandiose wave, his handsome face splitting into a grin. The girl, however, hung back.

She was dressed in her school uniform: navy-blue skirt that came to just below her knees, white blouse untucked. Her hair, which was cut short, framed her round face like a halo. Sunny judged her to be around the same age he was.

There was nothing shy in her smile when P' Bas beckoned her forward and introduced her: "This is my girlfriend, Jun." The declaration was met with cheers and wolf whistles.

Sunny could only stare at Jun as she greeted everyone as though she had known them all her life. He couldn't imagine himself being that comfortable and confident. Not in a million years.

As his girlfriend made the rounds, P' Bas sat down next to Sunny with a bottle of beer and slapped him on the shoulder. Sunny wished him happy birthday and they chit-chatted about nothing in particular, making jokes like they always did. The music from the stereo pulsed in Sunny's veins.

Sunny was on his third glass when P' Bas got up to sit with someone else, but his abandoned seat didn't stay empty for long. Sunny took another sip of his drink and then looked up to find himself staring right into Jun's huge, playful eyes. They sparkled with so much life.

"I don't think we've met," Jun said.

"Hi," he said. "I'm Sunny."

She tucked a strand of hair behind her ear. "Hi, Sunny. I'm Jun."

"Yes, I know." He couldn't look away, despite the burning in his chest. "It's nice to meet you."

He wanted to say, I saw your face in my dream. Or, this feels like a dream, and I'm reliving it all over again, just because you said my name. But it sounded foolish, like something a drunk, besotted, lovesick teenager would say. He wasn't his mother, he tried to remind himself. Her superstitions had caused them nothing but pain and deception – his father had seen to that. Since then, he had never believed in fate.

Jun was smiling at him, just like the girl in his dream smiled at him, so blazing it matched the searing heat of the alcohol on his tongue. That very same feeling he'd had in his dream was taking complete control of him.

And he found himself thinking: But surely there are exceptions to every rule, once in a while?

Dao

Dao and Jamie manage the rare and magical feat of making it to their third Tinder date. The fourth time they arrange to meet up, she sits waiting for him by the fountain in Princes Street Gardens.

The only person Dao has told about this fourth date is Sunny. She reflects on this fact as she surveys the marble angels glinting green and gold in the evening dusk. Yellow lights sparkle from the trees all around her, draping from branch to branch, and the Ferris wheel in the Christmas market is visible from where she sits. Couples and groups of friends stroll past. Some sit down on the benches next to hers, sipping hot drinks from plastic cups or chatting animatedly in low voices.

Dao stares at the time on her phone: Jamie is late, just like he'd been the last two times they'd met up. Their second date was at a small pub a ten-minute walk from Sunny's supermarket. On that day, after stopping by to visit Sunny, she arrived on time only to wait for nearly forty minutes. Their third was at another bar, in Old Town. He showed up an hour late. Both times he said he'd got held up at work.

She'd been too embarrassed to tell any of her friends. Even Simone, whom she's been confiding in ever since she started using dating apps, remains oblivious to these new developments. But for whatever reason, she'd told Sunny. When he'd heard of the plans for today, he'd remarked: "I really hope he'll get it together and show up on time for a change."

Dao thinks of those words while the moon begins its climb up the sky and sunlight begins to diminish. As she waits she listens to the sound of the fountain, the faint noises of the crowds and the carols drifting from the market, watches the lights in the trees.

An hour and a half passes.

She takes out her phone, sends a text, and puts it away.

For a long time, she sits by herself, watching people milling around the fountain and the lights sparkling off its marble surface. The cold bites her cheeks and she tucks her gloved hands into her coat pockets. The wind blows lightly against her face, rustling her hair and stinging her eyes.

She senses someone sitting down beside her. She looks up to see who it is and lets out a sigh of relief.

"You really didn't have to come," she says.

"I know," says Sunny. "But I wanted to."

"What about the supermarket?"

"Noon is taking care of my shift for me," he replies. "It's not really busy at this time."

"Thank you."

"So," says Sunny, his eyes on the fountain, "he didn't show."

"Nope, he didn't. And I don't think he's going to."

"Have you texted him?"

"Of course. And he hasn't replied."

"I'm sorry, Dao."

"Just my luck," she says bitterly. She removes her hands from her pockets and lifts one to brush the hair from her eyes. "Did I do something wrong?"

"No! You didn't do anything, don't blame yourself."

"Maybe I was trying too hard."

"Were you?"

She shrugs. "I like him a lot. I guess I thought it could be something. Maybe I got carried away too quickly."

"Did he give you reasons to get carried away?"

"We always got along really well on our dates. We really enjoyed each other's company."

"A guy can enjoy your company and still—"

"Yes, I know," she says, a bite to her voice. "I've seen it with Teoy. She's always dated these shitty guys who string her along, cheat on her or leave her without any explanation. I just thought with this guy…"

"That it wouldn't be like that?"

"I just thought he liked me."

The moment the sentence drops from her lips, she immediately feels pathetic. Like one of those weak girls who's always waiting around for a guy to call or message them back. A failure of an independent woman.

Sunny begins carefully: "There are certain guys who know the right things to say and do to get a girl attached or interested."

"Guys like you?"

"Is that what we're doing right now?"

"I'm sorry." She can see the flash of hurt in his eyes and feels guilty. "I don't mean anything by that. I just don't understand what happened." She lets out a groan and lifts her hands to cover her face. "Oh God, I even told you about my stupid dream and that card reading. I really did think everything was going to work out because of that. I'm actually so mortified right now!"

Sunny knows that feeling all too well, and here's another opportunity for him to tell her so. He can tell her of his mother's dreams, his own dream about Jun, or even the dream he had right before he came to Edinburgh. But all he says is: "You're not stupid, Dao. You just wanted to believe in something good, so you got swept up in it. There's no shame in that. Loads of people believe in all that stuff about dreams and tarot cards and destiny."

"I should have known better."

"Don't be too harsh on yourself."

"Maybe he really is busy. Maybe he's not doing so well."

"Come on, Dao…"

"Sunny—"

"Do you really think that's the case? That he's suddenly so busy he can't even send you a quick text to cancel your plans?"

Dao hates herself for wanting to cry. It shouldn't be this big of a deal. They only had three dates. They hadn't even kissed. So why does she feel like she wants the ground to swallow her up? She hears herself say, "No one has ever told me they liked me before…" She trails off and finds her gaze wandering to the bench next to hers, where a mother and a little girl are tying their shoelaces.

"Don't think too much about it," Sunny continues. "It's nothing to do with you. The guy's probably an asshole."

"You're just saying that to make me feel better."

"Yes. But I do mean it. It has nothing to do with you."

"Am I not good enough?"

"Don't be dramatic." The sentence rubs her the wrong way a little, but when she turns to him, she sees that he's simply teasing her, trying to make her laugh.

"Look," Sunny says, his voice now completely serious. He leans back and stretches his right arm across the bench, the tips of his fingers brushing against her shoulder. His voice softens. "Don't blame yourself. I'm speaking from experience. He probably did like you, he enjoyed your company, but he just…didn't like you enough to want to give this a go."

"That sounds awful." She sucks in a breath. "Oh, God, maybe I'm too sensitive to date. Maybe I need to develop a thicker skin."

"Yeah, I mean it's possible. Things like this happen all the time, and this might not be the last time it'll happen to you." He shrugs. "But how you are is just…who you are. You can't change the fact you're sensitive, or romantic. Besides…" – he stalls, a cautious note stealing into his voice – "…*I* like who you are."

At his words, everything around them seems to slow down. Dao feels a blush creeping up her cheeks, and is extremely grateful that they are both looking straight ahead and not at each other. She doesn't know what to say. Is he teasing her again or simply trying to be nice?

Before she can come up with an adequate response, she senses Sunny removing his arm from the back of her seat. "Come on," he says, "let's go explore the Christmas market. We can't have you being all doom and gloom for the entire night on account of some *boy*." His voice has shifted back to normal, with that cautious, soft tone completely absent.

Dao takes her cue from him. "I don't want to go to the market," she snipes back playfully. "That's where I was supposed to go for my date." Perhaps he really was just being nice, offering a friendly, comforting comment, and nothing more.

"Well, plans change," Sunny says. "Why would you want to waste a perfectly good Christmas market?"

"We can go another day."

He rolls his eyes. "I came all this way from Haymarket! I even got Noon to cover my shift. I don't want to waste the evening sitting with you as you look glumly at a fountain for hours on end."

"Are you trying to guilt-trip me?"

"Is it working?"

Dao laughs, shaking her head with mock exasperation. "Alright," she says. "You win. Let's go to our very first Christmas market."

Sunny gets up and offers her his hand. For a brief moment, their fingers are entwined as he pulls her to her feet. Then they drop away.

They walk side by side as they leave the park. She steals a glance over at him: his handsome face silhouetted against the night and the bright lights from the trees. There's a thoughtful look in his eyes and a solemnity to his expression that reminds her of that peaceful, happy dream.

For the first time, she wonders to herself: *Have I been getting it wrong this whole time?*

Sunny

Sunny buys Dao a vanilla donut coated in pink icing, while she treats him to his very first cup of mulled wine. The air is filled with the smells of grilled sausages, waffles, strong coffee and hot chocolate. A giant Christmas tree in the middle of the market shines with bright neon lights, yellow, green and red. Carols blare from the stereos. There's a Ferris wheel and a merry-go-round, and beyond it a path that winds up the hill, leading them through the market from Princes Street up to Old Town.

Sunny is still not accustomed to how different everything is here from what he knows back home. Yet he can tell, from Dao's glowing expression, that she loves it.

"Thanks for bullying me into coming here," Dao teases him. They're standing near the merry-go-round, sipping their hot drinks while they watch a family of five entering the ride. "I would have gone home and wallowed by myself, and I would have missed all of this."

"Well," he smiles, "the market is going to be here for a while, you can always come back."

"Yes, but I would miss the magic of *this* particular moment." She grins, exaggerated and cheesy, and takes a sip of her hot chocolate. "I can't get over it. Everything here looks like a postcard."

The merry-go-round begins to spin and play a happy jingle. Both of them automatically move closer to lean against the railing. They watch the family laughing and teasing each other as the ride spins. He steals a glance at her that she doesn't notice. She has a smile on her lips and a dreamy, faraway look in her eyes, and he thinks she's never looked more beautiful.

With an inward groan, Sunny recalls that he had all but told her that he liked her, right by the fountain. It'd slipped out before he could properly think it through. He was afraid that she'd laugh at him, or, worse, get angry. But thankfully she'd taken it as one of his friendly compliments and nothing more.

"So," says Sunny, "does this mean you're feeling less sad?"

"A little," she replies. "But at the end of the day...I have to get used to this kind of rejection, remember? If I want to keep going on dates? Most of them aren't going to work out. The odds are *supposed* to be stacked against me."

"Why do you want to date so much?" he asks curiously.

"I don't want to date *that* much," she clarifies, "but...I don't know...I've never put myself out there. I used to close myself off to people, and it just made me feel like shit about myself."

"And you think dating is going to make you feel differently?"

"I think it's going to give me more confidence. I want to be able to talk to guys without being absolutely terrified that I'm going to humiliate myself."

"So do you get terrified talking to me?"

She considers him for a few seconds. "No, I don't get terrified talking to you," she says simply. She holds his gaze and everything stills around him; all he sees is her. And the words he'd uttered by the fountain nearly escape his lips again: *I like who you are*, he'd said. *I like you. Just as you are.*

With a startling, almost overwhelming sense of clarity, he allows himself to fully accept the truth: there is something between them. Something real, exhilarating, frightening, that should be snuffed out immediately, if he were to listen to his head. All this business about dreams and cards and meant-to-bes – he would be walking down a path he already knows would end badly.

The music plays. All the lights around them shine. And Sunny breaks their eye contact.

"Let's go and see those little stalls up there." He gestures up the hill. "Maybe there'll be some fun souvenirs you can buy."

"Okay." She finishes her hot chocolate, tosses the cup into a nearby bin and puts her gloves back on. "Let's see what we can find."

He lets her walk ahead a few steps, and turns around for one last look at the merry-go-round.

//

After the market, Sunny walks Dao all the way to her dormitory. It's a forty-minute walk from the centre of town, but they're both warm from the exercise and the extra round of hot drinks they've had.

During the walk, they talk of his recent English classes and more ideas for her final thesis, which will be her own photography project displayed at an end-of-year exhibition at the university. He tells her a bit more about his mother and sister. The subject of his father, mentioned briefly before but never really discussed at length, rises to the surface.

When she asks what his father is like, he says: "Stubborn, hardworking, tough. I don't think he ever once gave me a compliment."

And before Sunny knows why, he's telling her of that rainy day when he was younger. Of the woman in the silver Citroën and his father secretly drawing her inside.

Dao's eyes widen in shock. "That's...terrible, Sunny, I'm so sorry. Do you think it's still going on?"

"Yes," he replies grimly. "I have no doubt it is. I can tell from how he behaves."

"Does your mother know? Your sister?"

He shakes his head. "I think Fai suspects something, but my mother definitely doesn't know. I've made sure not to give anything away. It would destroy her."

"So you've been carrying this secret by yourself for all these years?"

He shrugs. "It's just how it has to be."

Dao is an extremely good listener, he reflects. She doesn't interrupt, but simply lets him talk. When he struggles to explain himself, she stays silent and gives him time to find the words. And when he doesn't know what else to say, she asks him questions that unlock an entire compartment within his mind that he hadn't known existed.

Everything he's telling her, he has never told anyone else before. The knowledge both intrigues and confuses him. He hasn't fully experienced it until now: how comforting and freeing it feels to be heard.

As they approach her building, he spots a Christmas tree in a second-storey window. A female student, wrapped from head to toe in a giant winter coat and beanie, lets herself out of the building. They side-step away from the entrance to make way for her and end up standing awkwardly next to each other on the side of the pavement.

"So," Sunny begins, "are you feeling any better?"

Both of their hands are tucked inside their coats.

She shrugs. "A little. Maybe I was being too dramatic. But thank you for today. You've really been there for me. It means a lot."

"Don't worry," he says. "We help each other. You've been there for me too."

She laughs. "When?"

"You've just been a friend. That's all. I haven't found it easy over here. It means a lot to have someone to talk to."

She hesitates for a fraction of a second. "Oh. Okay. I'm glad I've been of help."

A gust of wind blows past. She brushes her hair away from her face, and looks at him the way she was looking at him at the merry-go-round.

A few seconds pass in silence.

"What?" she asks hesitantly. Then she grins at him, trying to make him laugh. He doesn't, though, but simply removes his hands from his pockets. It'd be so easy, he thinks, to reach out and take her hand. It'd be so easy to even...

If only he could move a step closer. Or if she were to do the same. But neither of them does.

No, it's better this way, he thinks. Nothing has gone wrong yet. Let it stay this way.

"Goodnight, Dao," he says.

A look he can't read fades from her eyes. "Goodnight, Sunny."

The weather turns colder as he walks home. Yet strangely he's in no hurry to quicken his steps and rush back to the warmth. It's a clear, cloudless night, and he can see a few stars appearing in the ink-black sky.

PART TWO

The Falling

Sunny

It was New Year's Day, and the garage was packed with more people than usual. Since it was the holidays, Sunny's parents were more lenient and had allowed him to stay out late. They thought he was watching the fireworks by the river with friends from school.

After the countdown, there were no fireworks or even firecrackers at the garage. A few people were already drunk, singing loudly to the music blasting from the speakers. Others were laughing hysterically, or barely managing to stay in their seats, while someone else was doing their best to sing an entirely different tune, an old Carabao country song, on a karaoke machine.

P' Bas was one of the drunkest. Whenever the older boy drank, he became even more exuberant. His friends and younger brothers gathered around him as he held court, throwing out jokes and telling stories. Sunny sat apart from them, sipping his beer, observing and brooding.

Jun sat beside him, like she always did whenever P' Bas got extremely intoxicated. She had a half-empty bottle of beer in her hand, and the alcohol gave a flush to her cheeks and a shine to her eyes.

Jun wasn't like any of the girls Sunny usually went after. She was much shorter than him, for one, her head only reaching his shoulders; he preferred girls that were slimmer and willowy. She smoked and drank with him and his friends at the garage, and never shied away from giving them grief. Although she was never brash or mean, she was loud, and laughter shot from her core like lightning.

But she was going out with his older brother. Sunny loved P' Bas. From the very first day, the older boy had taken Sunny under his wing. What kind of younger brother would he be, if he were to make a move on his girlfriend? Every time he and Jun talked or exchanged messages online, he felt guilty.

Sunny spared a glance in P' Bas's direction. "How will he get home?"

"Oh, easy," said Jun, smiling. "One of you will be driving us home. This isn't our first rodeo, you know."

"How long have you been seeing him?" Sunny asked, though he already knew the answer.

"Nearly a year now," she said. There was a pause as she took a sip of her drink. The way her gaze lingered on P' Bas made Sunny feel as though he were intruding on something private. "He takes care of me," she said.

"You don't strike me as the kind of girl that needs a guy to take care of her."

"Have you ever been in love?" she asked.

Sunny thought about it for a few seconds. "No," he said. "There were times when… No, I don't think so."

"There were times when what?"

"It doesn't matter. The answer is no."

She looked like she might press the point, but didn't. "Well," she said, her eyes going back to P' Bas, "then you wouldn't understand."

"Try me."

"Love complicates things. You tolerate things you never thought you would, just because you think there's even a slight chance that the person you love feels the same way."

Sunny didn't want to offend her, so he said, very carefully, "Well, there shouldn't be anything complicated about being with you."

"What do you mean?"

Maybe it was the alcohol talking, but he knew it wasn't. "I think you're kind of amazing," he said, looking down at his beer. He could hear P' Bas's laughter rising above the buzz of conversation. "There shouldn't be anything complicated about that."

She didn't say anything in response. Later, one of them grasped a different, more ordinary topic out of thin air, and they continued chatting casually as though Sunny hadn't said anything that could be construed as crossing the line.

An hour or so later, P' Bas strolled over to Sunny and Jun, barely able to stand. He tossed his car keys to Sunny. "You're driving me home, little bro," he said. "And then you're dropping off my girl."

Sunny put down his beer and stood, the car keys gripped in his hand. "Yes, sir," he said.

He knew which car was P' Bas's and headed straight for it, taking care not to look at Jun. She and P' Bas got into the backseat.

The ride to P' Bas's house, which wasn't far from the garage, didn't take long, and P' Bas was too drunk to make conversation.

As Sunny drove, he couldn't help but steal glances at Jun in his rearview mirror. A couple of times, he caught her looking back.

P' Bas stumbled out of the car when they reached his place, a three-storey convenience store with the shutters pulled down. Jun reached out of the car's window to squeeze her boyfriend's hand. "Be careful," she told him tenderly.

Then P' Bas gave a wave and stumbled towards his front door, fiddling with his keys. Jun didn't move to the front seat. "We can go now," she told Sunny.

Sunny stepped on the accelerator. The silence in the car was unbearable. He reached over to turn on the radio and a soft rock song that had been popular a decade before, when he was in primary school, started playing. A song by a band called Taxi. Do you miss me when you don't see me? When you have no one to argue with? Do you think of me, when you want a shoulder to lean on?

Occasionally, Jun would speak up to give Sunny directions, but everything she said was minimal: take a left, another right after the light, up the bridge.

Finally, they arrived at their destination. Her home was a two-storey townhouse far down a narrow side street. But she didn't move to open the car door. He switched off the music.

"Thanks for driving me," Jun said. She pushed herself forward to rest her arms on the back of the front seats, her right hand grazing his left shoulder.

He made a point of staring straight ahead. The dream he'd been trying so hard to forget – her face, bright and luminous, smiling into his – filled his entire vision.

"It's nothing," Sunny replied. "P' Bas is my big brother. I'd do anything for him."

He felt her fingers tugging at the sleeve of his shirt. "I'm sorry if I've been weird or cold with you at times," she said.

"That's okay."

"I don't want you to think that I don't like you."

"I'm trying to be respectful to P' Bas."

"And you are." Her fingers brushed lightly against his shoulder. "Ever since we left the garage, you haven't looked at me. Why won't you look at me?"

"That's not true. I've looked at you."

"Then look again."

He turned, and saw how close her eyes were to his own. Her eyes, her nose, her mouth, parted slightly in annoyance. "I'm looking," he said, a note of challenge in his voice.

And then suddenly she was moving closer to him. Or he was moving closer to her. What did it matter? He tasted the beer on her tongue, and beneath it all a sweetness that reminded him of candy and mint. Her hand found the side of his face, his neck, the plains of his chest.

When they finally broke apart, she rested her forehead against his and they breathed together. He felt like his heart was hammering outside of his skin.

"We shouldn't have done that," he said.

Her hand took hold of his. "We've just been drinking," she said.

"That's not an excuse."

"No, you're right." She sighed. "It's not an excuse."

But then she turned her head again, and he turned his. And together they fell.

//

After that moment with Sunny in front of her house, Jun stopped showing up to the garage with P' Bas.

She and Sunny kept in touch via phone calls and texts. She asked him often: "Can we meet?" But he couldn't bring himself to say yes.

One night on the phone, he once again lapsed into silence at the question. She let out an exasperated sigh. "Do I have to do everything?" she asked.

When he couldn't come up with a reply, she hung up.

Two evenings later, when Sunny was hanging out at the garage on a Friday night, P' Bas came through the gate on his motorcycle. Everything about him was tense: the look in his eyes, the set of his shoulders, his strides when he walked towards Sunny.

All conversations died away. Sunny put down his drink and stood up, bracing himself for whatever might happen. P' Bas rushed towards him, and for one terrifying second Sunny thought P' Bas was about to hit him in the face. He told himself not to flinch. But what P' Bas did was much worse.

He looked Sunny straight in the eye and simply asked: "Is it true?"

The noise Sunny made was half a sob, half a choking sound. "Sir, please—" A surprise: he hadn't expected to hear himself so desperate. "I didn't plan anything…it just happened…"

P' Bas's face darkened, and Sunny realised that his brother had been expecting an excuse. Even a lie. "If I were to ask you to never speak to her again, would you do it?"

Sunny thought of his dream and a recklessness seized hold of him. "I'm sorry, sir," he heard himself say, "but I don't think I can."

P' Bas's eyes hardened. "We're done, then."

"P' Bas, please, I'll...I'll never bring her around. You don't ever have to see us together—"

"This is not about the girl," P' Bas snarled. "There have always been others, you know how it is. But you disrespected me. I took you in and treated you like you were my real brother, and you went behind my back like a coward. You understand that what's about to happen here is entirely your fault, don't you?"

Sunny's eyes scanned the faces of the other boys arrayed behind P' Bas – boys he'd drunk, laughed and shared secrets with. Some looked away from him with pity or shame. Others looked at him with the same anger as P' Bas. He'd never had brothers before.

Sunny swallowed. "Yes, sir," he said. "I do understand."

He walked out of the garage that day with a bust lip, a black eye and the beginnings of a bruise on his forehead, and he never saw his brothers again. He would have new friends, but he never again experienced the closeness he'd had with P' Bas's gang as a teenager.

But he gained something else in return.

//

Things properly began for Sunny and Jun on the phone late that night, and during evening trips to malls and strolls through night markets on weekdays. She successfully snuck him into her bedroom twice. They rented a car for a day, and he drove them to Bang Saen beach, an hour from Bangkok.

They sat on the sand as the sun went down, their hands

entwined and her head on his shoulder, and he thought, Is this what it's supposed to be like?

They never talked about what they were. Never gave a name to it. He didn't even know if she had stopped talking to all the boys who were always messaging her and asking for her number. He told himself it didn't matter either way. He still answered messages from girls, after all, but he knew with certainty that she was the only one who meant anything real to him, and he didn't want to lose her. He still didn't know if his mother's dreams really meant anything, but now he was starting to think that his might.

Jun told Sunny she loved him as they sat together on that beach.

"You don't have to say it back," she said. Then her eyes twinkled. "But I'd be very mad with you if you didn't."

He remembered the garage and the laughter of the boys who'd raised him. Was this all worth it? But she was looking at him, all mischief and heat, and he could feel his heart beating uproariously against her skin as she lifted up her face to kiss him.

So what else could he say but that he loved her too? He thought he did. So very much. For what else could this be except love?

Dao

Dao doesn't quite know what to make of their situation. She asks herself, *Am I happy? I'm not unhappy,* is the answer. There's enough good to outweigh the uncertainty. It is enough.

She replays the moment in front of her dormitory building over and over again in her mind: the tension in the air, that look in Sunny's eyes. It would've been so easy for her to embrace him or simply take his hand. It felt unbearable to be so far apart.

Something has shifted after that night. Her conversations with Sunny now contain more depth, or at least, it feels to her as though they do. She begins to look for a deeper meaning behind everything he says – his choice of words, his tone, even a slight inflection – which might hint at something more.

Christmas comes along, and she spends it in the flat with her friends; they've all decided not to go home for the holidays. It's a small, but warm affair: wine, a roast dinner made mostly by Ella and Simone, and an exchange of presents. Dao gets cards, a knitted scarf from Cady and a deck of oracle cards from Ella. Dao marvels at the beautiful illustrations. They're all done in watercolour style, each containing an affirmation, such as *"There are always shadows that come with light. Do not be scared of your own darkness"*, or *"I am free of all emotional baggage, I now enjoy a state of peaceful balance"*.

"In case you want to do your own readings one day," says Ella, and Dao thanks her excitedly.

They end the night with hot chocolate and a drunken singalong of Christmas classics.

On Boxing Day, Sunny calls to tell her of his own festivities: a subdued, grown-up dinner with his aunt and uncle, followed by a quick evening walk in the park. "It's not too bad, but it is a bit lonely," he tells her. "And the dark doesn't help. I still can't believe it gets dark at 4 p.m. here."

"Really?" she says. "I love it here at Christmas. I wish Christmases in Thailand were like this."

"It would be better if I had more friends to spend it with."

"What do you miss most about home?"

"The food." He chuckles. "My friends. The language. Everything. You?"

She thinks about it for a second. "This might sound strange, but I miss watching old Thai movies and listening to Thai songs with Thai people."

"That's not strange," he says. "I miss that too."

"I really want to see *Pheuan sanit*. I haven't seen it in ages. Oh, and I miss moo ping and sticky rice. I can cook a few basic dishes, but moo ping is too difficult."

"Hang on," says Sunny, his voice perking up. "I actually have an idea."

"What idea?"

"If I said meet me at my place tomorrow evening, would you be up for it?"

She grins. "What are you planning?"

"Yes or no?"

"Can I trust you?"

He laughs. "Don't be silly, of course you can. Yes or no?"

"Yes. Tomorrow evening, right? I'll be there."

//

The next day, Sunny greets her outside the supermarket, leaning against the door and smiling widely and mischievously. He's dressed in a pair of faded jeans and a large grey hoodie, with his hair untidy and falling casually into his eyes. She thinks he's never looked more adorable.

He brings a finger to his lips. "You have to be quiet. My aunt and uncle don't know you're coming."

"So you're trying to get me into trouble, is that it?" But she, too, is smiling from ear to ear.

He shrugs, his eyes alight with excitement. "Let's live a little." He cocks his head towards the entrance. "Come on, let's get inside, it's freezing!"

The supermarket is dark and silent, and Sunny has to use the flashlight from his phone to guide their way up the stairs. "I think this is the first time I've ever been inside a guy's bedroom," Dao whispers.

He blushes and whispers back. "It's nothing shady, I promise!"

After two flights of stairs, they reach his room. He snaps the door shut quietly behind them and switches on the lights.

It is the first time Dao has ever seen where Sunny lives. The place is considerably smaller than her studio flat in the student accommodation, and the only two pieces of furniture in the room – bed and closet – are old. The maroon wallpaper is faded and falling apart, not unlike the brown carpet beneath their feet and the blotchy green curtains he pulls together to cover his single window. She spots a medium-sized suitcase tucked under the bed.

Yet what is truly out of the ordinary is the blanket spread out on the floor. On top of it are two bottles of Oishi green tea and two plates of food. She gasps. "Is that moo ping and sticky rice?"

Sunny is grinning like a little boy now. "Yes, it is. When you mentioned missing it, I asked my aunt to make some. I told her it was for my friends at the language school."

"How did you know I love Oishi green tea?"

"Oh, that's easy," he replies. "You buy it every time you come into the supermarket. I thought we could have some moo ping and sticky rice, and watch *Pheuan sanit* on my laptop. It might help both of us miss home a little less."

She has no idea how she can sum up what this means to her without embarrassing herself. So all she says is: "Sunny, this is amazing. Thank you."

For a second, it looks like he's about to take her hand. Then the moment passes. "Come on," he says. "Try the moo ping. I'll fire up the movie."

They spend the night eating, watching the movie,

laughing and talking in hushed tones so as not to alert his aunt and uncle to her presence. His room is small, but for some reason, it doesn't feel cramped with the two of them. They both drift off to sleep around the same time – him curled up on the floor, her on his bed with his duvet pulled over her head.

Before sleep completely takes her, she hears herself saying, faintly, as though from far away: "It's nice to be here with you."

The sound of his voice echoes back: "It's nice to have you here."

She repeats those words back to herself, time and time again, as she slips into a dreamless sleep. Holds them close to her chest, like a prayer. It's nice to have you here.

//

They wake extremely early the next morning, sneaking downstairs without getting noticed by Sunny's aunt and uncle, and decide to walk the twenty minutes to Dean Village.

It's a cold and windy day, but the two of them are chatting and laughing still, high from the intimacy of last night. There aren't many people out on the streets, and many of the shops and restaurants are still shut for the holidays, but the sound of their voices rings in the air in a way that makes Dao feel young and hopeful.

Dao has been to Dean Village a few times before during her early days in the city when she went out exploring often. She has fallen in love with the statue of the goddess of healing, a regal marble woman holding a cup in her hand, with her face turning to the side in serenity. Dao loves the cluster of classic brick houses, with their brightly coloured doors and their chimneys. The Water of Leith winds its way through. At certain points, it rushes by like a beast; at others, it trickles like a lullaby. The grass beneath their feet is frozen, bits of snow, sleet and fallen leaves clinging to it.

It's the first time Sunny has ever been here. She finds herself observing his reaction as they walk down the path by the water together, wanting him to be in awe of the place as much as she is. She has brought her camera with her, and sometimes she lifts it up to capture his expressions as he studies a particularly beautiful spot.

"I know you're homesick," Dao tells him, "but we don't have places like this back home."

He gives her another of his adorable smiles. "You're right, we don't. You win this round."

She urges him to stop where the path expands into a small field. There's a wooden bridge in the distance and a waterfall to their right. On the banks of the water, there is a memorial carved into stone. They read the words engraved there together: *If I should ever leave you whom I love, to go along the silent way, grieve not, nor speak of me with tears. But laugh and talk of me as if I were beside you there.*

She takes a step back and lifts her camera. He turns sideways to look at her, smiling against the backdrop of the trees and the river and the clear blue sky.

"Do I get paid for this?" he asks, teasing.

"Shut it, you." She lines up her shot. "This is an artistic process. Don't you want to be part of an artistic process?"

"I'm not a model."

"You don't have to be. As the photographer, it's my job to capture the essence of who you are."

"The essence?" He grins, his eyes shining playfully. "Why are you being so dramatic?"

"Shut up," she says again. "Do you want me to take a bad picture that ruins your essence?"

He laughs, and she clicks the shutter once, twice, thrice. "Now turn to face me fully," she instructs him.

He rolls his eyes, but obliges.

Afterwards, she walks up to him to show him the pictures. They're all close-ups of his face, every line of his expression bold and pronounced. He doesn't speak for a few seconds.

"What?" she asks, her heart sinking. "Do you hate them?"

"No." He shakes his head. "Of course not. It's just…I don't think I've ever seen pictures of myself like these before."

"Is that a good thing or a bad thing?"

"It's a good thing."

"How so?"

"I look…" – he furrows his brows – "…not like myself."

"Really? What do you mean?"

He stops at one particular picture. "I look…I don't know…all put together. I look…happy. I look…" – he rubs his jaw, his eyes intently focused on the camera – "…like someone with substance."

"You *are* someone with substance," she assures him. For whatever reason, every time he seems upset, she feels a strong desire to remedy it.

"I don't know, I hope so," he replies hesitantly.

She tosses her head back and turns her chin up resolutely. "Well," she says, "I like these pictures. Especially the ones of you smiling. I like your smile. You look…kind."

She can't tell what he's thinking. But then he shakes his head and takes the camera from her, his eyes sparkling again. "It's my turn now," he says. "Let me take a picture of you."

"Sunny, no! That's not what's happening here!"

"Come on! You've taken nearly twenty pictures of me! How is that fair?"

"I'm not a model! I'm a photographer!"

"Well, I'm not a model either! Come on!" He takes her by the arm and drags her to the spot where he'd been standing earlier, with the waterfall behind her.

She rolls her eyes and pouts. "I can't believe you're making me do this."

"Start posing." He steps back and lifts the camera. "Come on, let me capture your *essence!*"

She laughs. "You're terrible!"

He starts snapping. "Yes, like that! Keep laughing!"

She covers her face with her hands. "This is so embarrassing! Don't make me look ugly, please!"

He scoffs, lowers the camera and fixes her with a look. The corners of his mouth curve up in a smile that makes her stomach do somersaults. "That's literally impossible," he says.

She is quite sure that she is floating. She holds his gaze and smiles back. Feels the spark crackling through her entire body from the way he's looking at her.

And she tells herself: surely now, they aren't *just* friends. Her dream has to be coming true.

//

After Dao gets home that evening, she takes out the oracle cards Ella had got her for Christmas.

It's her first time doing a reading for herself, but somehow, she's not nervous. She sits down cross-legged on the floor, in the middle of her room, and shuffles the cards before spreading them out face down in a half circle as she'd seen fortune tellers do.

Then she shuts her eyes and breathes in, out, in, out, focusing intently on the scrambling, desperate *need to know* what's inside of her.

She pulls out one card and flips it over. When she opens her eyes, she sees a picture of a field of sunflowers, growing on the side of a hill. Behind the hill is a blue sky, the sun as bright as the flowers beneath.

The message on the card stares up at her like a beacon: *Believe in your dreams. The impossible is more possible than you think. Have faith that Divine Timing is in control of your life.*

And she lets out a long, calming breath.

Dao

Dao and Shane quickly became inseparable, eating lunch together every day in the school cafeteria, sharing late-night phone calls, and spending afternoons and evenings together at malls. But most of all, they obsessed about photography.

Dao started with Shane's film camera first, quickly learning to master its many quirks and moods. Before long, it became more natural, even easier, for her to see the world through its lens. Everything that felt too wild and unkempt made more sense when she could confine the vastness of life into a single frame. Her very existence felt richer when she could capture something profound – an expression, a place, a moment – with just a movement of her finger.

She and Teoy became closer, too. And it was the first time Dao ever felt like she had a best friend. But Teoy never took much interest in Dao and Shane's obsession with photography.

"I much prefer to do something fun," Teoy explained. "Not something so...contemplative. Besides..." – she looked at Dao with a meaningful glint in her eyes – "...I don't want to get in between you and Shane."

And Dao would always look away and mutter in response: "There is nothing between me and Shane."

But if Dao were to admit it to herself, deep in her heart of hearts, she knew that that wasn't entirely true. However undefined or subtle, there was, undeniably, something.

With other people, Shane was shy and quiet, just like he was when Dao first met him. He rarely betrayed what he was thinking or feeling through his expressions, always a cool, silent mask that only rippled in annoyance or subtle humour. But with Dao, he found a comfort that made him come alive.

Whenever they were together, they always had something to talk about. Their thoughts connected and flared into sentences, like a match catching fire with a strike. They shared and discussed various topics without reservation – their past, present, future. Prompted by her careful questions, he let himself be cracked open.

"What do you think of this?" he asked her often, whether about a photograph he just took, a movie they just saw, a lesson they just learned or something new happening in their lives. And then he would listen while she unburdened her mind.

She found herself opening up to him more than she ever had with anyone in her life. And the more she did it, the more she felt as though she was sharing things she had wanted to share all along. She'd just never had anyone to share them with.

She told him about the girls in school who made her life such misery. He reassured her that they were nothing but bullies. "They're jealous, like Teoy said. You're smarter than them. A better person."

He couldn't see it, but she blushed. "Thank you for listening," she said.

"You're welcome," he said. A pause. "I've never been able to talk to anyone like I can talk to you."

"I feel the same way," she replied, and her heart took flight.

It felt dramatic – all teenage angst and pretentiousness – to say so many of these things out loud. But it felt freeing, too: knowing, for the first time, that someone is capable of holding all your messy thoughts in their hands without wanting to crush them or laugh at them.

He showed her a photograph he took once: of her sitting in the school cafeteria, her face turned to the side as she chatted with Teoy, who wasn't in the frame. Dao had always hated seeing herself in photos, and thought that her side profile looked unattractive. But the way Shane had managed to capture her was surprising. For the first time, she liked her own smile, even the shape of her cheeks, and there was a warm, radiant quality to her eyes that spread to the rest of her face.

Later that night, after he had given her the photo, they talked on the phone. He said: "That's my favourite picture of you so far."

"I like it," she said. "Even though my hair looks a bit weird."

"It's not weird." A pause. "I think you look pretty."

It was the first time anyone had ever said that to her. It made her glow from the inside, a soaring, giddy sensation that came from feeling like she was finally special to someone. She wanted to see him in that very moment, to touch a hand to his cheek and sink into his skin, and tell him all the things she whispered to herself in the night.

//

When they were sixteen years old, Shane and Dao went to a movie together at Major Ekkamai, a small shopping mall not far from their school and Dao's home. Afterwards, they had dinner at a Japanese restaurant and then went to a bowling alley so she could try her hand at it for the first time. He taught her how to hold the ball, how to aim and swing her hand back, and the precise moment she should let go.

They played one game, and then, after he beat her thoroughly, another. She was atrocious; so many of her throws went down the gutter. He, on the other hand, was able to rack up the points.

Midway through their third game, they sat down for a break, ordering cans of Coke and nachos. She moaned about her losses, teasing him that she'd done so badly because of his terrible coaching. It felt so easy, how he laughed along with her and teased her back.

"This was fun," he told her when they said goodbye at the Skytrain. "Thanks for inviting me. The movie was okay, but the bowling was fun."

"Thanks for coming," she replied, a huge smile plastered on her face. "I was bored, and there was nothing else to do, so...you know...it was alright." She shrugged and made a face to mock him.

He rolled his eyes. "You keep telling yourself that. But I know you had fun, too."

Had she been that transparent with her feelings? She stammered in a slight panic: "Why do you say that?"

"Easy," he said. "I make you laugh."

All the fear went out of her, and her smile returned: perhaps there was hope after all. What an immeasurable high, she marvelled to herself later, when you could simply be this close to someone without touching them.

She drifted off to sleep that night to the sound of his voice ringing in her ears.

But then, in the early hours of the morning, just when her body had been lulled into a state of complete surrender, she dreamed.

A new dream this time, but no less terrifying.

For once, she was no longer being chased. Instead, the dream started out as peaceful and comforting, with Shane's smile filling her entire vision. The sight of it seemed to burn a hole inside her chest, the excitement pulsing along with the beating of her heart.

His touch was a breeze on her skin. She felt him moving closer and closer...

Then suddenly the dream changed...

The colours, like in the dream about her father, faded away. She could feel the presence of another person in the room with them – a stranger, whose eyes were drawing Shane away from hers.

Like it had done during her youth, darkness descended, and before she could cry out for help, the rain had already begun to fall.

When she woke, there were tears on her cheeks.

//

A week later, rumours began swirling among the students in the class: someone had spotted Shane at the cinema in Major Ekkamai with a girl from a different school.

The statement slipped from someone's lips so nonchalantly during English class, as though it didn't have the power to shatter Dao's entire world. "My friend in B Class saw him," said one of the popular girls. "They looked close."

Everyone began to speculate on which school the girl could be from based on the description of her uniform. Teoy turned to look at Dao with a worried expression. "Did he tell you about this?" Teoy asked.

It took everything within Dao to keep her face neutral. "No," she replied. "But the two of us are just friends. He doesn't owe me an explanation. He can date whoever he wants."

Later, Dao fled to the restroom, locked herself in a stall and pressed a hand to her mouth to stop a sob from bursting out. She thought of the dream she'd had a week ago and how it shifted from happiness to devastation so quickly. She'd thought he was moving closer to her in the dream – she could almost feel his lips on hers – but then he'd turned away.

She should have known then. Her dreams had always meant something.

Dao didn't talk to Shane in school that day, but she couldn't resist texting him that night. It was about something mundane, like how good her dinner was. Anything just to start a conversation. But he didn't reply until the next morning. When he did, it was a short and abrupt: That's nice. *And nothing more.*

They didn't talk for the next three days. Her parents began to notice that she was feeling down, but there was nothing they could say to make her reveal the cause of her misery. Dao already knew that her having feelings for a boy would be something they would disapprove of. Dating while still at school had been strictly forbidden since the day her mother had taken her to buy her very first training bra.

On the fourth day, Shane found Dao at recess and asked if anything was wrong.

"Nothing," she said, attempting a smile. "Anything wrong with you?"

"No," he replied, "but listen…"

She asked him point-blank: "Are you seeing someone?"

He looked down. "Yes," he said. "She goes to my brother's school."

"How long has it been?" she asked.

"Three months," he said.

"Three months?" Dread and embarrassment washed over her. "Why didn't you tell me?"

"I didn't know how to," he mumbled. "I'm sorry."

"Aren't we friends?"

"Of course," he said.

"Then you should have told me."

"I'm sorry," he repeated.

She, too, looked down at the ground. They were standing a few feet apart, near the traditional Thai house the school had converted into a stationery shop. The sounds of chatter and laughter from the cafeteria filled the air.

"Are we okay?" Shane asked.

Dao swallowed and nodded. "Yeah, we're good."

//

After that, more dreams about Shane began.

Not very often, but enough. Just short, fragmented ones. There were dreams in which Dao would feel the warmth of his smile, the softness of his voice, and everything felt easy and simple. Yet she had no way of knowing if it was her hand he was holding in those dreams or someone else's.

A few months later, Dao asked Shane again about the girl. He shook his head, avoided her eyes and said they had broken up.

Hope ignited within Dao. But then, a few months after, the cycle would repeat itself: another girlfriend, another lapse in their friendship and then another break-up, and then the two of them would reconnect.

She quickly learned that, as quiet as Shane was in large crowds, girls were drawn to him, and he to them, and, as a result, he was rarely unattached.

He never discussed who he dated with Dao, and she resisted the urge to ask. It was one of the very few topics they never talked about.

"You're my very first guy friend," she told him once. They were spending the day together, slipping in and out of art galleries by the Chao Phraya river so she could take some pictures. "But I'm glad you're someone else's headache."

He laughed, and they both pretended that the joke was sincere.

"Yeah," he said, "but I'm not close to anyone else like I'm close to you."

And that made her think: So this has to mean something more, right? It has to.

Sunny

Sunny feels as though he's caught in a constant battle between his head and his heart. There's an ease and comfort in his relationship with Dao that he's never experienced with anyone else before. He knows, without a shadow of a doubt, that she cares deeply about him, and that if he's ever in trouble, she'd climb into the trenches with him in a heartbeat. Yet somehow that knowledge terrifies him.

Is he even a man who's capable of doing the same for her? What if, somewhere down the line, her feelings for him were to change? And his for her? He tries to imagine a universe in which the two of them could walk in a shopping mall or down the streets of Bangkok together, holding hands.

The world simply gives way to people like Dao. Everything she wants, she can get at her fingertips. He remembers when she first stepped inside his bedroom: he thought he saw a look of surprise on her face. His little room must be a complete contrast to her swanky, expensive student accommodation. He tries to imagine a scene in which he brings her back to his family's hardware shop, so different from where she lives in Ekkamai. Their two families sitting down together for dinner and it being a normal, ordinary, everyday thing. He tries to imagine what it would be like – all that she is, alongside someone like him, their two different worlds colliding. No matter how hard he tries, he can't picture it.

Yet he finds himself being swept up by all the little things, like talking to her on the phone until they both fall asleep, and making her laugh. He likes being near her. In her company he's never invisible, never an afterthought, and the grey of Edinburgh fades in her presence. She brings more colour into his world, more life. A light, breaking through the fog that often clouds his mind.

He could have made a move to kiss her anytime during the night that she came over. But he did nothing.

"Lately, I think you've become my best friend," Dao tells him.

He smiles into the phone. "I think you've become mine as well."

And he thinks of his dream, coiled deep inside him, the one that sounds so similar to Dao's, which he hadn't been brave enough to share.

He'd been foolish many times before by allowing himself to believe that something could be written in the stars – first with his mother, then with Jun. He will never do so again.

//

One evening, Noon calls Sunny out of the blue while he's walking home from his English class.

Usually, they would only text, either late at night or early morning. Confused, Sunny picks up as fast as he can.

"What's wrong?" he asks at once.

There is quiet at the end of the line.

"Noon, what's going on?" he asks again. "Talk to me."

A few more seconds of silence. "Where are you, P' Sunny?"

"I just left school, I'm walking home. I'm near the Meadows. What's going on?"

He hears her breathe in a ragged sob. The sound alarms him; he has never heard her voice so much as tremble with sadness. "Noon, what's happened?" he presses.

"Can you come over?"

"What's wrong?"

"This guy…I've been sort of seeing…he…"

Sunny quickens his pace. "Are you alone?"

"I am now. He just left. He got angry."

"About what?"

"Does it matter? Men like this always find a reason."

"Did he hurt you?"

"He…took my arm…and he pushed me down…then he grabbed me and…" She trails off, but the implication of what happened next is heard loud and clear.

Sunny increases his speed to nearly a jog. "Send me your address."

When Sunny gets to Noon's flat it's nearly nine in the evening.

Noon only opens the door for him after he's knocked several times and called to tell her that it really is him standing outside. Her eyes are red and puffy from crying, her hair in disarray and her face starkly pale. He notices, right away, a bruise starting to purple around her jaw.

"I'm sorry, I didn't know who else to call," Noon says, her voice shaking.

It feels strange and awkward to be alone with Noon in her flat: a one-bed studio with a small sitting area and an even smaller kitchen. The place is a mess, with clothes and empty meal boxes strewn everywhere. An old, lumpy brown sofa is in front of the TV. She sits down on it and grabs a bottle of cheap wine from the floor.

He takes off his shoes at the door and joins her there. "Have you eaten anything?" he asks.

"I'm not hungry."

She doesn't look at him, but begins to pull up the sleeves of the oversized jumper she's wearing to reveal more bruises along her arms. The rage that cuts through him makes him feel as though his head might explode from the pain.

"Who's the guy?" he asks through gritted teeth.

"It doesn't matter."

"Noon—"

"It doesn't matter," she bites back. "I didn't call because I needed you to be heroic. I called because I needed someone to come and just sit with me."

"Has this ever happened to you before?"

"Once. Years ago." Noon's voice is strangely steady. "I didn't think it'd happen again. But I'm lucky. It could have been much, much worse."

He can't explain all the emotions that are battling inside of him, only that the rage is giving way to a heavy, familiar fear pushing down on him like a sudden fever. He's thinking of his father's closed office door and his mother's downward glance at the dinner table whenever her husband's voice is raised. Silence in the family car and his father's long and unexplained absences. Fortune tellers flipping over tarot cards and looking at his mother with pity in their eyes.

Noon wordlessly passes Sunny the wine bottle. He doesn't really drink wine, but takes a sip anyway. The unfamiliar taste causes him to wince.

"Why don't you go home?" he asks. He knows that Noon's mother, stepfather and stepsister live on the outskirts of Edinburgh, although he doesn't know exactly where.

Noon shakes her head. "Too many questions. I don't want them to worry." She turns to him. "Can you stay for a while?" Her voice is uncharacteristically small and uncertain.

He nods. "Of course. I can stay for as long as you need me to."

//

Sunny gets home at just after six in the morning, after Noon has finally fallen asleep.

It's after midday in Bangkok. He's exhausted, and functioning on less than an hour of sleep, but after crashing on his bed, he calls his younger sister, Fai.

"Hello?" His sister sounds confused. "What time is it over there now? Why are you up so early?"

"I just wanted to check on you and Ma."

"P' Sunny, are you drunk?"

"A little," he admits. The wine has given him a headache. He presses two fingers to his temple, massaging it.

"We can talk tomorrow," says Fai.

"How's Ma? I was helping a friend out, so I didn't get the chance to call her yesterday."

Fai sighs. "She's the same. Nothing's different here except that Father seems angrier than he usually is."

"Did anything happen?"

"You know Father," says Fai. "But if I were to bet money on it…he's been angrier than usual since you left. He's just taking it out on Ma because he can."

Sunny swallows. "It's not her fault. It was her idea, but I was the one who made the choice."

"I think Father is punishing her for it by ignoring her. I've tried to talk to him, but you know how he is. Also…" Here, Sunny notices the caution seeping into his sister's voice. "He's been gone from home a lot. We don't know where he goes."

The memory comes to Sunny: the woman, in the Citroën. Sunny tries to keep his voice normal. "He's always done that, gone off on his own. You and Ma shouldn't worry."

"I know, but lately he's been gone a lot more."

"Keep me updated, okay, Fai?"

"Do you know something?"

"Just keep me updated."

"P' Sunny, I doubt anything could get worse."

Sunny shuts his eyes. "It can always get worse."

//

Thankfully, Sunny isn't on shift the next day, so he's able to sleep as long as he wants. He wakes to find that it's almost three in the afternoon. His headache is now gone, but he's desperately thirsty.

He drinks an entire bottle of water in one go, brushes his teeth, showers, puts on fresh clothes and arrives downstairs to find his Aunt Oom behind the till. He gives her a *wai* in greeting by bringing his hands together in deference.

Sunny is struck, again, by how very different his aunt is from his mother. Even though they're sisters, they seem to be complete opposites.

Sunny's mother is short and petite; Aunt Oom is considered tall for a Thai woman. Sunny's mother has white hair, her movements careful and considered, while Aunt Oom's hair is dyed jet black, her energy always sharp and no-nonsense. Sunny can't imagine his mother ever moving to another country and opening her own business like his aunt has done.

When Ma had suggested that Sunny should come to Scotland to stay with Aunt Oom, she'd said regretfully: "I didn't raise you as well as I should have. Look at my sister's children. They're happy. Content. They seem to adore her."

"I adore you," Sunny had replied.

"You love me," she corrected him. "There's a difference. You love me, you dislike your father, and you resent both of us." And he couldn't tell her she was wrong, because she wasn't.

"You look terrible," Aunt Oom tells him matter-of-factly. "What were you out doing last night?"

"Nothing bad, Auntie, I promise."

"You know I hate to ask. So don't make me have to quite so often."

"I understand. I'm sorry if I made you worry. There's really no need to."

His aunt flips over the page of the magazine she's been reading. She looks at him with scepticism, and then shakes her head. "Off with you," she says. "Just don't come home late again."

"Yes, Auntie."

He practically dashes out of the supermarket. The weather is colder than usual today. He pulls his gloves out of the pocket of his jacket, puts them on and starts to walk, though he has no idea where his feet will take him.

Before he knows it, he's at the door of Dao's building. He calls her and she picks up after the second ring.

"Sunny?"

The sound of her voice stumps him for a second.

"Sunny, are you okay?" she asks. There's a trace of anger, of annoyance in her voice. He realises she's probably mad at him for not replying to any of her messages. Still he doesn't say anything.

"What's wrong?" Dao presses. Then her anger is replaced by concern: "Sunny, what's the matter?"

He swallows. "I'm just outside your building. Are you home? Can I come up?"

A pause. Then..."Alright," she says. "Hang on, I'll come down to get you."

"Thank you."

She comes down bundled up in a grey winter coat so huge it reaches below her knees, and opens the door of the building to let him in.

For a second, they stand there awkwardly in the empty lobby, looking at each other uncertainly. Her hair is pulled up in a sloppy ponytail, her face bare, except for a thin sheen of gloss on her lips. He can tell that she wants to ask him why he's here, and he realises he doesn't really have an answer. He only knows that there's no one else he wants to talk to right now except her.

"Are you okay?" Dao asks again.

He shakes his head. "I don't think I am," he replies.

A look of understanding appears in her eyes. She nods, as though landing on a decision, and takes a step towards him.

He has no idea what she's about to do; everything is happening too fast. Before he can gather himself, she's wrapping her arms around his neck and pulling his head to rest on her shoulder. It's the first time they have ever embraced. The first time anyone has held him in…he can't even remember how long.

He feels a tide of emotions rising up. He clamps down on them, burying his face in her skin. He doesn't know how long they stand there, holding each other. But he can feel her heart beating fast through her chest.

When it's time to let go, they do so simultaneously. Yet her right hand is around his wrist. Yet she is standing in his space. She stares at him with a look he can't read. And he decides that, whatever the consequences, he no longer cares about what might happen next.

He reaches out a hand to trace the bottom of her chin – tenderly, reverently – as her face lifts up to his in surprise. Then he bends down and kisses her.

Dao

It's Dao's first kiss, and it doesn't last very long. She starts laughing and he pulls away almost immediately. "Is this okay?" he asks, concern flooding his face.

"No, no, it's fine," she says hurriedly, laughing still. His hand is in hers; it's calloused and rough, but she grips it tight. "I just wasn't expecting it, that's all."

She's lightheaded. Dazed. She brings his hand up to her lips and holds it there.

His expression shifts, confusion giving way to urgency. "Come on," he says.

They walk through the lobby and take the lift up to her floor, hands clasped, arms entangled, lips brushing against skin. The clinking of her keys as she lets them in. She kicks the door shut behind them with her foot. They remove their shoes, shrug off their coats and hang them on the pegs next to her wardrobe.

A standard dormitory studio, with a desk, a bed, a cubicle-sized bathroom and a small kitchen area with a window that overlooks the courtyard. Still, she reflects, very different from his small, worn-down bedroom in the Thai supermarket.

She lets go of his hand and spins around. "So this is me," she says, trying to sound casual. She waves her hand at the room. "Welcome."

She expects him to reply, but he's moving towards her. Then his hands begin to trail up her arms until he's cupping her face close to his.

This time, the kiss lasts much longer. She lets her mouth open for his, lets him lead. Then lets herself push back and take him wherever she wants to go. He makes a noise in the back of his throat, and the sound spurs her on and wakes something within her that she hadn't been sure even existed.

Eventually he pulls away, grinning. "I can't believe that was your first kiss."

Her eyes grow wide. "Was it bad?" she asks, her heart sinking.

"Of course not," he says. "It wasn't bad at all. In fact, it was quite the opposite."

She breaks into a smile. Once again, she's lightheaded. Dazed. He caresses her cheek gently. "You can trust me," he says.

She sees the light dancing in his eyes, and she nods.

Then they're kissing again. And then they are drowning, all the thoughts – the hows and the whys, and whether this is a good idea – fleeing from her mind. And then she is the one pulling him to her, wanting them to be closer. She's tugging at his shirt, at his wrist, leading him to the softness of her bed. They're both laughing. She'd never imagined there'd be so much laughing.

"I'm telling you right now," she says, in between them catching their breaths, "if this turns out to be an unenjoyable experience, I'm never going to speak to you again."

His smile mirrors her. He's so handsome, she thinks. "You can trust me," he repeats.

His mouth finds the spot below her right ear, then her neck. Her hands bring him to the rest of her, her fingers guiding him as he undresses her. The yellow light from her night lamp shines against her skin, which pulses and comes alive with every one of his touches. It still feels too soon for her to go all the way – there will be time for more, much more – so she whispers to him all the things she's ready for and all the things she isn't, what she wants and how she wants it.

Afterwards, they lie curled up next to each other in bed. They don't talk about anything serious, simply make each other laugh with sweet compliments, jokes, random observations. Their entwined hands rest on top of the duvet, and occasionally she brings his up to her lips. His arms continue to hold her, and she feels like she might float up to the ceiling and never come down.

As it starts to get late, their conversation ceases. She leans in and kisses him again. "I don't want to leave," he tells her.

"Then stay," she says.

A little while later, as she's lying still in his arms with her eyes closed, she can feel herself drifting off to sleep. The sound of his breathing gives the silence a safe and peaceful rhythm. The world begins to turn unimaginably soft.

And then she hears her own voice, faintly, as if from a great distance, unbidden and unrehearsed: "I think it was you. It was you all along…the one in my dream."

Sunny

At first, Sunny thinks he must have misheard. Her voice is so low, barely audible, the words coming out muffled against the duvet she's pulled up to her chin. She doesn't open her eyes, and he lies completely still, pretending to sleep, too shocked and scared to move, until she eventually falls into a deep slumber.

Dao's bedroom is exceptionally comfortable, much larger and more modern than his, and she's decorated it with lights, pictures and little trinkets that make the place feel personal, like a real home. So unlike his own.

As he lies awake, he goes over what happened earlier in the night in great detail. He remembers how he and Dao had laughed in between their kisses. How every time they broke apart, he could still taste the sweetness of her laughter on his tongue.

His mother would have said: "Now you have found her. The girl in your dreams." He can almost see the knowing, pleased look in his mother's eyes. Or are these simply his own thoughts, playing tricks?

The visit to Noon has saddened him. The phone call with his sister has somehow made it worse. He's done it all without thinking, he realises – showing up at Dao's flat, kissing her and everything that had happened after.

Is he supposed to say something now, after she's woken up? With girls he'd been seeing over the last few years in Thailand, they'd simply left after the encounter with the unspoken understanding that this wouldn't turn into anything more. A casual friendship, maybe, or a good time. Nothing serious or meaningful.

But Dao has told him about her dream and what she believes it to mean. Did she intend for him to hear what she said? Does she really think that he's her 'pair', as the fortune teller had predicted?

He already knows the answer to that. This is Dao, of course she would want more than a casual fling. She deserves more. It *should* be more. Shouldn't it?

The responsibility and expectation descend on Sunny like the gloom of Scottish winter. With them comes a fear that makes him think of his mother and his father, sitting on the edge of his bed that rainy day after he saw the woman in the Citroën.

Do we really have any say at all in choosing our own lives and loves? Or is everything already pre-determined and written – by our parents, by past lovers who've damaged us, or by a higher power, perhaps, meticulously slotting us into a grander narrative of which we have no understanding?

Or is everything, Sunny thinks, simply a product of us tripping over our own feet and grabbing hold of each other in the dark, trying to give shapes and names to meaningless things?

He can't sleep.

He reaches for his phone, which is on Dao's bedside table, moving carefully so as not to wake her. It's four in the morning.

Dao

Dao has never slept in the same bed as a man before. And she doesn't understand why, now that it's happened, she feels a sense of accomplishment. She replays certain moments from the last few hours as she lies curled up in Sunny's arms. Every part of her body hums with electricity, yet she feels safe and at peace.

For what seems like the hundredth time she thinks of the dream and the reading that came after. The man she saw: it has never been Jamie. It's Sunny, she thinks. It's been Sunny all along. She's sure of it.

She dwells on the dream. The warmth and light of it, the inevitability of the two of them finding each other. And the comfort of that vision lulls her to sleep.

//

Dao wakes in the morning to find Sunny sitting on the bed. The sound of him putting on his clothes and his shoes. "What's going on?" she mumbles. She's immediately aware of how dry her mouth is. It's still dark in the room. "What time is it?" she asks.

"It's nearly five." He's sitting with his back to her as he grabs his shirt from the floor. "I need to go back home and get ready for my shift."

"Oh." She hears the disappointment in her voice. She sits up, clutching the duvet to her chest. "There's still time…you can stay…"

"I need to go back and shower." He sounds abrupt. Exhausted. "And I didn't really sleep that well last night, so I might catch a nap in my own bed."

All she can think to say is: "Okay."

He looks over his shoulder at her. "Go back to sleep," he says.

"Are you sure you're alright?"

"Yes, I'm alright." He leans over and kisses her on the cheek. "Go back to sleep," he repeats.

She lies back down and watches as he puts on his coat, opens the door and steps out of her room. He pauses to give her one last look, but it's too dark, and the moment too brief, for her to read his expression.

"I'll see you," he says. And then he's gone.

Sunny

The world is waking up slowly as Sunny emerges out of Dao's building and into the cold. A few cars are already on the road and early morning buses zoom past. Commuters on their way to work trudge along, faces devoid of emotion.

As Sunny joins them, despite having been in a warm room for hours, the cold quickly latches onto him. He sticks his hands into his jacket pockets, and the breath he lets out turns to fog in front of his face.

He has barely slept and is tired to the bone. But what exhausts him more are the thoughts in his head.

Thankfully, his aunt and uncle haven't yet come down to open the supermarket, so he's able to make his way upstairs without having to answer questions. He takes a long shower and stands under the hot water with his eyes closed in an attempt to quieten the scurrying inside his mind. Then he towels himself dry, pulls on a pair of boxers and a hoodie, cranks up the small portable heater his aunt had dug out of the attic for him and crashes on the bed.

His shift starts at eight. He has less than three hours to catch some rest.

In the comforts and familiarities of his own room, he finally succumbs to the fatigue, and sleep takes over.

Dao

Dao wakes again a little after noon to a roaring headache. For a second, she's disoriented. Then her eyes land on the spot next to her where Sunny had been. She checks her phone. No messages.

She rolls over to lie spreadeagled on the bed. Thinks. Is there some sort of protocol to all of this? This is her first experience; she can hardly be expected to know.

Then she texts Simone: *So Sunny stayed over last night…*

Out of all her friends in Edinburgh, Dao knows that Simone is the only one who would immediately understand the significance of what has happened. Even though they grew up half a world apart, there are many overlaps in the way they were brought up.

Sure enough, Simone replies almost immediately: *Are you okay?*

Dao has to think about the answer to that question for a couple of minutes. Then she types back: *I feel a bit weird. Don't know why. Not sure if I'm happy or sad or a bit of both. And then I'm confused about why I feel anything at all. Shouldn't it be no big deal?*

Simone texts back: *But maybe it is a big deal to you.*

Dao has no answer to that.

Simone texts again: *Do you want me to come over?*

No, that's okay, Dao replies. *I'll see you in class.*

She takes her time going through her morning routine, humming absentmindedly. The more she thinks of Sunny – the things he'd whispered, his touches and caresses – the more she feels herself to be glowing, and smiling to herself in the mirror. She feels strangely sensitive, as though she's floating outside of her skin, fragile and wonderfully breakable.

Sunny

Sunny is woken by the sound of his aunt and uncle walking down the stairs to open the supermarket. His head is foggy, as if he has a hangover. The events of last night rush back to him, and he checks his phone to see if Dao has messaged him, but she hasn't.

Instead there's one from Noon. *Thank you for staying with me last night, P' Sunny*, she'd texted. *I really appreciate you being there for me.*

A wave of shame washes over him. What happened with Dao had consumed his thoughts so much, he'd forgotten the whole ordeal with Noon. He sends her a quick reply, *No worries. Let me know how you get on*, and gets up to get ready for his morning shift.

He keeps thinking about what he should say to Dao today. Is there anything he's supposed to say?

He'd told her she could trust him. But now, in the cold light of day, he's not sure what he meant by it. She could trust him with what? Is he even a trustworthy person? Looking back at his track record with women, he's afraid that he's already fallen short.

Most of all, should he address what he'd heard her say,

just as they were falling asleep? The weight of her dream and the pedestal it places him on has become no lighter after he's slept. The memory of her words still terrifies him.

He takes the stairs down two at a time. He can hear his aunt talking to her husband in a quiet voice, but not so quiet that he can't make out what they're saying. "Where is that boy?" his aunt is saying. "He better not be late. Sometimes I worry about what it did to him, growing up in that house."

Dao

When she sits down for her afternoon lecture, Dao's mind is still racing with thoughts of last night with Sunny.

As the lesson progresses, she's unable to retain any of the information her professor is delivering. Instead she begins to think about the fact that half the day has gone and Sunny has still not reached out.

Yes, he'd left early, without saying much, but wasn't that because he was tired and he had to go to work? He'd told her that nothing was wrong, but did *she* do something wrong? Did he feel so uncomfortable in her room, in her bed, that he couldn't rest?

And then a memory from when she was at the edge of sleep comes back to her. *"I think it was you. It was you all along...the one in my dream."*

Dread overwhelms her, and she wishes nothing more than to cover her face with her hands and disappear.

After the lesson, Ella, Cady and Simone come up to ask if she wants to join them at a nearby pub for food.

Dao declines. "I have somewhere I need to be," she tells them.

She checks her phone. Still no text from Sunny. This makes her even more anxious, but she recalls the dream and tells herself: there must be a perfectly good explanation.

And if he'd heard what she'd said last night, she could let him know that she really didn't mean to pressure him or scare him away; she was simply caught up in the moment. If he has feelings for her too, he'll understand, won't he?

On the walk to the supermarket, Dao decides to call him.

Sunny

Sunny is grateful that the supermarket is busy today. The more he has something to focus on, the more he can avoid thinking about everything that's happened.

A few of the customers come to the till to chat to him about Thai food and their trips to Thailand. He stammers through their conversations. His aunt comes in from the back room around noon to make an order on the phone. Then she's gone again, breezing out the door to meet with her Thai friends for an event at the temple.

Around three in the afternoon, when the shop is relatively empty, Dao rings him.

Sunny doesn't know why he's surprised to see her name flash across his screen. But he stares at it, and doesn't pick up. The words he'd heard her say last night – *"It was you all along, the one in my dream"* – echo loudly.

Eventually, the ringing stops.

Sunny curses himself, thinking: *Do you have to be cruel as well as a coward?*

He steadies himself for a few seconds. Then calls her back.

"Hey, sorry," he says, once she picks up. "I had a customer."

This, too, is another lie.

Dao

Sunny sounds different on the phone, all tense and strained. But at least he's called her back, right?

Dao hears herself stammering: "Oh. It's okay. I was just calling to check up on you, that's all. I haven't heard from you since last night."

A few seconds of silence. She stops as the light turns red for pedestrians.

"Where are you?" Sunny asks. "Don't you have class?"

"I just finished," she says. "I'm…actually on my way to see you at the supermarket."

"Oh."

And just from that single syllable, she knows: he hadn't wanted to see her at all.

The embarrassment is much worse than the initial panic. Things aren't supposed to happen this way. Eventually, she manages to say: "If you're busy, I can just go home?"

"No, no," he says hurriedly. "You've already come all this way, it's okay."

"I don't want to come if you don't want me to."

"I didn't say I didn't want you to."

She bites down on her bottom lip to stop her voice from shaking. "Okay," she says. "I'll come. And...can we talk?"

"Alright," he says. "We'll talk."

"I'll see you in a bit."

"See you," he says, and hangs up.

She stands and waits for the light to change.

Sunny

Sunny and Dao end up talking after his shift has finished, at Dao's favourite spot in Harrison Park by the Union Canal. They sit on one of the benches that looks out towards the water and the boats, over the top of the red-brick houses with their quaint little chimneys. Fallen leaves decorate the ground around them in patterns of brown, red and orange.

Sunny has never seen Dao so nervous. He makes himself sit down and take her hand. Both of them keep their eyes straight ahead.

"Do you regret it?" she asks.

He hasn't thought everything through properly. But the truth, he realises, is still what it is. "No, I don't regret it," he replies.

"Did I do anything wrong? I wasn't sure—"

"No, you were great."

"Then why did you leave like that?"

"I told you, I was tired. I needed to sleep."

"If anything was wrong you would tell me, right?"

"Of course I would."

Silence for a few moments, but he knows there's no escaping it. "Actually, there is something," he says. "I don't know if you meant to tell me this, or you were just talking in your sleep, but I heard you. You said that you think I'm the guy in your dream, the one predicted by the fortune teller in your card reading. Me, not Jamie."

An intake of breath from her. The hand he's holding flinches. "I thought maybe you were already asleep."

"Well, I wasn't." He hears the resentment in his voice, but it's too late. "You know how I feel about these dreams and card readings. I don't think they lead to anything good. Look at my mother's superstitions and my parents' relationship. If you believe in your dream, then maybe you'd have...unrealistic expectations based on it, and I don't know if I can be who you want me to be."

Dao closes her eyes briefly, then opens them. "I shouldn't have said it, I'm so sorry, I wish I could take it back." He detects a slight panic in her voice. "If you don't want me to talk about my dreams again, or if you want me to put all these superstitions aside, I will. I don't want them to come between us. Sunny, I like talking to you, I like being with you. I have feelings for you."

He doesn't think he's ever heard anyone say how they feel so bluntly before. Her searing honesty floors him, especially since he doesn't know if he's capable of it himself.

And he hears himself say, as though from a great distance, "I have feelings for you too."

He looks down. "But I'm scared," he admits.

"Of what?"

On impulse, he nearly says: *Of everything going wrong.* He nearly says: *My ex, and everything that happened with my ex. Of believing in stupid dreams again.* He nearly says: *All the women who have come into my life before, and all the people I've let down.* He nearly says: *Myself. I'm afraid of myself. And you.*

But he can't say any of that, so he just shakes his head. "I don't know," he replies.

"Well, I'm afraid too," she says. "I've been afraid since I first started to get to know you. But since last night has already happened, I don't want to be afraid anymore."

"You don't know what you're talking about," he mutters. "I've been in a relationship before, you haven't." He hears the desperation in his voice as he says: "And I don't want to hurt you. That's the last thing I want."

"Sunny, listen." She grips his hand even more tightly. "I'm not talking about a relationship right now."

"Then what are you suggesting?"

She searches his face. "We can…just see how it goes? Get to know each other more? And if either of us isn't feeling it anymore, we can just talk about it. I don't want to lose you and I don't want you to have to lose me. But I'm afraid that might have to happen if you're not going to do anything, at all, about us."

He sees all the options clearly: it's either one extreme or another. What they have can't survive if it's something unsteady, half-baked, hovering in between.

"Sunny, I think what we have is worth a try," she says. "I want to be with you. I'll forget about the dreams, I won't do any more card readings, if that's what you want."

"You would do that?" he asks, surprised.

"Would that be better for you?"

"Well...yeah, I mean...I think that might help," he admits. "It just reminds me too much of everything back home."

"If it'd make things easier for you, then I promise. No more. We can go at our own pace."

He wants to tell her how her feelings for him are too overwhelming, like a tidal wave, and he's flailing about in the water, swept away by the current. He has nothing to give in return; his hands are completely empty. He can't see how things can possibly change. Worse, he doesn't know how to make her understand any of this.

Yet for all his doubts, he's sure of one thing: he doesn't want to lose her.

He knows there's only one answer he can give. And so he gives it.

Relief breaks through her expression.

He takes her other hand. Her eyes fall shut just as he kisses her. And he thinks to himself: *I don't know what I'm doing. I have absolutely no idea.*

Dao

Dao has never had *someone* in her life before. A person she talks to every day, who comes over and spends the night with her. Someone she thinks about during the day, more times than she can count.

She becomes obsessed with every little thing: when they will see each other again, when they will speak to each other again, what he's thinking about when he's silent. Practically everything reminds her of him, and she finds herself thinking in detail how she'll describe it all to him afterwards.

She takes pleasure in telling him about her photography project as it begins to take shape. She sends him portraits by other photographers she hopes to emulate, as well as different backgrounds or location ideas. He asks the occasional question and makes the occasional remark, but mostly he just listens. But everything in her brain, she feels, only comes alive once he's heard it.

She tells Simone about this as they eat dinner together one evening. "It's not like having someone who's just a friend listen to you," Dao explains. "I don't know how to describe it."

"Of course it's different," says Simone. "You have *feelings* for him."

"I hate it," Dao grumbles.

"Of course, everybody hates it when they catch feelings," Simone says. "The last guy from Hinge that I went on a date with was too much my type, it terrified me, I had to ask Ella to physically restrain me from texting him first the next day."

"It makes you feel like you're going crazy!" says Dao. "You start to wonder, are you being too much if you show him you care? Should you be playing hard to get cause guys only want what they can't have? But then you question whether your expectations are too high, so you try to be less needy. But then is that you being a pushover? You constantly overthink everything, it's ridiculous! It's like we can't win."

"Exactly," says Simone. "And you keep being told to just be yourself. Like it's *that* easy."

"And I don't like that word: *feelings*," Dao says derisively. "What kind of *feelings* are these feelings supposed to be anyway?"

Simone shrugs, though her eyes shine with playfulness. "Obsession?" she suggests. "Infatuation? Love?"

Dao blushes. "I don't think we're at the love stage just yet."

"But don't you want to be?"

Believe in your dreams, the oracle card had said. *The impossible is more possible than you think.* Dao had promised Sunny that she would put the dreams aside and do no more card readings, especially not about their relationship.

But she can still think about readings she'd done prior to their conversation, can't she?

Dao avoids Simone's inquisitive gaze. "Don't we all want to be in love one day?"

//

The next time Sunny comes over, as he takes her face in his hands before he kisses her, Dao thinks of her conversation with Simone. *Do I love this person?* she asks herself. *How would I know?* And more terrifyingly: *Would he love me back?*

But then his mouth meets hers, and then he's telling her how beautiful she is. He's kissing her neck, holding her so tenderly, and, later, listening to her attentively as they lie in bed.

Dao tells Sunny about the idea she has for her photography project. It's a little after one in the morning. The lamp beside her bed is on, bathing them in a yellow light.

"It's going to be a series of portraits," she says, lying with her head on his chest, her hand playing with his. "I've been thinking a lot about international students in Edinburgh," she says. "Asian students, specifically, who are living away from home for the first time in a country that's so…*different.*"

"Hmm…okay…"

"Young people. Expected to make the most of this once-in-a-lifetime opportunity. People like us."

Sunny frowns. "We're both Thai, Dao, but I wouldn't say we're alike."

"What do you mean?" she asks, confused.

He has a specific expression whenever he wants to say something but feels that he shouldn't. She rests her head on her hand, looking up at him. "You can tell me," she urges him. "Even if we disagree."

"Well…" He looks uncomfortable. "You come from a family with money. My family's…alright, but nowhere near as well-off as yours. Yours is able to pay for you to do this degree and live abroad by yourself. Even if you can't find a job in photography that pays well, you have your family to fall back on. You don't have to juggle multiple jobs while you're here. It's different for me, for Noon, for so many others."

She finds herself disliking his mention of Noon, but tries to brush it aside.

"Don't you have a family business?" she asks.

The incredulity in his gaze makes her blush with embarrassment.

"I'm sorry," she says quickly. "I know it's different, with my mum's family money and everything. But with how hard my father worked, how *constantly* he worked, it never really felt like we're…different."

"Trust me, you are," he says, smiling sarcastically. "And it shows."

She doesn't know what to say to that. She puts her head back down on his chest.

"Are you angry?" he asks.

"No, I'm not," she mumbles. "I just never thought about it like this before."

"Hey." He strokes her head. "I didn't mean to upset you. I didn't want to say anything, but you told me to—"

"No, you're right, it needed saying." She sighs. "I don't want my project to capture just one singular experience. But sometimes I forget."

"You're really okay?"

"Yes." She plants a kiss on his chest. "Do you think I can do it? Make it something meaningful? Something great?"

He shrugs. "Of course you can. You're the smartest person I know."

He says this with no sweetness or charm, but rather in a matter-of-fact, straight-shooting manner. And it means more to her that way.

In the morning, she wakes to find him already out of bed and making her a cup of tea. He chooses the green tea she likes and makes sure to put honey in it, just as she does, and she reflects on how nice it is to be considered in such a way.

She thinks about the conversation with Simone again as she walks him to his English class near the Meadows. In a move that surprises her, he pulls her to him and gives her a peck on the lips.

"What's that for?" she asks, a bit breathless. He's rarely affectionate in public, and she feels like she hasn't done anything to earn it.

He shrugs. "I don't know. I suppose that was for how good you are to me."

Her curiosity makes her want to interrogate him further, so she can better understand every facet of his feelings for her. Instead she burrows her face in his chest as his arms wrap around her. She can hear his heart beating through his coat, while her own aches in a way she finds almost sweet.

Oh it might be possible. It really might.

Sunny

A few weeks into seeing Dao, Sunny feels very much as though he's test-driving a new sports car. Everything is a whirlwind; he doesn't think he's ever felt this high before. Yet he keeps expecting a sharp turn in the road. A crash, somewhere up ahead. He doesn't know where he's going, or whether he's going anywhere, let alone what he's doing. He thinks of Jun, his father and mother, and it feels impossible to imagine that anything good could ever come out of this.

Is he happy? *Sure*, he tells himself. *I am happy. How can I not be?*

Dao is gentle, understanding, caring. The mischief in her smile, its underlying sweetness. The curves of her body and how she moves; the seamless way in which Sunny and Dao move together. She holds him without him ever having to ask her to. He loves the way she cradles his face and runs her hand through his hair. He feels like he could sit in silence with her for as long as he wanted to, or tell her everything that was going through his mind, and she would still be able to hold space for him.

One night, he comes to visit her after his shift has ended, and falls asleep while she's working on an assignment. He wakes to warm yellow lights and the press of her body against his. Her hand trails down the side of his face as her mouth wakes him. He can feel his body responding to her touch. "I have something for you," she tells him as they kiss.

"Something more than this?" he asks. He loves how her eyes shine playfully whenever he teases her.

"This," she says, giving him another kiss, with her hand running down the side of his body. "And this." Another kiss.

His hand gets tangled in her hair before it slides down to make her moan against his mouth. "You're distracting me," she says.

"You're the one who woke me," he retorts, and he turns her over so she's lying beneath him. "I was sleeping peacefully when you disrupted me."

Her hands make wild, curving shapes across his back. Then her legs. Before he knows it, he's pulling off her shirt, her bra. Then her hand finds his, her prim little mouth wrapping around his thumb. He lets out a groan against her neck. He hears her say: "I've thought about you all day today." And he says: "I thought about you too."

Hearing her say that gives him a strange feeling of pride. And suddenly a memory he'd forgotten comes to him: the sight of Scotland when he first saw it from his plane window. A stretch of green and brown, the sea of clouds and the dark blue of the ocean. When he laid his hand on the glass, the freezing cold seeped into his skin. *I'm in an entirely different world*, he'd thought to himself, marvelling at the view. At how extraordinary his circumstances were, how they were almost too good to be true.

Afterwards, she gets out of bed and pulls on his winter coat to shield her naked skin from the cold. She looks so tiny and endearing in it, he almost wants to pull her back down.

She returns a little while later with a folder. She hands it to him. "These are the portraits I took of you along the Water of Leith."

He takes out the photographs. There are five of them, all printed out in vivid colours. He stares at them, lost for words.

He picks up one of the portraits to look at it more closely, staring into his own face as though he were looking into the eyes of a stranger. "You said I look kind in these photos," he says. "Do you still think that?"

"Yes, I do," Dao replies, very easily. Too easily, in his opinion. She looks at the photograph he's picked, smiling.

He chuckles dryly. "I'm flattered you see me that way."

"I see you that way, yes," she says. "But that's also who you are."

He can't even begin to tell her why she's wrong. He wants, so very much, to say: *You deserve to meet someone better than me.*

But she kisses his forehead, both his cheeks, his eyes. He closes his. "You are a good person, Sunny," she whispers. "A good person, with a good heart."

Is he happy? Of course, he thinks. How can he not be?

It's been a long time since he's felt such tenderness. So why would he want it to end?

//

One night, after Sunny has closed up the supermarket, Aunt Oom comes downstairs to tell him that there's food left over from the temple in the fridge for him. "If you happen to get hungry at night," she adds.

Sunny thanks her politely, expecting her to walk back upstairs. But she lingers, watching him as he tallies up the day's earnings by the till. "Am I doing something wrong?" he asks cautiously.

Aunt Oom shakes her head. "Oh no, not at all." She walks over to look at the numbers he's written down in the accounts book.

"Your accounts are very much in order," she says as she leafs through the book. "You have a head for this sort of thing, your uncle says so as well."

"I've had training," Sunny replies stiffly. "For all his faults, my father is a good businessman."

"Ah. Your father." Just from the tone of Aunt Oom's voice, Sunny knows she disapproves. There is softness in her eyes when she looks at him. "He knows how to make money but, if I'm honest, I've always thought he might be a better businessman than he is a husband or a father."

The shock must be evident on Sunny's face, because his aunt gives a little smirk. "Are you surprised?" she asks. "I prefer to say things as they are. The man has never been good news. It doesn't take a genius to work that out."

"It's funny," Sunny says. "Despite all my issues with him, I still find it hard to admit to other people that he's a terrible father."

"You've learned that trait from your mother." Aunt Oom's smile is tinged with sadness.

As Aunt Oom has lived in Scotland for many years, Sunny hasn't often seen the two sisters interact, nor has he spent much time with his three cousins, Aunt Oom's children, who were all born here. He pauses his calculations to ask his aunt: "What was my mother like? Before she met him, I mean? To us, she's only ever been…Ma. The way she is now."

Aunt Oom sighs. "She was funny. She loved to laugh and eat and make jokes. Even after our father died and it was just Mother and the two of us against the world, she never flinched. She did everything with extreme precision and purpose."

"I've never been able to understand why she married him," Sunny admits.

"Oh, you know why," says Aunt Oom. She flips the accounts book closed. "We all follow our hearts instead of our heads when it comes to love. Even the best of us." She looks at him curiously, gently. "Don't you think?"

Sunny is caught off guard. He never expected such a question from his aunt. Vulnerability feels very much like balancing on the edge of a knife.

"I don't know anything about all that," Sunny stammers, sheepishly trying to smile.

"Are you seeing anyone? I've never asked."

"Me?" He scoffs, shrugging as nonchalantly as he can. "I'm very single, Auntie, there's no need for you to worry."

But it's obvious from the way she's looking at him that she doesn't believe him. "Well, whoever she is, make sure you take good care of her. Don't be like your father."

The joking smile slides off his face. "I won't," he promises, words coming out like scratches.

//

Is he happy? Of course, he thinks. Especially when he has someone who takes such an interest in him.

Dao seems to want to know everything about him. She asks him so many questions, he thinks she'd go on forever if he let her. She asks if he wants to go to Portobello beach. "You need to see what the ocean looks like here," she tells him.

And so one Sunday afternoon, with the weather beginning to grow warm, they rent bikes from the city centre and cycle down to the beach. They zigzag through residential areas, a park or two, and a long-abandoned railway tunnel that reeks of moss and decay. It's all downhill, so they take their hands off the handlebars and let the bikes roll down while a cold, refreshing breeze blows into their faces, tangling Dao's mane of black hair into an ungodly mess.

The beach is packed with people. He and Dao take their shoes off and walk into the shallows of the water, feeling the cold current against their skin. It's different from any beach he's seen in Thailand. The sky, as always, is overcast, though not completely, and the sand feels scratchy beneath his feet.

She holds his hand as they stroll, asks him questions about where he's travelled to, knowing he'd never been outside of Thailand before.

"We went to Hua Hin once when I was very young," he tells her. "Fai was only five or six years old, I think. And that's kind of it. Father has always talked about us travelling together as a family, but his plans never actually materialised."

"Maybe he's just trying to save money."

The thought of Dao knowing anything about saving money irritates Sunny a bit. He shakes his head. "Let's talk about something else. We're at the beach and it's not raining for once. Don't you want to hear about happier things?"

Dao gives a teasing smile. "Well, if you want me to speak about happier things, why don't we talk about your birthday?" she says. "It's in two months, right? April? What do you want to do?"

"I don't know. I haven't really thought about it."

"Don't you plan ahead for your birthday?"

"No. Do you?"

"I like to plan fun things to do on the day. Things I know I'd enjoy."

"I've never done that before."

"Why not?"

He is genuinely perplexed. "I don't know," he replies. "I'm not really used to planning for good things to happen."

She laughs. "Such a dramatic explanation!"

"You think I'm a sceptic?"

"I think you believe that the less you expect good things to happen, the less disappointed you are if they don't."

He winces. "When you say it out loud, it doesn't sound very healthy."

She laughs. "I suppose not." She runs a thumb across his right cheek. "But you can now, you know."

"I can what?"

"Dare to hope for good things."

He's quiet for a moment, thinking of that possibility and all the horrors it entails. He brushes his lips against her nose, then her chin. "I want to," he says quietly. "Maybe you should teach me how."

He wants to believe, so badly. He likes the idea of being a person who can.

PART THREE

The Trying

Dao

As Dao, Shane and Teoy grew older and university loomed, their bond was strengthened by Dao being moved to Shane's class for the last three years of secondary school. Not only was she happy to be around him more, she was relieved to be rid of the bullies who had plagued her life for the past few years. She tentatively began to make new friends. But still no one was as close to her as Teoy and Shane.

Teoy asked Dao more than once: "Do you like Shane? Cause I think he likes you."

"He told you that?" Dao always asked, trying not to smile or appear bothered.

"No, he doesn't have to," said Teoy. "It's obvious."

"He has a girlfriend," Dao reminded her friend. "Don't forget what he's like." There was always "someone".

"What's going on between the two of you?"

A bunch of signs and codes, Dao wanted to say. A lot of reading between the lines. Catching small, precious, meaningful moments that evaporated as quickly as they came. But all she said to her friend was: "Maybe there really is nothing."

"Maybe he doesn't want to risk your friendship," said Teoy. "Or he thinks you're too good for him."

"Why would he think that?" asked Dao.

"Because you are."

They were sitting on Dao's bed. It was the height of summer, with the glaring rays of the April sun baking the house. The windows were thrown wide open and the fan was on, but sweat still clung to their foreheads and necks. In Dao's lap was her very first camera, bought with the money she'd saved from Chinese New Year over the years. Dao began tinkering with it to avoid looking at Teoy.

"It doesn't matter," Dao said resolutely. "All these girls he dates and we're still friends. We can talk. Maybe he's just not ready."

Teoy shook her head. "Yes, but doesn't it bother you when you guys are this close but he says you're nothing more than a friend? That he chooses to be with other people and lie to you about it?"

"He doesn't lie to me," she said, looking at her friend.

Teoy gave her a pointed look. "Of course he does," she said.

"No, he doesn't. We just…avoid talking about them." Dao lowered her eyes once again.

"Doesn't it hurt?" asked Teoy.

"We have no obligations to each other in that way."

"Yes," said Teoy. "But does it hurt?"

Dao picked up her camera and took a snap: Teoy staring into the lens, her expression screwed up in frustration, her lips parted in expectation.

"Of course it hurts," Dao admitted quietly. She lowered the camera.

"So you like him then?" asked Teoy. "You're finally admitting it? After all these years?"

"It doesn't matter if I did have feelings for him," Dao muttered. "I don't know how he feels, so I don't want to do anything that would risk our friendship. Maybe it's better for things to just remain as they are."

Teoy looked at her for a long time. "Like I said," Teoy repeated, her mouth set in an angry line. "I think you deserve better."

But to Dao, her friend's statement made no sense. How could she deserve better when someone she wanted so badly (yes, despite what she might tell Teoy, she did want Shane very badly) didn't think she was worth having? Where was the logic in that?

//

A few months later, Dao and Shane found themselves standing next to each other as the entire classroom erupted with cheers and screams. Balloons filled the ceiling, and confetti exploded from crackers and rained down to litter the floor. There was a cake and more than a few half-empty boxes of pizza. All the desks and chairs in their classroom were pushed against the walls, and even their teacher had a party hat on.

Both Dao and Shane's school uniforms were covered with scribbles from their classmates: colourful markers – black, orange, green, blue – creating a plethora of well-wishes. It was tradition for seniors to have their shirts signed by friends on their last day of school.

Dao had already written on Shane's earlier that morning. Aware of the fact that others would be able to read her message, she'd written: Thank you for being such a good friend. Best of luck with your future! And signed her name with a smiley face at the end.

Shane was holding an orange marker in his hand. "My turn," he told Dao.

She couldn't hide her smile when she turned around so he could find an empty space on her back. He put his free hand on her shoulder as he wrote. "There," he said when he was done.

"What did you write?"

"Oh, well, I just wrote what I was planning to tell you anyway."

She turned around to face him. They were so close, she could have breached the distance between them and touched his cheek with her lips.

She asked: "What were you planning to tell me?"

He replied, a little sadly: "That I'll miss seeing you every day."

//

Three days after Shane said those words to her, Dao consulted a fortune teller for the first time.

Dao met the fortune teller – a woman who looked to be in her thirties – at a night market. She had set up a table next to an accessories stall, with a placard showing her prices ("Three questions for one hundred and fifty baht", "One question for sixty baht"), along with three decks of tarot cards and two stools.

Dao was by herself, and was already a few stalls down when she changed her mind, walked back and took a seat. Her parents would be both scandalised and saddened if they knew: this is not the power of God, they'd say. But Dao needed answers, and she needed them in a way that was clear and precise.

"One question, please," Dao told the fortune teller.

The woman began shuffling her cards. Her smile was warm and welcoming, as if she knew that Dao was nervous. "What do you want to know, little sister?"

"I had a dream a few nights ago," Dao said carefully. "I want to know what it means."

She could still recall the emotions she'd experienced while she slept, and even after she woke up. The fear and terror she'd felt while she was trapped on that airplane, high up in the sky. The storm pressing in so close that the entire cabin shook and shuddered.

The woman nodded and spread out the cards in a semicircle. "Think about the question and pick three cards."

Dao did just that. The woman let her flip the cards over herself. Two were upside down; the other was face up. Dao marvelled at the beauty and intricacy of the drawings. The redness of the heart and the blue of the water. The sharpness of the swords.

The look on the fortune teller's face was contemplative, curious. She touched the three of swords with a gentle hand, and looked at Dao with a small, sympathetic smile. "This reading is about love," she said.

//

Two weeks after that reading, Dao told her parents that she wanted to stay in Thailand and start a photography course at the same university as Teoy, who'd decided to pursue architecture.

Her father, however, didn't understand her choice. The debate raged on for days.

"We have the money to send you abroad," Father said, glowering. "We can afford to pay for the best education for you, so why aren't you taking it?"

"Your father is right," Mother chimed in. "So many of my friends' children study abroad. The UK. America. Australia. Ploy's daughter is in Canada!"

"You have friends whose children go to Thai universities too," Dao countered.

"You'll have better teachers abroad," Father said. "A new experience that can help you mature. And if you stick with it, you might even have the chance of an international career."

"I'm fine with just working in Thailand."

"But you've always loved the idea of going to Europe!" Mother said. "When you were smaller—"

"Well I'm not a child anymore."

"Is there another reason for why you're staying?" Father asked.

Dao disliked the fact that he knew the right question to ask. Still, she shook her head stubbornly. "I told you why I want to stay. I want to be with my friends. I want to stay home."

Her father's disapproving expression cracked, and an unfamiliar sadness appeared in his eyes. "Dao, I know we don't always find it easy to talk openly, we're not that kind of family. But I hope you know we're making these suggestions because we want what's best for you. The reason why I've worked so hard all these years is so that we can afford to give you opportunities like this."

Dao wanted to tell Father that he'd worked so hard mostly to prove himself to the world and to Mother's family. That he was the one who had created this distance between them. But she knew it was futile to say so, and that she had to pick her battles. "Father, I understand what you're saying," she told him. "But I've made my choice. This is what I want."

Her father was in a terrible mood for the next few days. But for the first time in her life, Dao found the courage to dig her heels in.

If she and Shane lived in different countries, they'd drift apart: she'd seen it in her dream. That's what her reading with the fortune teller had been about: a long-awaited love fading away, separated by distance.

The cards had been clear about the dream's interpretation. "The relationship is not yet over," the fortune teller had said. "There is still hope. A possibility. See this card here? He is confused, distracted. But there is something still connecting the two of you. A thread."

Dao swallowed. "If it were to be over...I mean, over for real... how would I know?"

"Oh, you'd know," the woman replied. "It'd be truly over if the two of you no longer live in the same country. That's what your dream means."

So when Father finally relented and let Dao stay in Thailand, she didn't feel victorious or even excited at the prospect of this new chapter of her life. All she felt was immense relief.

Dao

Sunny lets Dao hold his hand while they walk to the pub together.

It's Sunday evening, and Edinburgh, with its stone buildings and mountains in the distance, is basking in a golden sheen of light. The pub is on Rose Street, just down from Princes Street, and there are lights strung up along the path, reminding her of Christmas. Sunny is silent for most of the walk.

"Are you sure you want to come with me?" Dao asks. It's the third time she's asked since inviting him.

"Of course," he replies. He squeezes her hand. "Why would I come with you if I didn't want to?" This is how he's responded each time she's mentioned meeting her friends over the last two days: "If you want me to come, then I will."

"You'll like them, I promise."

"Oh, I have no doubt," he says. And she lets herself be reassured.

The pub isn't very busy, but the vibe is lively, with an '80s pop tune playing from the stereo. There are stragglers at the bar, chatting, drinking, trading laughs with the bartender. Simone and Ella are amongst them.

Ella has just dyed her hair dark brunette, and is wearing bright red lipstick. She's sipping on a martini and laughing at something Simone has just said. Simone is dressed up in a chic, sequin top, with leather trousers, high-heeled boots and hoop earrings. Her long black hair is braided and swung across her shoulder.

Simone spots Sunny and Dao first, and waves them over.

Ella spins around, grinning excitedly. "There you are!" she cries. "Finally! We get to meet this mysterious man who's been taking up so much of your time!"

Sunny smiles sheepishly as Simone wraps Dao in a quick hug. "Our table's at the back," Simone says. "Cady is already there." Simone shifts her attention to Sunny. "Nice to meet you, Sunny, I'm Simone. But you probably already know that." She sends a wink to Dao over Sunny's shoulder.

Dao stands to the side and observes Sunny's exchanges with her friends. His smile is shy and reserved, and he looks uncomfortable when Simone and Ella both embrace him briefly, with Ella giving him a kiss on the cheek. His English comes out haltingly, and heavy with uncertainty. It is strange to see him this way, so out of his depth and extremely guarded. Every action premeditated.

They order drinks and take them back to the table. Cady stands up immediately to greet Sunny. Cady is less boisterous, but Dao watches the same interaction unfold: Sunny's awkwardness as he trips over his words.

Dao takes the seat next to Sunny while he nurses a pint. She reaches under the table and lays a hand on his knee.

At her touch, he jerks away, as though caught by surprise. Then he gives her a look: *What are you trying to do?* She grips his knee as if to say: *Don't worry, I was just trying to let you know that I'm here.*

He relaxes, but his demeanour is still stiff. Conversation swirls around them. At first, the topics are their major projects and upcoming exhibition, then they shift to Cady trying to ask Dao and Sunny questions about the best places to visit in Thailand. Sunny hesitates, so Dao steps into the awkward silence and answers for both of them.

"If you're visiting Bangkok, the malls are the best places we have. Thai people love malls. There are some cool cafes, some bars with amazing live music…but if you want to go to other provinces, Krabi is a great place if you love the ocean. We have a lot of beautiful beaches down south."

Dao turns to Sunny in an attempt to prompt him to chime in. His smile appears strained. "Yes, I've heard that Krabi is beautiful. Many tourists like Phuket, too."

Ella turns to him and asks more questions. He stumbles through his answers before looking to Dao so she can continue on his behalf.

Eventually, the topic changes to their lecturers' ethnicities – whether learning photography through the lenses of white mentors is something they want to be doing. Ella says that, as a white person, she's never thought about it like that before, which makes her feel ashamed. Cady agrees.

"And all these photographers we're studying in class," says Simone, "not one of them is Asian! There's one black photographer, but everyone we've analysed so far has been white."

"And old," Dao chimes in. "Diversity in age is just as important as diversity in race. With social media, especially Instagram, the way we consume photographs is so different from how it used to be. The ways we share and admire them are different too."

Ella lets out a laugh. "Can you imagine if we studied influencers?"

"Why not?" says Dao. "I've seen some Thai girls' Instagram pages that are cooler and more interesting than actual photographs hung up in galleries!"

"What do you think, Sunny?" Simone asks.

Sunny lowers his glass and looks caught off guard. "I'm sorry," he stammers. "What's the question?"

"Sunny doesn't know much about photography," Dao says hurriedly. "He always gets bored whenever I talk about it."

"I don't get bored," Sunny says in a strained voice. "I enjoy listening to you."

"What do you think of what Dao said?" Simone asks. "About how some Instagrams can be more interesting than portraits hung up in galleries?"

"I don't really know," says Sunny, an uncertain, polite smile fixed on his face. "For me, a photo is a photo."

Cady chooses that moment to gracefully swoop in and introduce a new topic. Soon they're discussing the TV shows they're watching, the latest celebrity gossip, their most recent personal revelations and the triggers that have led them to those realisations. Dao offers her comments, her jokes, and laughs along with her friends.

Occasionally, Dao turns to Sunny to whisper a quick translation for what's being discussed. He nods and smiles indulgently. Yet she can't tell whether he understands anything that's going on around him. The longer the evening progresses, the less his forced smile appears and the more he drinks his beer. Translating for him starts to feel more awkward. Her friends, too, begin to involve him less and less in their conversation – a question here and there, but it's obvious that they're trying to be polite more than anything.

Dao takes her hand away from his knee. Sips her own drink. Lets out a peal of laughter when Simone says something funny. The whole table joins her except for Sunny.

Dao turns to check on him, her hand reaching out for his. But he pulls away and whispers into her ear: "I'm just gonna go outside for some air."

"Alright," she says, flustered. "Do you want me to come with you?"

"No, it's okay, I'll be back soon."

Sunny stands up, offers what she can only describe as an apologetic grimace to her friends, and makes his way out of the pub.

Dao lets out a long breath. Her face feels numb. She sips her beer. Simone notices and grabs her hand. "Don't worry about it," Simone says. "Nothing's wrong, you're okay."

Dao is surprised to hear how shaky her voice is as she whispers back: "He looks like he wants to be literally anywhere else."

Cady casts a glance towards the door. Her voice is kind: "He's probably just nervous because we're all speaking in English."

"Should I go check on him?" asks Dao, looking from one friend to another.

"What did he say to you before he walked out?" Ella asks.

"He said he'll be back soon, he's just getting some air."

"Then give him some time," says Ella.

They continue talking, but Dao can no longer concentrate. She slips in and out of conversation absentmindedly, checks her phone and sips her beer. Then she gets to her feet. "He's been gone a while now, I'll go check on him."

Simone looks concerned. "Dao, I don't know if that's a good idea—"

"I'll just be a few minutes."

Outside the pub, Dao can't see Sunny anywhere. It takes her a couple of minutes to finally find him a few shops down, smoking a cigarette while scrutinising a menu in a restaurant window. As she approaches, she sees that it's a Japanese fusion place, with plastic cherry blossoms decorating the doorway.

She tries to keep her tone light. Breezy. "I don't think I've ever seen you smoke before," she says.

Sunny turns, surprised. From the look that passes across his face, Dao gets the impression that he hasn't wanted to see her. She suddenly feels embarrassed, like an immature little girl.

"I just wanted to make sure you were okay."

"I told you I was okay," he replies sharply. He stubs out his cigarette in an ashtray balanced precariously on the windowsill. "You didn't have to come get me, I'm perfectly capable of finding my own way back. I just wanted some air."

"I know," she says. She should be saying something more, but she can't think of anything else. This is all going horribly wrong, she thinks.

"Do you even want me to go back in?" he asks.

The sting in his voice takes her aback. "What? Why wouldn't I want you to?"

He shakes his head. Smirks. "Alright. Whatever you say."

She doesn't understand what's going on. "Sunny—"

"Come on, let's just go back inside."

He doesn't say anything else and starts walking back towards the pub. She hurries to catch up with him. She wants to reach out and take his hand, pull him back and give the two of them more time. Then tell him how she doesn't understand why all of this has to be so complicated.

Instead, they just keep walking.

The night ends half an hour later. She and Sunny part ways with her friends in front of the pub. They all say goodbye to Sunny politely, telling him how happy they are to have met him. He nods and smiles cordially, shaking their hands and receiving their perfunctory embraces. "Goodnight," he says. "Goodnight."

Finally, Dao and Sunny are alone. Wordlessly, he lights another cigarette and takes a long drag. He doesn't look at her. "I'm sorry for smoking," he says. There's an edge to his voice. Not an angry one, but a harshness nonetheless.

She finds herself unable to stay angry with him. "That's okay. It feels like a long night for you. Thank you for coming."

He smokes for a while in silence. Eventually, he asks, "Do you want me to walk you home?"

"Do you want to talk about tonight?"

"Dao, I don't want to talk about tonight. I'm so tired. Do you want me to walk you home?"

She notices his set jaw and the flash of fire in his eyes. She feels like crying and doesn't know why. "Yes, of course," she says. "Let's head back."

Sunny

Sunny and Jun ended up taking the same course – computer science – at a university near the old airport. She chose it because she was genuinely interested in programming and all things IT. He chose it because he thought he would find it easy, and it meant he would be close to her.

Becoming a university student meant more freedom. Sunny didn't have to lie to his parents as much about coming home late. His mother even offered him the choice of staying with his grandmother at her house in Bang Na, so he'd be closer to campus. Sunny turned her down. The thought of sharing space with his grandmother without exchanging so much as a word to each other every day, while she kept track of his comings and goings, felt like an avoidable discomfort.

He preferred to alternate between home and the small one-bedroom apartment Jun had started renting in a student housing complex, a mere fifteen-minute motorcycle ride from campus.

Sunny knew Jun's mother had been experiencing some financial struggles, so he asked Jun how she could afford to pay the rent for the place.

"My mum's not paying," Jun told him. "I am." And, when

pressed, she wouldn't tell him where she was getting the money from.

"Don't you trust me?" she asked.

"Of course I trust you," he said. "But—"

"If you trusted me, you wouldn't be asking all these questions," she said, glowering. She was so upset she wouldn't talk to him for a day.

In the end he had to apologise, and he promised never to ask her about it again.

Sunny had always fancied himself relatively confident when it came to girls, but with Jun, he seemed to always find himself a few steps behind.

When she broke up with him a month into their first term, he didn't see it coming. Leading up to it, she did nothing that was out of the ordinary. But then, in the middle of the night, she woke him up out of the blue and dropped the bombshell.

"I think we should stop seeing each other for good," Jun said. "Something's not right between us, and I want to focus on my studies."

Her words were so simple and vague, yet they hit Sunny like a body blow. When he asked what she meant by them, she couldn't even explain. She, who had always been so unflinching, averted her eyes at his questions, and still did not look at him when she asked him to leave her apartment. She didn't pick up when he kept calling that night.

He spent the entire next day in bed, drinking. He thought that this must be what other girls he'd toyed with had felt when he had ended things with them – so casually, like the whole thing had simply been an afterthought. His younger sister Fai knocked on his door, but he told her to go away.

Three days later, he returned to university and didn't even spare Jun a glance.

He began talking to someone a year older: a shy, quiet but incredibly beautiful girl who laughed prettily at everything he said and brought him food and snacks every time he came over to her place. He heard that Jun might be seeing a guy two years above them, who drove to campus in a white Honda Civic. He pretended not to care.

But three months into his time with the nice, beautiful girl with the tepid kisses, Jun called him one night out of the blue.

"What are you up to?" she asked, and the sound of her voice woke up something inside him.

"Not much," he said. "What's wrong?" He knew right away that something was amiss.

"I just miss you," she replied. That was all the explanation she gave.

They met up in a mall the next day and talked for two hours, but they both danced around the question of their break-up or who they were seeing now. He walked her back to her place and lingered in her doorway. She pushed herself up to her tiptoes, put a hand behind his neck and pulled his lips down to hers. "Stay," she said into his mouth, completely unguarded. He stumbled into her room with his hands in her hair, inside her shirt.

He left the next morning with the feel of her skin still burning on his, and texts left unanswered on his phone.

Within a week, he and Jun were back together. He never did ask her about the guy with the white car, nor did she ask him about the kind girl who had cried for two weeks straight after he suddenly disappeared from her life.

//

During their four years of university, Jun broke up with him twice more.

Every break-up felt final and dramatic, and they would attempt to not talk to each other for a few months. But something would always happen – one of them would do something, see something, hear something – that reminded them of each other. A call or a text would be sent and, like clockwork, they would be back in each other's arms.

"It's just poor self-control and discipline on my part," Jun once remarked, while Sunny laughed into her hair. She burrowed her head into the crook of his arm. "We're too used to each other," she said. "But you do make me laugh."

Later that night, Sunny was awoken by the sound of footsteps.

After his eyes had adjusted to the darkness, he saw Jun slipping outside to the balcony. She stood with her back to him, her hand gripping the railing. She was on the phone.

He pretended to be asleep when she slipped back into bed a little while later.

In the morning, he asked her who it was that she'd been talking to.

Her eyes widened. "Don't you trust me?" she asked.

"Yes," he stammered, "but I just thought it wouldn't hurt to ask."

"I know other people besides you, you know," she said. "I have friends."

"I'm not disputing that."

"But you don't trust me," she said, her voice breaking. "I knew it. You told me you do, but I think you're just saying that.

Why would you want to be with someone you can't trust?"

Her eyes began to well up. She made to stand, but he gripped her hand.

"Jun, of course I trust you," he said at once. "I don't want you to doubt that. But it's just—"

"If you trust me, then why are you trying to ask me all these questions?"

She looked at him with such hurt that he felt extremely guilty. "Jun, I'm so sorry," he said. "You're right. We shouldn't even be together if I don't trust you, so of course I trust you. We never have to speak about this again."

And they never did. Yet the memory had sunk its teeth in him, no matter how hard he tried to banish it away with excuses.

He strived to remember that dream about Jun he'd had all those years ago. It had come true, hadn't it? The two of them, together...this was exactly how it was supposed to be. So why couldn't he just let it be?

Sunny

Another day in Edinburgh, another day of steady, unending drizzle.

Sunny is on the early morning shift. The city is only just stirring from sleep, with a slash of pink and gold beginning to emerge at the edge of the sky. He stands under the awning of the supermarket, hands in the pockets of his coat, brooding and leaning against the closed shutters. He is both amused and frustrated by his capacity for rumination.

His phone rings. It's his mother. He picks up and tells her good afternoon.

"You sound glum today," she says right away. "Is everything alright?"

"It's raining," Sunny says. "It always rains here."

"Oh, darling, I'm sorry. Were you planning to go somewhere today?"

"No, I'll be at work all day."

"Oh, that's good, at least."

"Yes, but when it rains like this, the mood is different."

His mother starts telling a story about a friend of hers whose son studied abroad in London, and that friend's experience of what it was like visiting her son there. Sunny listens patiently, makes the odd comment, laughs in all the right places. But once the story ends, he doesn't make any effort to continue the conversation. He watches the bakery on the other side of the road opening up for the day.

"Ma," Sunny says, "have you ever thought about what our lives would be like if we had more money?"

His mother sounds taken aback. "What's brought this on?"

"You've always talked about your friends and their children who have these top-earning careers. The reason I'm even in Scotland is because you admire Aunt Oom for moving and for putting her kids through school here. Is that what you would have wanted for me, if we'd had more money?"

His mother is silent. He brushes a few droplets of rain from his cheek.

"Your father," his mother says eventually, "has given us an amazing life."

"This has nothing to do with him," Sunny says irritably. "I'm not blaming anyone."

"Then where is this coming from?"

"I've just been wondering, that's all. Would I be able to speak English fluently? Learn to love Edinburgh? Would I have different friends? Would I be someone completely different if I'd grown up like your friends' children?"

"Sunny, dear, do you want to be someone else?"

He lets her question hang in the air for a moment. He checks the time. Looks up at the sky to see the dark clouds gathering above. "Never mind," he says.

Sunny still flinches with embarrassment every time he thinks about his experience meeting Dao's friends. He wants to kick himself for agreeing to go. Who did he think he was? Someone educated like Dao, who could speak English flawlessly and engage in intellectual conversations like he belonged there?

He dislikes how they all tried to coax him to engage in what they were talking about as though he were a child. Then the topics they were discussing – they nearly made him laugh out loud. Pretentious crap, he wanted to say. Just people spewing rhetoric that they thought made them sound smart while being completely removed from reality.

When he'd left to get some air, Dao had come looking for him – she's that kind of person. But when he saw her walking towards him, her pretty face filled with concern and apprehension, he'd felt a stab of annoyance. *Why can't she leave it alone?* he'd thought. *Why must she make a big deal out of everything?* Coming to collect him as though he were a lost puppy?

They had walked home that night in icy silence. He'd expected her to prod him with questions. Yet the only thing she said once they'd arrived at her place was: "Call me tomorrow."

He didn't call her the following day, only texted in the afternoon to ask how her day was going. And everything resumed as normal. Or as normal as was possible, under the circumstances.

//

Sunny's mother is speaking to him: "That dream you told me about before you flew to Scotland. The dream about the girl. Have you met her yet? Does this have anything to do with her?"

Sunny bristles. It's a conversation they've had so many times before. "Ma, dreams are not real life."

"I'm simply asking a question. I thought maybe you were feeling down because you were unhappy about something in your love life."

"Ma, I have to go open the shop now," he says. "I'll speak to you later. But call me if anything's wrong."

"Oh, Son, everything's absolutely fine here, you don't need to worry."

He pauses, then decides to test the waters. "That's not what Fai told me."

His mother's voice turns strict. "Sunny, what has your sister been telling you?"

He feels a rush of anger. "So something is wrong then? What has he done this time, Ma?"

"Sunny, your father and I are fine."

"Ma, you don't have to lie to me."

"I'm not lying."

"I don't believe you."

A pause. Then he hears his mother say, in nearly a whisper: "If anything were to happen that you should know about, I would tell you."

"Do you promise?"

"I promise."

"Good."

She sighs. "You're still as stubborn as ever. Go do your

work. I love you."

"I love you, too."

He hangs up, but continues to stand there for a while longer, breathing deeply and letting the cold chill his lungs.

A small laugh escapes his lips, ironic and almost cruel, the sound blending in with the pitter-patter of rain.

He had been such a fool.

No matter how much you wish otherwise, some things, he concludes, are meant to repeat themselves.

Dao

Dao's university was right in the centre of Bangkok, flanked by the city's two largest shopping centres. It was a prestigious establishment, which meant that the girls had to wear uniforms that were crisply ironed, their skirts no higher than their knees, their feet clad in white nursing shoes and white stockings, and their shirts always tucked in.

Teoy blossomed at university. People gravitated towards her straight-talking personality and, before long, she had cultivated a posse of girlfriends who were just as popular as she was. Dao found herself swept up in their friendship, feeling a little out of place yet grateful to be included at all.

Shane was still in Dao's life, but – she began to realise with a sinking feeling – only on the periphery.

He decided to study finance, just as his family wanted. He got into a university on the outskirts of Bangkok and moved away from home to rent his own dorm room near campus, an area notorious for the number of bars and pubs that lined its streets.

During one of their rare phone conversations, she told him how frustrated she was with her teachers. "Everything is theory-based," she complained. "It feels so traditional. Every time I go to class, I question whether this is what I really want to do."

"Maybe you're doing what you want to be doing, but you're doing it in the wrong place."

"Wow. Dropping pearls of wisdom, huh?"

"Not pearls of wisdom," he said. "I'm just stating the obvious."

She paused. "When will I get to see you?"

"Soon," he said. "I'm sorry I've been so busy. There's been a lot going on."

"Okay," she said. "Hopefully soon."

But "soon", Dao quickly realised, meant months and months. He always had a perfectly understandable reason: he was too busy with coursework, he'd already made plans with his new friends, or he had to go home and visit his family. "Soon" also meant less and less texting between them. They used to talk almost every day, but now it was mostly: I'm so sorry I just got around to replying or I'm sorry I haven't been checking in, I hope you've been doing well.

When Teoy asked if she'd seen Shane lately, Dao would say: "He's just been really busy. But we'll hang out soon."

//

When "soon" finally arrived, it was late one night at an outdoor bar in Thonglor.

It was Dao's birthday, and Teoy had insisted they celebrate in style. Shane, surprisingly, decided to show up, joining her, Teoy and their new uni friends.

Dao was so happy he was coming, she couldn't find it in herself to be mad at him when he arrived nearly two hours late, or when he spent most of the hour that he was there sitting quietly in the corner of their booth, sipping on a beer. The only person he talked to was Teoy. But even then, it wasn't for long.

At around one in the morning, Shane put down his beer and stood up. A look in Dao's direction said everything. She quickly got up, left her drink with Teoy and excused herself. She walked a few steps behind him as he made his exit, carving a path through the throngs of partiers. I could simply reach out, she thought, and grab the back of his shirt. No one would see.

Then they emerged from the bar into the glaring white lights from the streetlamps and clubs around them. She blinked a few times, adjusting her eyes to the brightness, while he glowered at their surroundings as though they had somehow offended him.

She stood with him as he waited for the valet to bring his car around. He drove a navy blue BMW that belonged to his father before the old man had upgraded to a newer model.

"Where are you off to next?" Dao asked, trying to keep her tone light.

Shane shrugged. "A couple of friends are out at this bar near my uni. I might join them."

It was a lie, she could tell. The chasm between them felt so wide, he could have been standing on the other side of a valley.

"Thank you for coming, though," she said.

He smiled wanly. "No problem. I had to come through eventually."

"Eventually?"

"I have to be reliable every once in a while."

They attempted to laugh together at the banter, but it felt forced and awkward. Shane's car pulled up. The valet stepped out, leaving the door wide open and handing him the keys.

182

The words came out before Dao could think too much about it: "Shane, I really wish…"

Shane froze. "You wish?"

She shook her head. "No, never mind," she said.

A look of annoyance flickered through Shane's expression. "Can we both finally just say what we mean?" he snapped.

Panic rose up inside her and she shook her head. She gave him a friendly push towards his car.

"It was nothing," she repeated. "I just wish…I wish we could see each other more. Like you said."

He stood there, framed by the bright lights. "Yeah," he said quietly, suddenly sounding exhausted. "Me too. I'll see you around."

He slipped into the driver's seat. But just before he shut the door, he paused to look at her for a moment, his head tilted, as though he were looking at a puzzle he couldn't quite solve. "Happy birthday," he said. And then he was gone.

Teoy found Dao there a couple of minutes later, still standing in the same spot. Teoy put an arm around her and squeezed fiercely.

More cars pulled up and more young people tumbled out, dressed to the nines and ready to party. But all of Dao's earlier excitement about her birthday had evaporated. She leaned in closer to Teoy, and was grateful that her friend pretended not to see the tears forming in her eyes.

Dao

Ever since the meeting between Sunny and Dao's friends, Dao's tendency to look for subtext behind Sunny's every tiny gesture or action has gone into overdrive.

She's not proud of it: she wants nothing more than to be a cool, collected, confident woman who is so rooted in her own worth, she remains unshaken. But almost everything Sunny does fills her with doubt.

He takes a long time answering his messages? He must be talking to other people or he's bored of her now. He's too busy or tired to come over? He must not have liked her that much to begin with. She has messed up. What if her dream no longer comes true?

She tries to throw herself headlong into her major project, especially since the portraits will be displayed at an exhibition at the university campus. She starts talking to students from other courses and convincing them to let her photograph them. Even Simone has agreed to sit for a session.

But no matter how many portraits she takes, or how happy she is with them, those worries about Sunny continue to weigh on her.

Dao quietly reveals these concerns to Ella one night.

They are the only two left in the common room past eleven that night. Dao is nursing a cup of lemon and ginger tea, a blanket wrapped around her, as she divulges the details of her fears in a trembling voice. Ella, in her hoodie and shorts and with her hair tied high in a bun, listens patiently.

"Maybe it was a mistake inviting him to meet you guys," says Dao. "It just seems to have driven him away. Ever since that evening, we've been talking less. I don't know if he's angry with me. But when I ask him if he is, he says he's not."

"He did look uncomfortable," Ella concedes, "but if he's going to shut down because of it, then that's his issue. He needs to let you know what's going on."

Dao senses the anxiety rising within her again, a tightness in her chest that makes her feel like she can't fully breathe in. In a tiny, desperate voice, she says: "Ella, can we ask the cards what I should do?"

Ella's eyebrows quirk up in surprise. "Are you joking?"

"I am, but also I'm not." If she does this, she would be breaking her promise to Sunny. She has asked without thinking, but now that she has it feels like she's already tasted the fruit and there is nowhere to go but forward.

"I've told you guys about the dream I had," says Dao. "Ever since then, I haven't been able to shake this feeling that something big is supposed to happen to me. I need to know if it has anything to do with Sunny." She doesn't mention the promise she'd made; she knows Ella wouldn't want to help if she did.

Ella looks uncertain. "Dao, I've met the guy now—"

"I don't think that matters. Please, I've been so anxious, I don't know what to do. I'd go to the fortune teller I saw before I flew here, but she's all the way in Thailand. I can do the oracle cards you gave me for Christmas myself, but you're the expert."

"I'm definitely *not* an expert!" says Ella, laughing.

"Come on, Ella, please! At least this way I won't be so anxious."

Ella looks at her for a moment, then groans. "Alright, let me go get my cards, we'll set it up."

"Thank you, thank you, thank you!"

Ella has a specific ritual for how she sets up her cards, starting with a small threaded mat, and then putting down four different kinds of crystals on each corner of the coffee table. She lights two incense sticks for cleansing then hands her deck of tarot cards to Dao. "I want you to play with the cards for a bit," says Ella. "Think of the question you're asking. Repeat it to yourself while you shuffle."

After Dao has done so, Ella takes the cards back, shuffles them herself and spreads them out, face down in a half circle. "Pick two," she tells Dao.

Dao's hand hovers over the cards. She pulls one from the middle of the pile. Then another one, less slowly, from the right side. Ella turns them over: "Temperance reversed," she says, "and the Knight of Cups." She frowns as she studies them, then shuffles the cards again, asking, "Can we have a clarifier for Temperance reversed?"

She pulls out a third card and flips it over to reveal a woman with long, flowing hair, sitting on a throne. At her feet is a river, in her hand a cup, tipped to the side, pouring water. She reminds Dao of the statue of the goddess of healing in Dean Village.

"The question I asked," Dao says, "is what should I do with Sunny?"

"Then according to the cards," Ella says, "there is nothing you *can* do. This is Temperance. It signifies balance, harmony, patience. But currently it is reversed, which means that there is a chaotic energy within you that is unstable. There's a lot of fear. Doubt."

"On his part or on mine?"

"Looks like it's on both. It looks like what you need right now is stillness. And here…" – Ella points to the other card – "…is the Knight of Cups upright. Someone is coming in with a strong energy. The knight is romantic, eager, charming. He comes charging in with an open heart."

"So he's coming back? Or he'll come around?" Dao asks, breathless.

Ella frowns, her eyes on the cards. "It would seem that way." She picks up the one with the image of the woman on the throne. "But here we have the Queen of Cups as a clarifier for Temperance Reversed. She signifies compassion, care, intuition. You in your true form. Once you've achieved the stillness we were talking about earlier," – she flips the Temperance card so it's upright – "you're going to feel collected, nurtured and secure in your power, like the queen in this picture."

"But what about the knight? What does he have to do with the queen?"

"All these cards are connected. You asked what you should do, and I think the key here is balance and moderation. You need patience. You need to be the Queen of Cups."

"But the Knight," says Dao. "It means someone's coming, right?"

"Yes, but—"

"So what I should focus on is being patient and keeping things in balance, and he'll come back?"

Ella tilts her head to the side. "Is that what you're taking away from these cards?"

"Yes," says Dao, confused.

Ella takes her hand. "Sometimes the cards just reflect the energy that's going on at the moment. The future can change."

"I know it can," Dao replies. "But with my dream, and with these readings...I can *feel* that there's still another chapter for us."

Ella looks at her for a moment, then squeezes her hand. "I don't know Sunny very well. From meeting him, he seems like a really nice guy. But Dao...try and focus on your project. Go do other things you love. Please do not wait around for him. Please remember to guard your heart."

Dao wishes she knew how. She looks down at the Knight and the Queen close together. Temperance upright stands beside them. A man in white, with wings sprouting from his shoulders, holding two cups, water pouring from one to the other, then down into the river.

Sunny

A few days before his birthday, Sunny's mother calls him at her usual time during his lunch break. He's sitting in the empty classroom with a pot of instant noodles and a Coke, while the rest of his classmates have gone outside to have their meals in the Meadows.

At first, his mother's conversation is nothing out of the ordinary: she asks how his lessons are going, what the weather's like, how Aunt Oom is doing, whether his mood has been improving. Then she updates him on some drama she's been having with a friend of hers, a disagreement over fortune tellers they've been seeing. Sunny lets his mother talk, like he always does, and gives her enough information about his life to appease her.

Then she lapses into silence, but like so many times before, Sunny is able to read her mood like the back of his hand. "What is it, Ma?" he asks. "Tell me what's bothering you."

A pause. Then, in a grave voice, she says: "Your grandma has been very ill. The doctor says there's an issue with her kidney. I didn't want to tell you because I didn't want you to worry, but yesterday her symptoms got worse, and Fai and I had to drive to Bang Na late last night to take her to the hospital. She might have to stay there for a few days."

"Does Aunt Oom know?" Sunny asks. Then, in a gentler voice: "Are you sure you're able to handle all of this, Ma?" Sunny has never been close to his grandmother, but he knows how much his mother adores her.

"I talked to your aunt last night when I took Mother to the hospital. And don't you worry, Son, I'm fine, and your grandma's going to be fine. She's strong, she'll be back home in no time."

"You and Fai drove out in the middle of the night?" Sunny asks, the frustration clear in his voice. "Where was Father? Why wasn't he helping?"

His mother sighs. "Sunny, you know how your father feels about your grandma," she says, as though Sunny is the one who's being unreasonable. "And it was no problem. Fai was a wonderful help, and I wasn't tired at all. Besides, your father has been very busy lately, he deserves some time to himself."

"Some time to himself?" says Sunny, aghast.

"Sunny, please. Let's not make this a big deal today. I knew you'd react like this, which is exactly why I didn't tell you anything when she started getting sick."

"Ma, what did he do?"

"Sunny, please, your father hasn't done anything."

"That's not what I heard from Fai."

"Sunny, listen to your mother." There's a desperation in her voice that he rarely hears. "Now, let's talk about something else. It's your birthday on Saturday. Just two more days. What are you planning to do to celebrate?"

"I...really haven't thought about it."

"What do you want for your present? I can get something sent to you, or I can talk to your aunt and she can help get you something from there."

"That's okay, Ma, I don't need you to buy me anything."

"You must want *something*."

"I want you to stop defending Father and letting him do whatever he wants! Do you have any idea how much—"

"Sunny, I keep telling you, I don't want to argue today."

Sunny bites down on all the harsh words that are resting on his tongue, gets up from his seat and walks to the window. From there, he can see his classmates in the distance, strolling back from the Meadows together – this group of strangers he sees every week yet chooses to know nothing about. Sometimes he thinks he's nothing more than a coward.

"Ma, I have to go," Sunny says. "It's almost the end of my lunch break."

"Are you angry with me?"

He lets out a sigh and pushes his fingers against his temple. "Ma, you said you don't want to fight, so let's not fight."

His classmates are crossing the road. He walks back to his seat.

"Alright, Son." Sunny can hear the tension going out of her voice, whether from relief or resignation, he can't be sure. "Call me tomorrow?"

"I'll call you tomorrow. I promise. And keep me updated on Grandma."

//

The day before Sunny's birthday, his father calls him.

Sunny is in the middle of his afternoon shift in the supermarket. At first, he's too stunned to pick up. He stares at the caller ID, thinking it must be a mistake. Then he quickly gathers himself and accepts the call. "Father?"

"Your mother reminded me that tomorrow is your birthday."

It's been months since Sunny last heard his father's voice, and after all this time it sounds like thunder in the middle of summer. "Yes, sir, it is," he replies.

"Well, since I'm going to be busy tomorrow, happy birthday."

Sunny is too confused to say anything except: "Thank you, sir." Is his father genuinely wishing him happy birthday without any ulterior motive? Sunny chooses to make an effort at conversation: "How is Grandma doing? Ma told me she's been in the hospital."

"Oh, the old woman?" His father scoffs. "She'll be alright, she'll stay alive just to spite me. How are things in Scotland? Have you come to your senses about coming back home yet?"

Sunny's eyes fall shut briefly, a cynical laugh rising to his lips. *There it is.* "I thought this was a birthday call," he says.

"Birthdays are a good opportunity to reflect on who you are, to think about where your life is heading."

"Sir, you've already made your opinion about where my life is heading loud and clear."

"You already know what I think of this little *adventure* you and your mother insisted you go on. I let you go because I knew, once you were there, that you'd come to your senses."

Sunny is too angry to speak. His father continues without even raising his voice: "How is that country treating you? You must be homesick. And how is that little supermarket of my sister-in-law's doing? Are you having fun working there as her cheap hire?"

"That's not how I see things at all," Sunny says through gritted teeth. "Aunt Oom is a great boss, a great businesswoman. I'm learning a lot from being here. Not everyone in Thailand gets an opportunity to do something like this."

"You're squandering the privileges we've given you. All the sacrifices we've made, how hard I've worked all these years to provide for you and your sister. I want what's best for you, but I'm not your mother. I am not going to mollycoddle you and treat you as if you were made of glass. I'm going to tell you the honest truth every single time because that's what men do."

Sunny's anger dissipates; now he simply feels numb. He takes the phone away from his ear as his father keeps on lecturing him. There is no point trying to explain that he needs to get back to work.

Eventually, his father is the one who ends the call, citing once again his busy schedule. By that time, all Sunny has been saying in response is "Yes, sir. Yes, sir."

Once Sunny is back behind the till, his aunt, who's rearranging the condiments close by, stares at him questioningly. "Who were you talking to?" she asks.

"My father." Sunny is in no mood to elaborate, but his aunt seems to understand. In a gesture that surprises him, she reaches out and squeezes his hand. The moment is brief, only a few seconds, but the tenderness in her gaze as she looks at him causes tears to sting his eyes. He blinks them away.

Then she pulls her hand back and nods. "Get on with your work," she says.

//

The next evening, Aunt Oom makes Sunny a special birthday meal: crispy northern Thai noodles in spicy soup with chicken drumsticks, called khao soi, pork larb fried in dumpling-sized bites, and hung lay curry with ginger slices and pork belly. She even makes a chilli paste, served with cucumbers and carrots and a warm bowl of jasmine rice.

Noon and his uncle Chang join them for the meal. It's a nice enough evening, one of the nicest Sunny has had in Scotland. He is loath to complain. Everyone is friendly, light. But no matter how hard Sunny tries, he can't shake that afternoon's conversation with his father from his mind.

Noon comes to help him with the washing up after the meal is over. She doesn't say anything, simply takes the cloth from its hanger and dries the dishes one by one. Once they're all done, she asks him: "Do you feel like going for a drink, P' Sunny?"

He shakes his head. "I have somewhere I need to be."

A flash of hurt in her eyes. But he doesn't care enough

to investigate why at this moment. He's tired, with another feeling he can't name taking hold of him.

Sunny walks away from Noon, says thank you to his aunt and uncle, and leaves the supermarket, pulling on his coat as he goes. Usually he listens to music while he walks, but this evening he prefers silence.

Dao welcomes him in the lobby of her building with a happy birthday and a huge embrace. He clings to her, and they hold each other longer than usual. She buries her face in his shoulder. "How are you?" she asks.

He lets out the breath he hadn't realised he'd been holding. "Better now," he says.

She doesn't ask him what's wrong, simply takes his hand and leads him up to her room. When she opens the door, he's lost for words. She has redecorated her place for his birthday, with fairy lights streaming down from the ceiling. There are hanging photos as well, and he realises that they're all selfies of the two of them, together. He hadn't expected her to take the time to print them all out like this. There's a small table in the middle of the room, and on it is a cake topped with candles. Two presents, both wrapped in gold paper and tied with red ribbons, sit beside it. "Open them," Dao tells him, her face alight.

Sunny moves as though in a trance. He unwraps the bigger present first to find a music book with the title: *Popular Thai Songs of the Early 2000s*. He turns to her, excited. "I can't believe you got me this!"

"For your guitar lessons," she replies, beaming. "I know you miss being home. So I thought learning how to play some of your favourite songs on the guitar might help.

Besides..." – she shrugs and walks towards him – "...I can enjoy some of the perks as well."

He breaks into a smile – the only genuine smile of the whole day – and kisses her. "Thank you," he says. Yet he feels as though those two words are insufficient.

"Now the second present," she says, handing him the smaller package.

Sunny puts the guitar book down and unwraps the second present to find... "A watch?"

Breathless, he stares down at the object in the little red box. A handsome, polished silver wristwatch stares back at him. Just one look at it tells him everything he needs to know. He nearly drops it. "This is too much, Dao. This must have cost...I can't accept this!"

"Don't be silly!" Dao swoops in and takes his hands, along with the watch. "Sunny, it's your birthday. The first one we're spending together! I wanted to give you something special, something you can really use! Don't you love it?"

He stares down at the leather strap, the gold numbers on the dial, its three tiny and delicate hands. "I love it," he admits. But his words ring hollow. "But Dao, you can't give me this. This is too... You shouldn't be spending this much money on me."

"It's my money and I'll do what I want." She pecks him on the lips. "Come on, try it on, I want to see you wearing it!"

Sunny sees that there's no point in negotiating with her, so he takes the watch out of the box and puts it on. The watch is light, despite how impressive it looks, and it tears at his heart that it fits him beautifully, both in weight and style, as though he had been there in the shop with her when she'd picked it out.

She's smiling at him expectantly. "Happy birthday," she says again.

Thank you for remembering my birthday, he might have said. For being so thoughtful. For caring. For being here, and allowing me to fall into your arms when life gets a little too tiring…

But all he can think of is the feel of the watch on his wrist. The light reflecting off the silver, glinting so finely when it turns, and he catches the time.

Sunny

After Sunny and Jun graduated from university, Jun got a job doing social media marketing for a website development company, while Sunny landed a low-paying IT support job at a Central shopping mall. She moved from her dorm to a larger one-bedroom condo near On Nut, while he continued to live at home.

Sunny's father told him in his hard, grainy voice: "It would make no sense for you to waste money paying rent, when you can stay here for free and learn more about the business for when you take over."

His mother, who had always sided with his father in everything, agreed: "I'd hate not to see you every day."

Sunny wasn't particularly happy with his new job. He knew he was smart enough to find something better, to do more. But the mall was close to his house, and he was content with just coasting by and occasionally seeing Jun. The future could wait.

A year into their respective jobs, Jun broke up with him yet again, this time over a hot pot dinner, with steam rising up and stinging his eyes. It felt like a joke.

"Why?" Sunny asked. To his surprise, what she said no longer felt like a gut punch.

"I just don't think we're right for each other," she said.

The memory of her phone call on the balcony reared its head. "Is there someone else?" he asked.

Her eyes constricted with hurt. "How can you ask me that?" she said. "You've never really trusted me. Not ever. This is one of the reasons why I no longer think this is a good idea."

She said a lot more after that, but everything sounded like a corporate email from an employer, hollow, with no real details or explanations given. He would forget all the words she used soon after. Should he cry? Beg? Storm off in anger? All he felt was numb. Maybe he'd become accustomed to this dance.

"We can be friends," she told him before they parted. But they both knew it was a feeble attempt at politeness.

Sunny spent the next few weeks thinking that they would inevitably get back together, like they had done on every previous occasion. But gradually, over six weeks or so, their contact diminished. She stopped initiating communication and took longer and longer to reply to his messages, until eventually she didn't reply at all.

Then one day Sunny heard from an old university friend: Jun had been spotted at a mall in Siam with a much older man. Someone who looked rich, was the report.

Sunny kept silent. The call on the balcony. The money. It all made sense. In fact, it had made sense all along, he had just refused to see it.

His mother had been wrong, Sunny thought. Their dreams led to nothing but disappointment. He had let himself be distracted and taken in by false hope, by Jun. He should've learned his lesson the day he'd found out about his father's affair: love never works out the way we want it to.

//

Cherry was the first girl Sunny started talking to after his break-up with Jun.

They'd met on a dating app. He'd swiped on Cherry's profile because of the low-cut dress she was wearing. On the first day chatting, he added her on Instagram; by the third, he dropped hints that he'd like to come over. By the fourth, he was in her queen-sized bed in her one-bedroom apartment in Phra Khanong. She was warm, eager, as desperate as he was. And he took her with thoughts of Jun fraying at the edges of his mind, which happened occasionally when he was with a girl he didn't yet know very well.

Afterwards, they lay joking about this and that, not speaking of anything deep or particularly interesting. She made a brief mention of an ex-boyfriend who'd got her the nightlight by her bedside. Sunny made a joke about how cute she looked in nothing at all.

Later, she asked him whether she'd see him again.

"You want to see me again?" he asked.

She laid her head on his chest. His arm rested on the headboard of her bed. "Maybe," she said, smiling mischievously.

"Why would you want to see me again?" He sounded a little bewildered.

"Well, you're funny. Not creepy. Not bad on the eyes."

He laughed. "Wow, the bar's that low, is it?"

"What can I say?" she teased. "I'm a simple girl." She pushed closer into him. "I just want to have some fun. And we have fun. Don't we?"

"Yes, we do." He traced his fingers up the side of her body until they were tangled up in her hair. "Of course I'd like to see you again," he said, and drew her lips up to his.

He thought, very briefly, of telling her that he had no intention of sticking around for long. But when she returned his kiss and ran her hand up his chest to grab the back of his neck and pull herself on top of him, his resolve evaporated.

The next day, she texted asking how he was doing. He took a day to read it. He kept his response curt: I'm doing okay, just been busy with work, nothing much. She read and replied within minutes: Oh, I've been busy too, but I'm going to be free next week. Maybe we should hang out again? And he chose not to read it.

It's for the best, Sunny thought, as he ignored a second text she'd sent. If they kept seeing each other, he'd inevitably end up hurting her. And if he'd just been honest with her, it would only have hurt her feelings. They had only been talking for a couple of days and met up once. It was easier to simply fade away. She'd get the message, but in a gentler, unobtrusive way.

A week after that, he started seeing someone else – a girl from work, who could talk his ear off and make him laugh – and ended it with her soon after. Then there was another girl from the app, for a short while: someone who cared about him just as little as he cared about her. And another, who walked away from him before he could walk away from her.

Weeks stretched into months, and months blended into a year. More people came and went from his life. Before he knew it, he had forgotten the sound of Jun's voice.

Sunny

The day after his birthday, Sunny returns home from Dao's and goes straight online to look up the price of the wristwatch she'd given him.

The search results leave him feeling extremely uneasy. He puts the watch back in its box and decides to keep it discreetly tucked away in his suitcase, which is kept under his bed. He never wants to bring it out again.

He feels disgusted that she's spent this amount of money on him. Even more disgusted with himself for feeling so uncomfortable with it. Is it because he himself is insecure? His ego too fragile? Or can he simply not reconcile himself to the fact that she's paid that much money as though it were no big deal? Buying a watch like this would mean throwing months' – no, years' worth of savings away, in his case. It's absurd.

But how can he tell her this, when she's so determined to get him something special? He doesn't believe he has the words to make her understand.

//

"Have you ever dated someone who's much richer than you?" Sunny asks Noon.

They're sharing a beer after work one evening. The supermarket is already closed, and Sunny's aunt and uncle have retired upstairs. He and Noon sit on the crates in the back of the store passing a can of beer between them, talking quietly. This activity has become a weekly ritual now, ever since that day Noon had called Sunny about her ex-boyfriend.

"How rich are we talking?" Noon asks.

"Like, significantly richer than you."

Noon laughs. "You mean like a sugar daddy? Or, in your case, a sugar mama?"

"Ha ha, very funny." He allows himself a small smile, rolling his eyes. "I'm being serious."

Noon looks at him sharply. "Are you dating someone right now, P' Sunny? Someone richer?"

"Just answer the question."

"It's unfair. You asked me first. Now I have to divulge my private experiences while you get to remain mysterious."

"Answer the question and I will tell you something in return."

"Now we're talking." She winks at him. "Alright...there was this guy when I was twenty-one. This hi-so kid a few years older than me. Handsome. Drove a fancy car, had a fancy house, took me to fancy restaurants, bought me brand-name clothes...I met him on the internet. We were seeing each other for a month or two, but then it just fizzled out."

"Was it difficult, the fact that your backgrounds and lifestyles were vastly different?"

"I didn't mind all the fancy stuff. In fact, I enjoyed it. It made me think…what a *life*, you know? Never to be stressed about money – to be able to do things and move through the world without that being a hindrance. What freedom!"

"You didn't feel…I don't know…that he was superior to you? Or all of that money was a bit obscene?"

"Not at all," says Noon. She gives Sunny a startled look, mixed with concern. "Should I have been? Is it weird that I didn't?"

He thinks about it for a second. Before he knows it, he's telling Noon about Dao and everything that has happened. Shock flitters across Noon's face, but she doesn't say anything until Sunny is done speaking.

"Way to keep things to yourself all this time," Noon mutters. She takes a swig of beer and hands him the can. "You have the rest, I don't want any more."

"Are you angry I didn't tell you?"

"No, P' Sunny, I'm not angry." She sighs. "I want a cigarette."

"We can't smoke inside."

"I know that, genius."

Silence. He watches her carefully. Her brows are knitted together, her lips pursed in frustration. Finally, she shakes her head and turns to him. "So you're feeling like you love her, but you're having doubts about this relationship because of your incompatible lifestyles and just how both of you are as people?"

"I never said I loved her," Sunny said.

"Not in so many words, but that's the gist of it, right?"

It's Sunny's turn to fall silent. He feels as though he's revealed too much, and takes a sip of beer. "Yes, that's the gist of it," he admits. Another moment of silence. Another sip. Then nearly in a whisper: "I don't think this whole thing with Dao is going to work out."

Noon's expression turns wistful. "I'm sorry to hear that, P' Sunny, it's not easy being alone." She looks away. "You meet someone you really care about, someone you click with, but there's no chance for you to be together... That's sad."

Sunny has never been able to abide other people's pity. "Don't be sorry," he says bluntly. "It's just life."

For a second, he thinks, he sounds exactly like his father.

//

"You haven't worn your watch," Dao observes.

The two of them are at dinner in Fountainbridge, a rare occurrence since they spend most of their time at Dao's place. Her camera and equipment are on the chair next to them. She's been spending the day photographing subjects for her exhibition, while he's been working a morning shift at the supermarket and attending an afternoon class.

Sunny looks down at his wrist, as though surprised. "Oh," he says. "I must've forgotten."

"Don't you like it?"

"I'm just not used to wearing watches." He shrugs. "Besides, I want to save it for special occasions. Don't want to damage it or lose it."

"Oh." She looks awkward. Cautious. He notices she's been like that since his less-than-stellar showing with her friends at the pub.

They spend the dinner discussing how her project is shaping up. He listens, mostly, giving his reaction here and there, but he finds his mind wandering.

"Sunny, is everything alright?"

Dao's question jolts him out of his reverie. She's staring at him, her face creased with worry. He realises he hasn't really been paying attention for the last few minutes. "I'm sorry," he says automatically. "It's just been a long day, I'm a little tired."

"It's been a long day for me too, but I did ask if you wanted to meet up and you said yes." She sounds hurt, which makes him feel worse. "Are you sure nothing's wrong?"

Sunny thinks of the conversation he had with Noon, and the doubts he'd quietly expressed as the shadows lengthened on the floor of the shop. But now, looking at Dao, Sunny can't bring himself to tell her the truth.

"Nothing's wrong, sorry. I'm just tired," he repeats, and decides to pivot: "What about you? Is there something you want to talk to me about?"

Dao is taken aback, and for a second she looks like she wants to say something. Then she gives a small smile and shakes her hand. "I'm alright, there's nothing major. I've just been worried about you, that's all."

"You really don't need to be," Sunny replies kindly. "Everything's good, I promise. We're good."

He thinks: perhaps things can still be different. Perhaps there's still time.

//

But that night, during the quiet hours of the early morning, when light has yet to touch the edge of the horizon, Sunny dreams...

He's a boy again, all the years turned back – a little boy traipsing around the house behind his mother. Younger, happier, more beautiful – she towers above everything and her smile is luminous, her laughter ringing out with joy. Sunny can't remember the last time he's seen his mother so full of life.

Then, without warning and as sudden as a flame, a shadow passes across his mother's face and her smile disappears. Sunny can feel the atmosphere in the room shift to a familiar feeling of fear that seems to always be hiding in the pit of his stomach, biding its time.

He tries to reach for his mother, pleading with her to pick him up, to tell him that everything is alright. But she's looking away from him, towards someone he can't see.

Sunny hears his father's voice, booming and loud, like the sound of a whip cracking through the air. Then, that sense of gloom, pressing down on his chest until air barely escapes his lungs. His mother cries out, full of despair and hurt. But Sunny is too small, too helpless and weak to help her.

His father's voice rises even higher. Then Sunny is falling, his arms flailing about in front of him, his childhood home fading into shadows. He tries to grab hold of his mother, but her cries are farther and farther away, and he can't reach her.

Suddenly Sunny hits the ground, and his world spins. There's thunder in the distance.

He staggers up and discovers that he's no longer a child, and now just a man, who is unsteady on his feet.

A woman is standing across from him.

At first he can't see her face through the mist, but he keeps walking closer and closer, a desperate *need to know* driving him forward. And then there she is, with her eyes burning fire and rain mixing with the tears on her cheeks.

Sunny hears himself call her name: "Dao…!". She doesn't reply, and so he calls out for her again, over and over, as if the sound has the power to stop the downpour.

But like his mother had done, the woman turns away, retreating further and further into the darkness. Sunny makes to follow her, but every time he puts one foot in front of the other, an invisible force pushes him back.

Then the water begins to rise, and he starts to sink, the flood pulling him down to its depth with greedy, claw-like fingers.

Too late, he thinks. All too late.

Sunny

When Sunny was ten years old, his father had taken him to buy a condo in the heart of Bangkok.

It was in the Sathorn area, where the traffic was always extremely busy during rush hour. The unit was on the twenty-second floor: a one-bedroom apartment with a balcony, a bathtub in the main bathroom and a living room large enough to entertain at least five guests. It came unfurnished, but Father was in no hurry to decorate the place. He took Sunny up to view the room late one evening.

While Father was examining the water and electricity, Sunny stood out on the balcony and wrapped his arms around the railing that came up to his chin as he stared out at the Bangkok skyline. Below him roads twisted and turned, the cars so small they were merely a crowd of red lights. There was a calm in the atmosphere that made him feel strangely safe.

His father joined him. "Great view, isn't it? You feel like you're on top of the world."

"Sir, why can't we live here instead of at the shop?" Sunny asked, imagining what it would be like to wake up to this view every day.

"One bedroom for the four of us?" said his father, laughing.

"Are you crazy? But I'm happy you like it up here. If you work hard like me, keep the shop running like me, you can buy a condo like this for yourself one day."

Father looked extremely proud of himself as he said this. His face, usually so stern and guarded, glowed with success. Along with how captivating Bangkok looked from this height, that look on his father's face was what Sunny remembered most from this experience.

//

On the night Father was told of Sunny's plans to go to Scotland, it was this memory – his father's pride, his child-like excitement – that Sunny thought of most.

Ma suggested that she go into Father's office alone first to gently broach the subject with his father. "If you come in with me right from the start," she told Sunny, "his first reaction will be that you want to work in your aunt's store, but not in his. He'll be angry. But his anger always passes. After I've laid the groundwork for you, you can come in and talk to him yourself. He'll be more understanding then."

Sunny agreed to proceed with his mother's plan, but the moment he heard the office door shut behind her, he crept down from his bedroom and sat down at the bottom of the stairs. Ever since he was very young he'd been using this spot to listen in on the low murmurs of what was said inside the office.

It wasn't long before Father's voice started to rise, and snatches of what he said began to filter through.

"So you're telling me," said Father, his voice thick with incredulity, "that what this kid needs is to go and live abroad with your sister? To go and learn English? How does that solve anything? How does that make him better equipped to do what he ought to be doing?"

Sunny heard his mother's muffled protestations. "Tone, he's still young. Don't you remember what you were like at his age?"

"I was making money at his age! Not wasting my time taking on shit IT jobs in malls and travelling the world! I paid for the boy's education! The education I never had! He keeps talking about doing things his own way. Having something for himself. But what are these things he keeps talking about? What is he doing that is of any substance?"

More low, fervent explanations from Sunny's mother. But Father's response was merciless and scorching: "It would be best if the boy knew the truth: he has always been useless! Ungrateful, spoiled and irresponsible! It's all your fault, you've been too soft on him – you, your mother, his sister! You, feeding him with all your nonsense about dreams and fortune tellers! Did you think I wouldn't know? This is what's come of letting my son be raised by women, he grows up without a spine, he might as well wear a fucking skirt!"

"Tone, please!"

"You know what?" Father laughed viciously. "The way he's turned out just proves what I've suspected all along: that I made the wrong decision when I chose you as my wife."

Ma's cries reached Sunny's ears. "Tone, you don't mean that, please, you don't mean that!"

"I've given you so many chances to prove yourself to me, and you've failed every single time! My family! A fucking disappointment!"

Then came the sound of Father's fist making contact with the desk, and Ma screamed. Sunny sprang to his feet.

"P' Sunny, wait—"

Sunny looked up to see Fai standing on the landing, her face pale with fear. But Sunny was already moving. His hand was almost on the doorknob when it swung open, and he came face to face with his father.

The older man's eyes were flashing with anger and distaste, his expression thunderous. In the corner of his eye, Sunny saw his mother slumped over in a chair, her head in her hands.

"Sir—" Sunny began, anger and fear and hurt warring against each other inside of him.

Father's look chilled Sunny to the bone. "You two do what you want," he said, turning away from Sunny and directing his words towards his wife. "But you will see that I'm right eventually and you will come crawling back. I'm done here." He pushed Sunny out of the way and marched towards the front door without a backward glance, grabbing the car keys from their peg on the wall.

Sunny rushed to his mother's side, with Fai following close behind.

At the sight of Sunny, Ma quickly brushed a hand over her face to compose herself, but she was shaking terribly. "I did warn you." She attempted a rueful smile. "He wasn't going to be pleased. Your father is a passionate man, he'll speak his mind."

"Ma, stop defending him!"

"Sunny, please, I can't have this conversation right now—" Her voice trembled and she was near tears again.

"Maybe my going is a bad idea," Sunny said, his words rushed and panicked. "I don't want to leave you like this, he's never been this bad, we don't know what he'll do!"

"Nonsense," his mother said. "Everything is arranged, this is an opportune time." From the use of that phrase, he realised

she'd consulted a fortune teller. That made him even angrier.

"Ma, that doesn't matter!" Sunny thundered. "We can't live our lives according to your dreams and your cards!"

"You heard your father when he walked out: he's going to let you go. I did tell you that he would get angry, but his tempers pass quickly."

"Ma, some of the things he said—"

But her expression was so broken that he couldn't say anything more.

Sunny and Fai went and wrapped their arms around her and she felt tiny in their embrace, cornered and quivering, a frightened child. They held her until her crying subsided. Until she was able to pull herself together and attempted to say that the whole episode had simply been nothing but a misunderstanding and the result of exhaustion.

Sunny's eyes found his sister's over their mother's head. It's no use, *they told her.* No use at all.

Later that night, once Sunny was alone in his room, he tried to pass the time by watching something mindless on TV. But still he couldn't shake the night's events from his mind, especially everything he'd heard his father say.

Even after so long, it was still a habit so ingrained in him, it felt like breathing: pressing Jun's number.

He thought about what he was going to say. I'm leaving Thailand, *he could start.* I thought you ought to know. *Or,* I've just been wondering how you are. *Or simply...*I miss you.

The line rang and rang and rang...but no one answered.

Dao

As Simone turns her head to the left to show Dao's camera her side profile, Dao's thoughts stray to that first camera Shane had put in her hands all those years ago. Her fingers shake, but just for a fraction of a second, and then she clicks the shutter.

Afterward, Simone comes over to look at the portraits in Dao's camera. Her eyes fill with admiration.

"Dao, these are great," Simone marvels. "I never thought I could look like this." She pauses at a particular portrait and smiles. "I love this one," she says.

They haven't really styled Simone for the shoot; she's wearing her usual clothes – high-waisted jeans and a white collared shirt – with minimal make-up and her hair tied up in a loose ponytail. Her smile is tense, more of a smirk, as though she's offering a challenge: *How close do you dare come?*

Simone takes Dao's hand. "Thank you," she says. "You've given me something so special."

Dao beams. She wishes she could condense everything she's feeling in that moment into a single photograph and send it to Sunny. But all she can do is send a series of excited texts. Before that, he had given her a very short update: he's going to be in class all day. So she doesn't want to think about when he'll reply, especially since he hasn't been replying much lately.

She and Simone are in the university's studio. It's a rare sunny day, but all the curtains are drawn; the only source of light is the spotlight Dao had set up for her shots. Dao's mentor – a tall, red-haired Scottish woman in her fifties – hands her a small pile of brochures for the exhibition.

"They finished the artwork yesterday," says the lecturer. Multiple silk scarves are wrapped around her neck, and her large hoop earrings glitter in gold and silver. "You can give these out to your friends or put them up somewhere. Invite as many people as you can to come see your work."

Dao thanks her profusely. She takes out her phone to take pictures of the brochures and thinks about whether she should send one to Sunny. But would double-texting him be too much?

"You're doing good work here," her mentor tells her. "But don't forget that essay you have to write." And Dao says that of course she won't forget.

Simone is kind enough to stay behind to help Dao pack up. By the time the two of them reach the nearby pub, it's dark. Cady and Ella are already there, each with a plate of food and a drink. Simone starts chatting with them right away and excitedly shows them the portraits Dao has taken of her.

Dao orders a small pizza and a rum and Coke for herself while she listens. She tries not to think about whether Sunny has texted back yet. An hour or so into the night she checks, and still there is nothing.

Then Cady is speaking to her, something about how many portraits she's taken for her project already and how many more are left. Dao feels her mouth move to answer her friend's questions, her hand drawing out the exhibition brochure from her purse.

Then she makes excuses about getting a breath of air and dashes for the door, pulling on her jacket haphazardly.

There's a group of students outside smoking cigarettes. She sidesteps them and sits down on a nearby bench.

Still…no messages.

Her fingers hover over the keys. Before she knows it, she's sending Sunny the picture of the brochure. Immediately, she wishes she could take it back, and she puts her phone away as though it were a piece of burning coal.

She continues to sit there and watch the students smoke. Ella is the one who finds her.

"Dao, are you alright?" Ella asks. Ever since their last reading, Dao has begun to notice that Ella will often look at her with concern – or pity? – and this has been happening more and more often, particularly when Sunny is mentioned.

Dao forces a smile. "Yes. Why wouldn't I be?"

Ella hesitates. "Is everything okay with you and Sunny? You just seem a little distracted, and last time we talked about him you were quite worked up—"

"Everything is fine," Dao says immediately. "We had a conversation. He just has a lot going on at the moment, but nothing's wrong."

The thought of admitting the extent of her worry

feels like conceding defeat. The Knight of Cups still has to come true; she's not ready to give up on her dream just yet. And Dao also knows, deep down, what her friend would say, and none of it would include anything positive about Sunny.

Ella looks sceptical, but tells Dao kindly, "Alright, if you say so. But come back inside, we all miss you."

Dao goes to bed that night having not heard from Sunny, and repeats to herself possible reasons for why he's been distant with her. Maybe he's just busy. Maybe it's her own insecurities making her more attached; they don't have to be chatting to each other all the time. He has a lot going on. And it's important to give each other space.

He'll reply, she tells herself. He always does.

//

The next day, Dao shows up at the supermarket when she knows that Sunny will be on his shift.

He looks up in surprise when she comes in, waving a brochure for the exhibition. "I have to give you this," she announces. "And I wanted to make sure you were doing okay."

"I didn't know you were coming." Sunny gives her a half-smile and puts away his phone. "Is everything alright?"

"Yes, of course!" She hopes her voice doesn't sound too high-pitched or forced. She approaches the counter and hands him the brochure. "Official invitation," she says. "Two weeks from now. I don't know if you'll be busy, but I want you to be there. You've been such a big part of what

I do. It would mean so much to me if you could see the whole project on display."

He takes the brochure from her and scans it. "Alright," he says. "I'll be there."

She can't read him. "Do you want me to stay with you?" she asks. "Keep you company for the rest of your shift?"

"No, it's okay." He reaches out to take her hand. One tiny gesture and her body softens. "It's boring here. You should go hang out with your friends. Enjoy your night."

"Sunny—"

"I'm fine, I promise."

"Sunny, I know you can go through things alone, but that doesn't mean you have to. I'm right here. I'm not going anywhere. If anything's the matter, you can let me be there for you."

A cloud falls across his face. For a second, he's unguarded. And she thinks: finally.

But then he gives her a smile. "I'm fine, Dao. Really. You don't need to worry." And he kisses her palm.

Dao

While at university, Dao and Shane kept in sporadic contact, but they no longer hung out in person or had any of the long phone calls that were synonymous with their schooldays. Yet Dao held on firmly to her faith in her dream of the airplane and the card reading that had followed. At least she and Shane were still in each other's lives; there was still hope.

Dao couldn't imagine Shane leaving Thailand. Of the two of them, only she had shown any interest in travelling the world. So as long as they were still keeping in touch, as long as they were in the same country, she was never going to lose him.

When graduation season rolled around, Dao did wonder…should she show up at his ceremony and take pictures with him as was customary with new graduates? In Thailand, graduation is considered a monumental event. She sent Shane the date and times for pictures at her campus in case he'd like to attend. He, however, didn't send an invitation to his graduation in return and didn't post about it online.

In the end, he didn't come to her ceremony.

When Teoy asked if Dao had expected him to be here, she looked at all the bouquets gifted to them from friends and relatives. The lie came easily now: "No. I'd assumed he'd be busy with his own graduation, and he was."

"Did you invite him?"

"Yes."

"Did he reply?"

"Oh, of course. He told me congratulations." This, too, was a lie.

When Shane's true congratulations came, it was two months too late. But it came with an invitation she had not been expecting at all.

I'm sorry I've been such a rubbish friend, he wrote. It's been so long since I last saw you. Let's meet up.

Dao's heart jolted. She quickly unlocked her phone, already forming an enthusiastic reply to send back when another message from him arrived. I've missed you, he said.

Those words opened up something inside her, and a restlessness she'd never felt before seized hold of her.

In that moment, she made up her mind: it was time. She was finally going to tell him how she felt. She had been waiting for much too long.

//

Dao and Shane agreed to meet by the Chao Phraya river, in a beautiful Chinese heritage building in the Talad Noi area. The old building had been converted into a cafe for Bangkokians to come and enjoy desserts and beverages, and take vintage-style pictures for Instagram. Ivy crawled up the crumbling brick walls and grey clouds dotted the sky, the city's usual humidity turning the air sticky.

Shane no longer looked like a teenage boy, Dao thought to herself, as she watched her old friend walk through the cafe to *where she was sitting. He had a more confident stride now, his pale, pointed face more angular, with his hair grown out and his muscles taut.*

Yet, like always, even though it had been ages since they'd met up, her stomach lurched at the sight of him – a habit she'd always been terrified of never being able to quit. She watched him make his way through the cafe, and for the first time since she'd made up her mind to do so, she felt excited at the prospect of telling him the truth. Perhaps this was how their story was meant to play out. After all these years of their timing not being right, perhaps now – now that they had spent some time apart, growing up as they each needed to do, putting the capriciousness of youth behind them – their paths would finally merge.

"Hi," Shane said when he reached her.

"Hi," Dao replied. She couldn't help it: her face broke into a smile.

They ordered tea, a coffee, a thin slice of cheesecake that only earned its steep price because of the surroundings. The rhythm of conversation was scratchy, like a record that still played but was just broken enough to skip occasionally: mutual friends, family members, the weather, politics, until eventually the topic came around to work.

"Are you going to look for a job in photography?" Shane asked, gesturing to her camera.

"Well, that's the plan." Dao blushed. "I still feel silly admitting that, for some reason."

"Oh, it's not silly at all."

"I don't know if I'd make enough money to get by."

"Well…" Shane offered a lopsided grin. "The good thing is you don't need to."

"That sounds awful."

"That's the truth." Shane shrugged. *"You should enjoy it."*

"My idea is...I only want to photograph people. Interesting people, you know. Capture them in a way that only I can see them."

"So strictly portraits?"

"Maybe. But I still doubt whether I'm good enough to do it full-time. As a career. It sounds so scary. So adult!"

He laughed. "It's strange, but I've always imagined you doing something like that," he remarked. "In school, you were into all that abstract stuff that was always too clever for the likes of me."

"Oh, no," she laughed. "I was just being a dramatic teenager. And you were always cleverer than me. I've always thought you were."

A pause: they looked at each other a little too long.

He picked at his half of the cake, sitting uneaten and forlorn on his plate, and then sipped his cappuccino. "Anyway, there's a reason why I invited you here today," he said eventually, drawing a breath. He didn't quite meet her eye. "I have something I need to tell you."

"I have something to tell you too," she said, smiling.

Is this the moment? *she thought, her heart hammering. She wanted to remember everything – all the words she'd secretly always wanted to hear him say:* I've realised now. It's you. I'm sorry I took so long.

But he didn't say any of these things.

"I thought you should know," said Shane. "I've been talking to my dad and he suggested...well, the thing is...I'll be leaving soon."

The smile slid off her face. "Leaving? To where?"

"America," said Shane. "For the business, you know. Dad says it's time for me to step in full-time."

Dao didn't know how much time had passed after he'd said those words; she must have been in complete shock. Then Shane said her name, and she noticed that his expression turned to concern. Panicking, she exclaimed: "Oh, that's great! That's exciting, I can't believe it! America! Wow!" And when he didn't look convinced, she rushed on: "When do you leave?"

"Next month. I already have a visa."

"But…I've always thought you'd take over the business here, in Thailand."

"Dad wants to expand what he started in Texas. And he thought it'd be a good learning ground for me. A father–son project." His voice was laced with sarcasm. "You know how my dad is, always picking up some crazy new idea."

"When will you be back?"

"Who knows?" He attempted a light-hearted smile. "Dad wants to try and get me to stay for as long as possible."

"Wow," she said again, feeling as if she were one of those dolls she had as a child, capable of repeating only one word over and over again when you pulled its string. "Wow. That's… you're going to do great, Shane, I know you will. Does Teoy know yet?"

"No. I wanted to tell you first."

"That's nice of you."

"I know we haven't been as close as we used to be," Shane said. "I'm sorry if things have been…weird since uni. But you'll always be my friend. That hasn't changed and it's not going to."

She didn't know what to say to that, so she didn't respond.

Shane, looking concerned again, asked: "You said you had some-thing to tell me as well? What is it?"

She shook her head and forced herself to give him a small smile. "Oh, I actually don't remember anymore," she said. "Maybe it'll come back to me in a little while."

Dao wanted to reach for his hand; after all, she had never held it before. All of these things between us, *she wanted to say.* Those longing looks, the secret smiles, the slip of the tongue when you said tender things to me. The enormity of who I am, given away, almost freely. What were they, then, if you've never chosen me? Not even now?

But all these questions could only be asked by another girl – someone braver, who cared less about what his answers would be – and Dao was not that girl, not yet.

So she smiled and told him exactly what he wanted to hear. "Don't worry," she said. "I'm not angry with you. We're okay."

//

By the time Dao got home, it was already dusk. She noticed her father's car parked under the tamarind tree. Her mother and P' Pun were setting the table for dinner. The scents of warm rice, garlic and chilli drifted out from the kitchen. She could smell her father's favourite dish through the half-open doorway – clear broth stewed with chicken drumsticks stuffed with Chinese herbs.

"Where's Father?" Dao asked, almost automatically.

"In his study," her mother replied. She nodded towards the closed door.

Dao felt a strange urge to go knock on it, but she stopped herself just in time. She told her mother, rather hurriedly, that she was going upstairs to change before dinner.

Once Dao was alone in her room, she sank to the floor and finally let the tears fall.

She noticed a picture taped to her full-length mirror: a snapshot from what felt like a lifetime ago when she went on a trip to the north of Thailand as a teenager. A cluster of mountains, with a sea of mist clinging to them. Her younger self stood in the foreground, smiling so brightly that she hardly recognised herself; her arm was slung over Teoy's shoulder. The person behind the lens, however, was who she thought about most. Shane had taken the picture with her camera. It was he who'd insisted the they capture the moment.

What, Dao wondered, was she supposed to do now? She finally realised: All this time, I've simply been waiting for nothing.

She thought of her dream from four years ago – of the plane, shaking in a storm, and the feeling of being close enough to touch the sky.

Maybe it's time, *she thought.* For something new, somewhere else.

Sunny

The next two weeks pass in a blur for Sunny.

He tries not to think of the nightmare he had and what it could mean. Even though it has left him with an uneasy feeling, he tells himself that he is not his mother. He is not Dao. He puts no stock in silly superstitions.

But he can feel himself pulling away from Dao regardless. He begins taking longer to reply to her texts and doesn't call to check in as often. He can tell from her constant questions – about what he's doing and how he's feeling – that she's getting worried. Her need for him seems to be laced into every word of encouragement she offers, in every question she asks.

He marvels once more at how easy it is for her to simply say exactly how she feels about him. It is one of the most terrifying things about her.

He feels guilty for thinking it, but the question has pushed itself to the forefront of his mind: *What more do you want from me?*

It shouldn't be a burden, should it? he wonders to himself. Being loved by someone? But no matter how many times he turns the thought over in his mind, the stone at the heart of it remains.

//

The day before Dao's exhibition, Sunny's father's name flashes across his phone.

There's no small talk, no asking after his well-being. Father, as always, gets straight to the point: "Sunny, your grandmother is dead. I need you home."

For a second, Sunny is too stunned to speak. Somehow, the only memories of his grandmother that are coming to him are the ones from his childhood: hours spent together in silence and stillness, with the TV humming in the background, and the old woman an immovable object, distant and untouchable.

He suddenly feels lightheaded and sinks to the ground. His first question is: "How's Ma?"

"Your mother is trying to arrange the funeral," his father replies, "but she is distraught and in shock. You know how your mother is, she's never good in a crisis."

Sunny swallows all the harsh retorts that come to mind and tries to keep his tone civil. "Ma kept saying that Grandma was doing fine, that she was going to get better."

"Well, your mother just didn't know what she was talking about. That's not news."

"Does Aunt Oom know yet?"

"Your mother would have told her by now," Father says. "Your aunt should be flying back to Bangkok for the funeral, that's what your mother said, so I want you to be on that plane with her."

"You want me home to help with Ma? Is this the angle

you're using now?" Sunny has been expecting Father to use this situation to his own advantage somehow; now he understands why he's getting a call about his grandmother's death from his father and not his mother.

"You're her son, she relies on you. You're refusing to fly home to be with your mother at a time like this?" Father's voice is laced with mockery, as though he's throwing out a challenge.

Dao's face flashes across Sunny's mind. "Every time I think that things could be different between us…"

"There's no need to be dramatic," says Father, frustrated. "Your grandmother is dead and your mother needs you home, so you're coming home. Even if just for a short time. I also want you back because your grandmother left her Bang Na house to you in her will, like your mother requested. I want you to sign the house over to me."

This information absolutely stumps Sunny. Father using Grandma's death to get Sunny to return to Thailand is very much in line with his character. But his sudden interest in owning the Bang Na house is completely unexpected.

"But that's Ma and Aunt Oom's childhood home," Sunny protests, confused. "Why would you want it?"

"I have my reasons."

Fear slides its blade into him. "What are those reasons, sir?"

"Are you talking back to your father?"

"No, sir, I'm simply asking a question." A bravery he doesn't recognise takes hold of him. "Since you're asking me to sign over a house that has great sentimental value to my mother, and a property that would be an asset to me in the future, I deserve the full story."

"I've talked to your mother," Father says curtly. "She's fine with it, she understands that I'm making the best decision for all of us. That building is old. We're not renting it out, no one is living in it. There need to be some changes. I already have someone I'm planning to give it to. Someone who can afford to take care of it."

Again, that memory: the silver Citroën backing into their driveway. The rain falling thick and fast. His mother crying out in his dream.

Sunny asks numbly: "Who are you talking about, sir?"

"A friend of mine. You don't need to know anything else. I only need you to sign the documents."

"Sir, I don't think I can do that."

"I just told you that your mother has already agreed," Father thunders. "Why must you make everything so difficult, boy?"

"Can you please put Ma on the phone?"

"Your mother is busy. And like I said, everything is already agreed."

Sunny's hand balls into a fist as anger and blind courage fuel him on. "Sir, with all due respect, I know for a fact that Ma, Grandma and Aunt Oom wouldn't want this house to go to a friend of yours. No matter how much you might like this *friend*."

"Watch your tone with me, boy!"

"Father—"

"I let you traipse all the way to Scotland to play at being a man! I watch you squander the education I've given you like it's nothing! I've had enough! Now you listen to me. I'll give you some time to cool down. But the next time we speak, you better talk to me with respect. I'll call again tomorrow and you will have an answer for me as to when you're coming back. Understood?"

Sunny swallows. "Yes, sir," he replies automatically.

"Good."

After his father has hung up, Sunny calls his mother at once. She doesn't answer. He tries again. Still nothing. He calls his sister, but that, too, goes unanswered. He has no choice but to leave a message: *I talked to Father. I know about Grandma. Call me back as soon as you can.*

He calls his aunt, which he has never done before. The line rings for a long time. He's about to hang up when she answers.

"Aunt Oom, it's me," Sunny says at once. "We need to talk."

//

A few hours later, Sunny is standing and smoking outside the supermarket with Noon. It's drizzling again, and pedestrians trudge past in long, hurried strides.

Sunny lets Noon talk about her day while he broods. The conversation with his father and his latest dream are lodged inside his chest, blocking air.

Noon sighs dramatically. "What I'd do for a plate of Bonchon fried chicken…"

"Well, I might be able to have some soon," Sunny admits quietly. "I think I'm going home."

Noon whips around to look at him. "What do you mean, you *think* you're going home?" Her eyes fill with alarm, and for whatever reason, it makes him feel terrible about himself.

He takes a sharp breath. "I am actually going home. It's just family stuff, it's nothing to do with you." Somehow, he feels the need to let her know that. "My grandma just passed away and I have to go home and take care of my mother."

Noon's expression turns mournful. "Oh, P' Sunny, I am so sorry. Your poor mother. And Aunt Oom!"

Sunny has never been good with sympathy or condolences. "Well, Grandma and I weren't that close and she'd been ill for a while, so..." He lets the rest of that sentence trail away uncomfortably. "I just talked to Aunt Oom, she's booking plane tickets for the two of us."

Noon pauses. "When will you be coming back?" She looks sad, and he tears his gaze away.

"As soon as I can," he assures her. "I won't be gone long, I promise."

For whatever reason, he hasn't told Dao yet.

//

The next morning, the day of Dao's exhibition, Sunny's sister Fai calls. "Have you booked your flight yet?" she asks.

Sunny tells her that, yes, he's coming home two days from now. He and Aunt Oom will be flying together, transferring through Istanbul. "How's Ma? She won't call me back."

"She's busy arranging the funeral," says Fai, "but I know she's taken the news badly. I've never seen her like this, P' Sunny. I'm so glad you'll be home soon."

Fai sounds like she's been crying. Sunny hasn't shed a single tear. It's been more than a year since he last saw his grandmother. They were never close, but he still feels like he ought to be sadder about her passing. Instead it's his guilt that feels more pronounced.

//

A few hours later, Sunny finds himself outside a pub with Noon.

She's finally managed to stop him drinking, and she stands beside him, holding him by the arm as he tries to catch his breath.

"When you told me you wanted to grab drinks," Noon mutters, "I didn't think you meant till the death."

"I told you to stop me at three drinks. Four, at most." His head is spinning, and he can feel the nausea building up.

Noon rolls her eyes. "Have you ever tried stopping yourself when you've set your mind on something? It's like trying to stop a tsunami. It's futile."

Sunny's words come out all slurred. "I think I have somewhere I need to be," he says.

Noon takes a firm grip of his arm. "You shouldn't be going anywhere but home in this state. Where are you supposed to be?"

He takes the paper out of his pocket. It is all crumpled up and wet around the edges, and he remembers that he'd used it earlier as a coaster. "University," he mumbles. "Exhibition. I promised."

Noon takes the brochure from him and studies it with a frown. "No way you're going to P' Dao's event while you're this drunk!"

"I have to go," Sunny says. "I promised. Take me to the bus."

"P' Sunny—"

"Noon, just do as I say. Please."

A little while later, the two of them are in the back of a bus. He closes his eyes and tries not to be too swayed by the motion of the vehicle. Noon sits beside him; he can sense her concern and disapproval even though he can't see her expression. "You should be going home," Noon repeats. "She wouldn't want to see you like this."

Dao wants him to be there, Sunny tries to tell Noon. She's told him multiple times. He's doing what she wants.

Next thing he knows, he's spilling out of the bus, his arms and legs all tangled, his vision blurry. The world turns upside down. Noon grabs his arm. "You can barely walk, P' Sunny," she says. But he insists they go inside the building. "Please just take me there, Noon," he keeps saying, "I need to be there."

Then he's walking into a large, white room, spotlights shining into his eyes. He catches a glimpse of portraits hanging on walls, glasses of wine in people's hands, confused glances.

Then his eyes land on Dao standing at the far end of the room. His brain briefly registers what she's wearing: an elegant strapless black dress, with her hair loose over her shoulders and a wine glass in her hand. She turns and spots him.

It's been more than a week since he last saw her. Or has it been more than that? He isn't quite sure, but he has known she'd be upset with him because of it and, sure enough, there's a sting in her eyes and a particular tightness in the corners of her mouth. She's hurt, and he detests himself. But then she says, "You're late," with an accusing tone in her voice that gets his back up.

"I'm here, aren't I?" he counters. "You wanted me to come, and I'm here."

Dao's stare pierces straight through him. "Are you drunk?" she asks.

He hears so much contempt and judgement in her question that he baulks. She moves quickly to take his arm and lead him outside. The cold wind hits his face, waking him up a little.

She sits him down on a hard wooden bench, and he dimly registers that they're right in front of the campus building. Noon is nowhere to be found. There are only a few students standing at the gate, talking and laughing. He's surprised by how gentle Dao's touch is when she sits down next to him and caresses his cheek.

"Sunny, are you alright?" Dao asks. "What's wrong?"

Somehow, her ability to put her own hurt aside and speak to him makes him feel more ashamed of himself and his situation. He opens his mouth to speak but no sound comes out.

Then Dao's eyes grow wide. "You're here with Noon," she says. "What is she even doing here? Did something happen between the two of you?"

He's too taken aback to form his sentences properly. "Is

that honestly what you think of me?" he blurts out. "Do you think I'm that much of an asshole?"

She begins to pace back and forth in front of him. "I don't understand why this keeps happening," she mutters to herself. "I don't understand what I'm doing wrong. I thought everything was supposed to align...I thought you'd come around."

The next thing he knows, words come tumbling out. "Dao, I have a lot going on," he says. "Things you don't even know about. But you...with your gifts, and your constant questions..." Somehow, he can't stop. "Maybe it would've been better for us to take things slow. I didn't want to rush, but you just had to go and get too invested—"

The look on her face when she turns around to face him makes him immediately regret everything he's said and wish he could take it all back. But there's nothing to be done now.

Dao's expression crumbles. "So all of this," she says, "has meant nothing to you?"

"Dao, that's not what I'm saying—"

"No, I hear what you're saying loud and clear. You said I got too invested. I thought maybe you wanted to take your time, that you were scared. But has this all been just a game to you?"

His brain scrambles for the right things to say. *Do something*, he tells himself. *Anything*. But all he can seem to do is sit there and watch her as she looks at him imploringly. He sees tears on her cheeks.

Then she's walking away from him and back into the building, her head bent and her steps quickening to a run.

Follow her, he urges himself. Do something. Anything. Fix this. But he does nothing and simply lets the time pass, until there's a careful touch on his shoulder.

"P' Sunny, how long have you been sitting here?" Noon asks, but he can't find the energy to reply. She crouches down so that their faces are level. "P' Sunny, where is P' Dao?"

He shakes his head. His mind is a forest of cigarette smoke and dead ends.

"Come on," Noon says, so gently. "I'll take you home."

Soon after, Sunny is lying on his bed. His eyes are open, fixed on the ceiling. There's something heavy on his chest: a very large crate, perhaps, like the ones they keep vegetables in for the supermarket, or a big boulder. He wants to drift off to sleep and not have to think about anything. But if he sleeps, the nightmares might come…

The next thing he knows, there's light breaking in through the curtains.

PART FOUR

The Breaking

Dao

After a dreamless sleep, Dao wakes with the determination to dwell only on the good parts of last night.

Her exhibition had gone down extremely well. The fight with Sunny, she tells herself, is just one unfortunate blip. She needs to focus on the applause she received from her lecturers and course mates at the end of the night, and how her portraits had shone under the spotlights.

Her parents have sent her congratulatory messages, wanting to hear about every little detail. She's sent them pictures from the night, including snapshots of her smiling proudly in front of her portraits, a glass of wine in her hand. Her parents show their pride and enthusiasm in multiple positive emojis. Her father even goes as far as reposting the pictures on his Facebook page.

It was a good night, she tells herself.

But she can't deny it: she had looked around, wanting to see Sunny standing at the back of the room. Maybe next to Simone, taking in her moment, smiling proudly. But he wasn't there.

He hadn't wanted to be there, she reminds herself, sitting up in bed. He'd shown up late, drunk, with another girl. He hadn't cared that it was an important night for her.

You had to go and get too invested. Those words make her burn with embarrassment. There is nothing, she feels – absolutely nothing – more humiliating than feeling so much more than the other person.

She sits through her lectures that day dazed and exhausted, emerging from the campus in the evening with a headache. Still no messages from Sunny. She heads straight home, microwaves a meal for dinner and then crashes on her bed.

When she finally awakes, the first thing she does is check her phone. It's nearly eleven at night. Still no messages.

She gets out of bed, splashes cold water on her face, and slips into her boots and her big coat with the hood.

The night has a certain charm to it, she notes, as she begins walking down the road towards Haymarket. A few stars have come out, the half-moon silver and bright. A few restaurants are still open; late-night diners clink wine glasses and chat under the glow of yellow lights. She walks on, trying to think of what she's going to say, and realises that she actually doesn't know. She only knows that she wants to see him.

As expected, the Thai supermarket is already closed. But then her eyes land on two figures huddled together outside, right by the door: a man and a woman.

The man's head is bent, a cigarette in his mouth. The woman's hand is on his arm, her face turned away from Dao's and lifted up to his, her lips at his ear as she talks. Her arm then wraps around him in an embrace, and he drops his head to her shoulder, and they stay like that for a few seconds, or minutes, weeks, months, Dao can't tell.

A moment of closeness and familiarity, and then suddenly it's over: the woman pulls back; the man smiles wanly and takes a drag of his cigarette.

Dao recognises them.

The next thing she knows, she's crossing the road towards them. The man spots her first. The realisation must have shown on his face because the girl he's with tenses up and turns.

"P' Dao," says Noon, stepping back to create space between herself and Sunny. "We were just talking—"

But Dao ignores her. Instead she studies Sunny's face. His eyes are bloodshot, and there's a smile on his face, that wan, thin smile she saw earlier after he and Noon had embraced. But his eyes are hard and cold, his demeanour defeated. He is deeply sad, she realises. Incredibly so.

"You always show up unannounced," Sunny tells her. His short laugh is not accusatory, just bitter.

Noon speaks up: "I'll just head home and leave the two of you alone."

Sunny gives Noon a nod. "Thanks, Noon," he says. "I'll call you later."

Dao doesn't want to look at Noon, but in the corner of her eye she watches her walk away. Once Dao is sure Noon is out of earshot, she says to Sunny: "I didn't know the two of you were this close." She's surprised to hear how emotionless her voice sounds.

"We confide in each other from time to time," Sunny says. "Just…similar backgrounds. Similar temperaments. I was feeling down today so we decided to hang out after work."

Dao flinches. "I didn't hear from you after last night. I wanted to talk."

"Well, I didn't."

"Sunny—"

"I'm sorry I was late. I'm sorry I was drunk. I'm sorry for all the things I said."

"Are you only saying what you think I want to hear?"

He hangs his head.

A terrible feeling is making its way up from the pit of her stomach. "Did something happen with Noon?" she asks.

His head jerks to the side, like he's shocked to hear her question. But he doesn't look up, and doesn't reply. She waits. Still he doesn't say anything.

She's reminded of Shane looking at her mutely in front of that club in Ekkamai. "Did something happen between the two of you?" she asks again.

He hangs his head. The next thing she knows, she's grabbing the cigarette out of his mouth. She drops it to the ground and stomps on it.

"Are you going to say anything?" she demands. "You're not even going to deny that something happened?"

"What do you want me to say, Dao? Tell me what you want me to say and I'll say it."

"Sunny, that's not how this works," she says despairingly.

He hangs his head, mute and unflinching.

The next thing she knows, she's turning away from him, not wanting him to see her cry like he did last night.

"Maybe we can talk later," Sunny finally says. "There are things…" He takes a deep breath. "There are things I need to tell you."

Dao shakes her head: "I don't think we should talk again. At least, not anytime soon." She swallows. "I'm calling it. This. Whatever this is, it's over."

"Dao…" he begins. But that's all he says. He hangs his head. She waits. "I don't want you to hate me," he says.

She closes her eyes briefly. "I don't hate you, Sunny," she replies. There's a spot in the wall above his head where the concrete fractures; somehow it's easier to look at it than at him. "I could never hate you. If you only knew how much I don't hate you."

He hangs his head, and then rubs a thumb back and forth across his chin.

Soon, she's walking home. She thinks – no, wishes – for him to follow. But when she turns around, she can still see him standing slumped against the wall of the supermarket. She quickens her pace.

There's a church in front of her, dark and ominous in this night light. A group of teenage girls stagger out of a nearby house, all dressed for a night out, their heels clicking and their voices raised in laughter.

She realises her hood has slipped down and pulls it back up to block her face against the wind.

Sunny

Sunny wakes up in his bed. Judging from the sunlight in his room, it's almost evening. He has slept nearly the entire day away. But it's Sunday, he remembers vaguely, which means he doesn't have to work today; his aunt usually takes on the Sunday shifts. He can go back to sleep and not think about...

He hears someone moving. He looks down from his bed and, to his surprise, finds Noon asleep on the floor, curled up in a blanket and lying on top of several of his coats and jackets. An overwhelming sense of guilt rolls over him.

"What happened?" Sunny croaks.

Noon's eyes fly open. He can see her taking in her surroundings for a second, recalibrating herself. Then she groans. "You called me late last night," she tells him. "You were pretty wasted. You didn't want to be alone."

Pieces of last night return to him in flashes: Dao walking away from him at the supermarket. The sound of Dao's voice, echoing repeatedly. *I could never hate you. I could never hate you.* The bottle of Regency brandy he'd unearthed from one of the boxes in the supermarket's stock room.

Noon sits up, wrapping the blanket around herself so that only her head is poking out. "So much for not wanting to get drunk last night," she says. "How are you feeling?"

He rolls over to the side so that he's looking at her properly. "My head hurts," is all he offers. He looks around at his messy room. "And I need to pack."

"When's your flight?" Noon asks.

"Early morning, the day after tomorrow." He thinks of the last phone call with his sister, and the way Fai's voice broke when talking about their mother's grief. "I should've known something bad was going to happen."

"P' Sunny, don't be silly, how could you have known?"

"I had this dream...a bad feeling..." Then he shakes his head, trying to clear the heaviness there.

"A dream?"

"It doesn't matter."

"Maybe you and P' Dao should talk," Noon suggests tentatively.

He finds his phone, resting on the table beside his bed. There are no messages from Dao. No calls. He hasn't even told her he'll be leaving.

"There's nothing to talk about," he says. "She called it off. It's over."

"Oh, P' Sunny," Noon says. "I'm so sorry."

"It's for the best," Sunny says. "It wouldn't have worked anyway. And I'm a mess. Clearly, it's for the best."

"It's okay to be sad."

"I'm not sad," he says.

He really isn't. Things have ended between him and

other girls many times before, haven't they? Why should this time be any different?

Noon is looking at him differently than she has ever looked at him before. There's softness in her eyes. Pity. Fondness. But also other things he finds he doesn't want to think too deeply about right now. "Thank you," he tells her, "for staying with me last night. I shouldn't have called you."

"You're a big baby," Noon scoffs. "I've got used to it."

They keep looking at each other. Then she reaches out and takes his hand, her fingers twining with his, firm and warm.

Without thinking, he moves closer to her. Then their foreheads are touching, and they stay like that for a few seconds. Another scene from last night comes to mind: they are standing close together in front of the supermarket, with Dao looking at them from across the road.

"You'll be okay," Noon whispers. "Everything will be okay."

That one beautiful dream, from what feels like a lifetime ago, appears in his mind. The woman standing in the distance, looking only at him, and the kiss they shared and the strange calm that came with the light. *What if I got it wrong?* he thinks. *What if it was supposed to be a different girl all along?*

Without thinking, his mouth finds Noon's, and almost instantaneously, she's kissing him back. He notes the differences immediately: the feel of her lips, the way she bites his. It's like a storm, rushing down a mountainside, when he's been used to summer rains and bright Edinburgh days. The thought of Dao makes him pull back. *What am I doing?* he thinks.

He'd had his eyes closed while they were kissing. Now that he's opened them, he sees that Noon is smiling. "What was that for?" she asks.

He doesn't say anything and looks down at the floor. There's a long, uncomfortable silence, and when Noon speaks again, her voice is brittle. "I've thought about what this moment would be like for a long time," she says, her smile turning sour and twisted. "But now that it's happened…I can't help feeling like it doesn't mean much to you."

"It means something to me! Of course it means something," Sunny corrects her at once. "You've been there for me all these months. Even last night, when Dao saw us standing together outside the pub, she thought something happened between us."

"You corrected her, didn't you?"

At Sunny's silence, Noon's eyes widen.

"You let P' Dao believe that something happened between us?" she hisses. "Why didn't you tell her she was wrong?"

A dozen explanations come to mind, but each feels as cowardly as the next. Because it was easier that way? Because Dao wasn't wholly wrong? Because he's deserving of such an accusation?

Noon's expression hardens. "So what happens now?" she asks.

He hangs his head. "I never meant to hurt you," he says.

Noon's voice cracks. "So what happens now?" she repeats.

He can't answer her, can't look at her.

Then he hears Noon sigh, followed by the sound of her getting to her feet. "This is my fault," she says, as though talking to herself. "I knew this would happen, and I still let myself…This is my fault."

"Noon, it's not your fault, please don't say that."

"It *is* my fault, because I should have known better."

"Noon, I want us to be okay," he says. "Are we okay?"

Sunny feels something shift between them. Noon stands in his doorway and looks at him for a moment before she slips out of his room. It's a look that reminds him of that Bang Saen trip with Jun, the beach and ocean basking in the light of a setting sun.

"P' Sunny," Noon says, "you really can't have it both ways."

//

After Noon is gone, Sunny considers going for a walk. But his hangover is still severe, and the longer he stays awake, the more he's plagued by thoughts he'd rather not entertain.

He takes a shower, smokes a cigarette with the window cracked open and takes a trip downstairs to steal an orange from his aunt's fridge. Then he goes right back upstairs to sleep.

No dreams visit him.

He's woken up by the sound of his phone ringing shrilly.

It's now dark. He realises he left the window open from

when he was smoking, so there's a chill in the room that makes him shudder the moment he throws the duvet off of himself. He leaves the phone ringing as he snaps the window shut.

When he finally picks up his phone, he sees his sister's name on the screen. "Fai? What's going on?"

Her voice comes through, angry and frantic. "Why'd you take so long to pick up? What's wrong with you?"

"I'm so sorry," Sunny begins. Again, he is so, so sorry. "Is everything—"

"It's Ma," Fai says, tripping over her words. "She...she fainted and...I'm with her now, we're at the hospital, we're waiting for the doctor. P' Sunny, I don't know...don't know what to do, I'm frightened, I don't know what's happening, I don't know what's happening."

Dao

Dao returns home after her encounter with Sunny and finds herself unable to be alone.

For the first time, her studio flat feels confining; it's too quiet, too still. She tries to watch a film, to put on music. Even go through pictures from her exhibition. Nothing helps.

It's past midnight when she texts the group chat. Ella replies immediately, followed by Cady and then Simone. Fifteen minutes later, Dao is on the sofa in the common room, wrapped in a huge blanket with a cup of tea that Simone has made for her.

Cady sits on the floor, wrapped in a blanket of her own, while Simone and Ella sit either side of Dao. Through tears and long-winded rants, Dao slowly divulges the exchanges she's been having with Sunny during the last few weeks, culminating in the moment with him and Noon outside the supermarket.

Aside from questions here and there, no one admonishes her or even Sunny. Her friends simply sit beside her and let her say everything she needs to.

"I don't understand," Dao says, the tissues Cady has given her clutched in her hand. "I had...the feeling was *so* strong. There was the dream I told you guys about. The reading I did back home. Then the reading I did with Ella. The Knight of Cups."

For the first time that night, Simone's expression tightens with anger. "I did tell you that believing in these dreams and these…readings might not be the best idea." She gives Ella an apologetic look. "Focusing so much of your attention on forcing things and trying to steer them in the direction you want…maybe it hurts more than it helps."

Ella throws Simone a warning look and then takes Dao's hand. "I did tell you," Ella says gently to Dao, "that our futures can change. We talked about patience. Balance. And you…"

"And I simply believed whatever I wanted to believe without actually listening to the true interpretation?"

Ella doesn't contradict her.

Dao feels fresh tears coming on. Her voice shakes. "I was…I am…so *sure*. I had this feeling…it was so strong. He has to come back, he has to."

"Maybe he shouldn't," Simone says stubbornly. "I have no problem with Sunny, I'm not even saying he's a bad guy, but this is not even close to what you deserve."

"And the thing with Noon…I don't know what to think."

"Maybe there's nothing there," Ella says.

"Then why didn't he deny it?"

Ella doesn't have an answer.

It's Cady who takes the empty cup out of Dao's hand and sets it aside. "It's going to be alright," she tells Dao. "You're going to be alright. You have us."

Dao doesn't think she will ever have the words to tell them how grateful she is – for the love and grace, and for this space they have afforded her so that she can be weak and broken. An act more intimate than any she has ever known.

She allows herself to fall, and her friends catch her.

//

A day later, Dao goes by herself with her camera to the Scottish National Gallery of Modern Art.

It's not too far from Dean Village, her favourite stomping ground. Unlike the galleries and museums near Princes Street, the Modern Art gallery is much quieter, with spacious grounds surrounding the main building. The rooms inside aren't packed with tourists, and she can stroll through without being jostled about.

The exhibition that's on display at the moment is about space: photographs and artworks of stars, planets, moons and suns, the empty spaces in the cosmos. The lights have all been dimmed to create the feeling of being flung out among the galaxies. She walks through a room with a giant disco ball in the centre; it spins around slowly in time with twinkling lights reflecting from the ceiling above. A sparkling moon surrounded by spinning stars.

The last room in the exhibition is filled with photographs only. Sunsets and sunrises, vibrant colours blending in with the white and blue of the sky and shifting clouds. Other photos show complete darkness, punctuated by tiny spots of light, or a streak of silver, gold or red.

Dao stands in front of one photograph: a resplendent view of the sea from atop a cliff, with a red sun sinking into the waters; orange, pink and purple swirling together in the foreground. Warm and calm, yet fierce in its beauty.

Somehow, it reminds her of the beautiful dream she had before she boarded the plane to come to this country. She had believed in its significance so fervently and had made choices driven by that belief because she had thought there was something special at work, no matter what name you might want to give it. But is something special because it truly is? Or because we have made it so, simply because we are creatures who will always yearn for meaning?

It is while Dao is standing in front of this photograph, dreaming of how she might try capturing her own sunset at Portobello beach, that Sunny's message comes through.

I'm flying back to Bangkok today, there's been an emergency in the family. I'm sorry, I should have let you know. I am sorry for everything. Please. Can we talk?

Sunny

Sunny and Aunt Oom go straight to the hospital from Bangkok Suvarnabhumi airport.

It's a medium-sized government hospital not far from Sunny's family home, next to the main road. The hospital has a sterile smell he detests, and as usual, there's a crowd everywhere he goes. Patients occupy every chair available. Those who haven't managed to find seats are sitting on the ground, slumped against pillars and walls.

Sunny is exhausted from the flight, his body reacting violently to the change in location. Everything about his home country – the brightness of the sky, the heat, the usual sights and sounds of Bangkok – feels jarring. He also keeps wondering when Dao is going to text him back, whether she will ever do so again. So when he arrives at his mother's ward, he does so in an exceptionally foul mood.

Sunny pushes the door open to find that his mother is sharing a room with three other patients. There's an old air conditioner in the corner, emitting a cranky rhythm. He spots his mother's bed immediately, farthest from the door, next to a window. Fai's sitting in a chair beside the bed, and she jumps up the second she spots him.

"P' Sunny!" A cry that sounds more like a screech. She wraps her arms around him. "I'm so happy you're here!"

He embraces his sister briefly and then his eyes land on his mother, asleep with an IV hooked to her right hand. He leaves his suitcase by the foot of the bed and takes the chair Fai has abandoned. Aunt Oom stands on the other side. The expression on her face as she looks at her younger sister is the softest Sunny has ever seen, but beneath it all, there is sorrow and anger.

His mother seems much older than when Sunny last saw her – more grey hairs on her head, a hollowness in her face, her arms much thinner. When Fai had told him that she'd collapsed while doing chores around the house amidst funeral preparations, he hadn't known what to expect. Now that he's seen her, he realises that she looks worse than he'd even imagined.

"She looks very frail," Sunny says quietly to Fai. She nods. His jaw tightens. "Where's Father?"

"I don't know," Fai replies. "He came the day before yesterday, but only for about five minutes. Then said he had to go back to the shop."

Aunt Oom flinches, her eyes still on her sister. "And the funeral?"

"Ma was handling all the preparations," Fai explains. "Now that she's like this…I don't know…"

"I'll take over everything," says Aunt Oom, the efficiency in her voice not unlike when she is assigning tasks to Sunny in the supermarket. "The two of you will focus on taking care of your mother."

"Have you talked to her doctor yet?" Sunny asks. In public hospitals like this, talking to the doctor in charge of the case can be a difficult feat since most doctors cover more than one hospital and are only available to each of their patients once or twice a week.

"On the first day, yes," Fai replies. "Her blood pressure was extremely high. She's malnourished and dehydrated. The doctor said the likeliest cause for all of this is stress. Plus, she's hardly been sleeping. They've had to give her something to help her rest."

Sunny runs a hand across his brow and feels a strong desire to smoke. "Why isn't Father handling things?" he asks his sister. "I don't understand why he's not here."

"He keeps saying someone has to work."

"You'd think his wife's well-being would be more important than his business."

"Then he wouldn't be Father, would he? And there's something else you should know."

Sunny frowns. "What else is there?"

"I went home for a couple of hours last night to sleep and get a change of clothes," says Fai. "*She* called the house."

"Who?" he asks, even though he already knows the answer.

"Father's...friend, a woman. She's the one he's giving the Bang Na house to."

Aunt Oom hisses. Her fingers tighten around her sister's wrist. "That *cannot* happen. It *will* not happen."

Sunny sees his last dream again: his mother's cries and his father's voice. The rain. Then the silver Citroën, backing into their driveway. "What does she want?" he asks Fai.

"She wants to know how Ma is doing."

"She knows Ma is in the hospital?"

"I reckon Father must have told her."

"I didn't think you knew about her," he says to Fai.

His sister's eyes darken. "P' Sunny, you aren't the only smart one in the family. Did you really think I had no idea?"

Sunny is too tired to process this information, so he instructs his sister to go home and get some rest. "I'll keep Ma company until visiting hours are over," he says.

After Fai has gone, Aunt Oom fixes him with a stare. "Sunny, you're going to take care of this business with your father." It is neither a question nor a request.

He nods to show that he understands.

After his aunt has left to sort out the funeral arrangements, Sunny continues to sit by his mother's bedside, scrolling aimlessly through his phone. Occasionally his mother shifts position slightly, lets out a breath, her eyes fluttering as though she is about to wake up. But each time she quiets down again, and falls back into her deep slumber.

A few hours later, around dinnertime, Sunny goes downstairs to buy frozen food from 7-Eleven. He's just leaving the store after paying for his sticky rice burger and Coke when he spots two figures walking in through the hospital entrance.

Sunny is too shocked by what he's seeing to register his actions. At first, he stops walking completely. He must have put his bag of food down somewhere, or else dropped it, because the next thing he knows, his hands are empty. He's striding ahead. Then his strides quicken into a run. He raises his voice.

Father turns, astonished. The woman next to him gasps and steps back.

Sunny rushes at his father: "You brought her here? When Ma is upstairs lying in a hospital bed?"

Sunny doesn't know if he's flinging out punches or curses, but soon he feels his father's strong grip around his wrists, and then his father's arms wrapping around him, restraining him in a tight boxer's embrace.

Father hisses in his ear. "You're embarrassing yourself, Sunny, people are watching. Control yourself!"

Sunny struggles, but his father is too strong. "Are we civilised humans? Or animals? Control yourself!"

Sunny lets the strength go out of him and Father's grip slackens. He shrugs his father off, but he has never in his life, never until this moment, felt anger like this. "You've been gone all this time," Sunny shouts, "and you're showing up now, with *her*?"

The woman flinches. Sunny looks at her properly for the first time. She looks to be in her early forties. Slim, with large, doe eyes, dyed brown hair and long legs, and with a designer bag clutched in one hand. She's wearing platform heels and a long, flowing white dress. So very different from his mother.

"You're not going into Ma's room with *her*," says Sunny, shaking his head. To his shame, hot, angry tears fill his eyes. "I can't stop you going in to see her because you're her husband, but you're not bringing this woman. As long as I'm here, you're not bringing her into this hospital."

"You're not the head of this family," says his father. "I am."

"And look where that's got us," Sunny retorts. "Sir."

Father's mouth twitches into a horrible grimace. "What can you do for our family that I can't?"

Sunny stands firm and lets that comment stab through him. Fully wash over him. "Well…" he says, "Ma wouldn't even be in the hospital if it weren't for you, so you've done a great job for our family, haven't you, sir? If I were you, I'd leave now. No one wants you here. Your family don't want you here."

His father appraises him for a moment. Sunny can't tell what he's thinking. Then, to his surprise, his father nods. "Okay. Alright. We'll leave for now. I'll come back another time."

Sunny swallows the lump in his throat. The instinct to apologise rises to the surface. "Father—" he begins.

But his father waves his words away. "We'll go."

Sunny stands there and watches until his father and the woman walk out of the hospital, heading in the direction of the parking building. He realises his hands are still shaking.

Sunny makes it back upstairs to find his mother awake.

Her eyes shine at the sight of him. "I can't believe you're here," she says, her voice raspy from disuse. "I didn't want you to come home like this, I didn't want you to worry."

Sunny takes her hand, bows his head so his forehead touches it. "There's no way I wasn't coming home," he tells her. "I'll take care of you, Ma. I promise."

She touches the top of his head and smooths his hair. They don't say anything for a while. But somehow that is enough. It is enough.

An hour later, she drifts back to sleep just as visiting hours come to an end. Sunny gathers up his things, preparing to leave.

His phone buzzes. He takes it out, stops in his tracks and stares dumbstruck at the name on the screen.

It's a message from Dao.

He can feel everything around him falling away, like an empty theatre before the light comes on.

Dao

The four friends are having a picnic in the Meadows. Simone has brought a big checkered blanket, Cady has brought a batch of homemade cookies and Ella has shown up with a can of cider for each of them.

They're not talking about anything serious. But Dao is getting a bit tipsy, the alcohol affecting her just enough that she feels warm and tingly. Cady is showing off her knowledge of all the lyrics to the song 'One Day More' from *Les Misérables*; she switches from one character to another deftly, assigning a different theatrical voice to each, making Ella hoot and cheer as though Cady were running the final stretch of a marathon. Simone throws a crisp at Dao, teasing her for already being mildly inebriated from just one drink.

Dao picks up her camera and snaps the shot. All her friends in the frame, lounging on their blanket. Laughing. Joyful. The sun in their eyes.

Her thoughts turn to Sunny, as they often do. She doesn't think she ever saw him this happy when he was in Edinburgh. She never saw him smile or laugh like this with a group of friends, his face alight without the burden that seemed to always cloud it.

Dao has been ashamed of how she'd reacted the night they last spoke, in front of the supermarket. While her friends had been there for her, she can't believe she'd allowed herself to crumble with such desperation. She'd cried so much that her eyes were swollen the next morning.

After she has finished the song, Cady takes Dao's hand. "How are you feeling today?"

Dao gives her friend a smile. "Better," she says. She leans in to show Cady the photos she's just taken.

But Sunny's last text message, still left unanswered, occupies her thoughts all the same.

//

The next morning, Dao decides to text him back.

She tells him how sorry she is to hear that there's been an emergency in the family, and that she hopes everyone is safe. A short, polite text. Formal. That ought to set the right tone, she thinks.

He calls her back immediately.

She stares at her phone for a few seconds as it rings. Then, just as she thinks he's about to hang up, she presses to accept the call.

"Hello?" Wordlessly, she curses herself for picking up at all.

"Hi," Sunny says. "I didn't think you'd pick up."

"I didn't think I would either," Dao says. A pause. "How are you?"

"I have…no idea." She closes her eyes at the sound of his voice. "I just left my mother in the hospital."

Sunny begins to tell her of his grandmother's upcoming funeral, his mother's condition and everything that has happened with his father, all while Dao lies on her bed, eyes fixed on the ceiling, listening quietly. There's a pocket within her heart that aches with every new revelation.

"Do you know when you're coming back?" Dao asks him.

"I don't know yet," Sunny replies. "I can't come back until my mother is well and this Bang Na house business is sorted with my father."

"What do you want me to do?"

"I lied," he blurts out. "That night outside the supermarket."

"You didn't say anything outside the supermarket that night. Nothing comprehensible, anyway."

"Yes, but I still lied. I let you assume that something happened between Noon and me. But nothing did."

"Sunny, I'm not blind—"

"I kissed her the next morning, after our fight, because I thought it was over between us. I kissed her because I was upset, and because I was lonely and she was there for me. I'm sorry."

She had thought that she couldn't hurt any more than she already did, but pain always finds new ways to wound you. "Sunny, why are you telling me this?"

"I wanted to be honest," says Sunny, his voice small and faraway. "And I wanted to apologise. You mean a lot to me. I care about you, even if I'm not always very good at showing it."

A few more seconds of silence. Then... "What do you want, Sunny?" she asks again.

"Can we...can we just go back to talking, like we used to?"

"We're talking right now."

"No, I meant..." Sunny sighs. Dao hears the frustration in his voice. "I meant...talking like we did before. I need...everything is so overwhelming right now and I'm not sure...with other people...it's not the same. I want it to be you."

It's the last thing she's been expecting to hear. A short laugh escapes her lips. "The Knight of Cups," she whispers.

"The knight of...what?"

"It's nothing," she says numbly. "What would happen if we were to be in each other's lives again? What would be different?"

"I would be less selfish," Sunny replies.

This time, her silence is longer than a pause.

"Dao, please say something."

This is it, she thinks. The moment she's been waiting for. He hasn't said anything grand, nothing that hints at much personal development on his part. But what he offers is of value to her all the same: an opening.

Dao admits quietly: "I've been waiting for you to come back."

Sunny hesitates. "So, is that a yes?"

It'd be so much easier for her to say yes. Yes, let's go back to talking like we did before. Yes, to the illusion of having someone. To the remote possibility of seeing him again, of holding him in her arms.

But something inside stops her. She remembers her friends gathered around her in the common room: Ella's grip on her hand, the stubborn look in Simone's eyes, Cady's gentleness. She isn't strong enough yet, she knows this well enough. But for her friends, through her friends, perhaps she could be.

What was it that Ella said? Our futures can change. She has a choice.

She takes a deep breath, and begins by saying his name.

Sunny

Sunny returns to the hospital alone the next morning, having lain awake the entire night after he and Dao ended their call.

He tells himself there's no point dwelling on things he can't change. Dao has made her choice. He apologised, asked for things to be different, tried his best. Still she said no. There's nothing else he can do.

Now Sunny would rather focus all his energy on making sure his mother gets back on her feet as soon as possible.

Ma looks stronger today, her eyes a little clearer, with a hint of their usual warmth when they look at him. Sunny tells her that Fai has gone to school, but will visit later in the evening.

"I'm very lucky to have such beautiful children," says his mother. "I must have done something good in my past life to deserve you and your sister."

"You're in a dramatic mood today," Sunny teases. "Have they been showing soap operas on the TV since I left?"

She cracks a smile. "I mean it."

"Well, we're lucky to have you too."

He starts cutting the chicken in the green curry the nurse has given her for lunch into smaller bites. His mother looks at the food with trepidation. She hasn't been able to eat much, and Sunny has been doing his best to make hospital food as appetising as he can for her.

"Have you seen your father yet?" his mother asks.

Sunny looks down at the plate of food and spoons the green curry from a separate bowl onto the rice. "Yesterday. Very briefly." He thinks of the scene that occurred and feels no need to elaborate; his mother should be spared the details.

"He came to visit me early this morning, just before you got here."

Sunny can't conceal his surprise. "He did?"

"Yes. And he has a black eye. Do you know where he could've got it from?"

Her inquiry is soft, coaxing; she knows the answer already but wants to hear him say it. Sunny rubs his forehead and grimaces. "Did he tell you that we had...an altercation?"

"Yes, he mentioned it."

"Did he tell you why?"

"Yes, he did."

Sunny stares at her, shocked.

"My darling boy," says his mother, sighing. "For all these years...do you really think I haven't known about that woman?"

The floor falls out from beneath him. The whole world, perhaps. Everything tilting on its axis. He thinks of what Fai had told him: *Did you really think I had no idea?*

His mother must have seen his feelings written clearly on his face. She squeezes his hand, her touch weak, barely a grip. She looks confused. "How long have you known for?"

"Since I was little," Sunny says, his voice breaking. "I thought I was the only one, and I was trying to keep it from you...I've tried to keep it from Fai...I thought that was my duty..."

Ma's expression falls. In the face of her devastation, Sunny tells her of that rainy day when he was a child, and the Citroën he saw from his bedroom window, the visitor his father tried to hide. The little moments of deception he'd noticed from his father over the years.

His mother listens without saying a word. When he has finished, she looks away from him, tears shining in her eyes. "I never wanted you to carry the burden that I was carrying. I see now that might have been another one of my mistakes. I seem to be making a lot of mistakes these days."

Sunny doesn't know what to say to that. He lets out a long breath. "How long have you known?"

"Oh, since he first met her. Back when you and Fai were children."

"Then why..." He stops, trying to choose words that would best soften his anger.

"Why have I never left him?"

"Yes."

"Because I've never been strong." Her voice trembles. "I'm not strong like Fai. Like my big sister. Like you."

"I'm not strong," Sunny whispers. He thinks of the phone conversation he had with Dao last night. When she told him that, no, she didn't think they should talk right now or be friends, he had been anything but strong. *If I were stronger*, he longs to tell his mother, *I would be better at being alone.*

For a brief moment, he nearly tells her what has happened. *The girl you said I dreamed about...I've met her, but I think I've lost her.*

Instead, what he ends up telling her is completely different. "I had a dream," he says, "not too long before I heard about Grandma." She looks up, intrigued, and he continues with his eyes fixed on her face. "In the dream, I was a little boy again, trailing after you around the house like I used to do when I was little. Everything was fine. Peaceful. I could see your smile. You were happy. But then I heard his voice. My father's voice ..."

"Oh, Sunny—"

He cuts her off: "When I was little, I believed in dreams because you did. You've always told me that they can mean something, or that our fates have already been written, and everything happens for a reason. But I found out about Father, and then a few dreams of my own turned out to mean the exact opposite of what I thought they did, so I started to believe that you were wrong. There's no order, no grander narrative, it's just us and our chaos. But with this last dream..." He looks around the hospital room, at the other patients in their beds and the IV hooked to his mother's arm. "...I had a feeling that something bad might happen, especially with you, and it did."

His mother bows her head. She is afraid, he realises. The knowledge both pierces and galvanises him.

"Ma, this cannot happen again," Sunny says. His voice hardens even more. "This *will* not happen again. You cannot let him do this to you anymore. Do you understand me?"

Tears roll silently down his mother's cheeks. She wipes them away. Once. Twice. Purses her lips to stop any more from falling.

Then, after what feels like hours to Sunny, she nods.

He takes her hand. "I'm right here with you, Ma," he tells her. "I'm right here. I will make everything alright."

Dao

The framed portrait arrives for Dao when the exhibition comes to a close, three weeks after it was first put on display.

Dao had forgotten about it in the wake of her decision to end things with Sunny. Now that it sits on her desk, leaning against her wall, she finds herself astounded by her own idea to have this portrait framed as a gift.

While she and Sunny were still seeing each other, it felt like a great idea. Sunny looks exceptionally handsome in the photograph, his eyes alight, his mouth curved into a smile. Behind him are all the autumnal colours of the Water of Leith. What was it that he'd told her? That he had never seen himself like this before?

Dao stands leaning against her kitchen sink and looks into his eyes.

She misses him, she realises. Not for the first time. But the portrait looks wrong in her room.

She stares at it for a few more seconds. Then she makes up her mind.

She takes it down from her desk and wraps it in the bubble wrap it came with. It's still two hours before she and her friends have to leave for their outing to Inverleith Park. She has time to spare.

Even though it was she who took the photo, it's not hers to keep.

//

It will be Cady's first time going to Stockbridge. The four of them have chosen the perfect day for it, just as summer starts to make its presence felt in full force, the temperature reaching twenty degrees. There's hardly a cloud in the sky. For the first time since she came to Scotland, Dao is able to wear shorts and a sleeveless shirt.

The entire city has come outside to enjoy the heat: crowds spill out of restaurants and pubs, and on every patch of green, there are people picnicking or sunbathing. Coming from a country where everyone shuns the sun, Dao would usually find the sight of people intentionally avoiding the shade a little strange. Yet the day is so beautiful, her beloved Edinburgh even more magical in the summer light, that she begins to see the appeal.

In Inverleith Park, the four friends set up their picnic blanket on a hill overlooking a large pond, with the view of the city reflected in the water and the castle rising high above it all. Like Dao had told Sunny long ago: a postcard. She looks around at her three friends, chatting and sipping their drinks, and tries to commit every moment to memory.

A cocker spaniel runs up to them, a tennis ball in its mouth. Ignoring its owner's call, it lies on its back for Cady and Ella to tickle its belly, barking and licking their faces.

Cady sings a short verse of a Wailin' Jennys song in her crystal clear voice.

Simone tells a funny story about the last date she went on – how the guy made her watch a two-minute video of himself trying a new protein shake. "I swear, I've given up on men," Simone says. Ella rolls her eyes: "I'll believe it when I see it." Simone gives a cry and begins to protest loudly.

Ella leans back on her hands, sunglasses perched on top of her head. "I've been reading this new book," she says. Her voice has a relaxing, soothing quality to it that reminds Dao of Teoy. The thought makes her smile.

As the evening winds down, Ella and Simone walk down to the edge of the pond to take pictures.

Once they're out of earshot, Cady asks Dao quietly: "How are you feeling today?"

Ever since Dao told them about her phone conversation with Sunny, her three friends have been going out of their way to support her. From trying to find new activities to keep her occupied to going on long walks so that she can vent, they have made it extremely clear that she isn't alone.

Dao manages a smile. "I actually feel great today."

She tells Cady of the portrait that had arrived earlier in the day, and what she'd done with it. "I think it was the right decision," Dao says, and Cady nods.

"Have you had any more dreams?" Cady asks.

"Yes," Dao admits, a little embarrassed. "I still dream about him sometimes."

"What happens in them? You don't have to tell me if you don't want to."

Dao blushes. "No, it's okay. It's just…they're mostly of him coming back, us getting back together, that sort of thing. Mostly nonsense."

"What do you make of the dreams now?"

Dao is silent for a moment, then shakes her head. "I try not to," she replies. "I thought my dreams meant something, just like I believed in all those card readings. But when it came down to it…" – she remembers Sunny's vague statements on the phone – "…maybe Simone is right. The dreams are just that: dreams. A manifestation of my fears and desires. Nothing more." She pulls a fistful of grass from the ground and begins separating it blade by blade. "Maybe, in reality, there's no such thing as 'meant to be', you know. Maybe that's just something we tell ourselves to help us believe it'll all be worth it."

The two of them look over at where Simone and Ella are taking pictures. Simone does a particularly extravagant pose, popping one leg up and holding her long ponytail high with one hand. Ella's laughter reaches over to where Dao is sitting, and she and Cady laugh along, the sound of their voices adding brightness to the day.

"Well, for what it's worth, your dream was right about one thing," Cady says. "As cheesy as it sounds, you did find love in Edinburgh. You found us."

//

The four friends begin walking back to their halls while the sun is setting, cutting a path up from Stockbridge High Street, stopping occasionally to look through shop windows and take pictures. It's nearly nine at night but people are still out on the street, taking in the summer evening. Dao sees her friends' faces glowing in the golden light.

Eventually, their path reaches Haymarket, and they would have to turn right in order to continue to their destination. But Dao spots the Thai supermarket on the other side of the road.

An idea enters her mind. She signals to Cady, who is walking closest to her. "You guys go ahead," Dao says, "I want to stop and get something." She inclines her head towards the supermarket.

Cady looks uncertain. "Are you sure? Do you want us to wait?"

"There's just something I need to take care of," Dao answers. "I'll tell you guys later."

Dao waits for her friends to walk a few paces away before crossing the road.

The bells above the door ring as she enters the supermarket. She immediately spots the one customer who's browsing the shelves in the back of the store, basket in hand. But the person she's hoping to find is behind the till.

Noon has already spotted Dao when their eyes meet.

Sunny

Grandma's funeral prayers start on Wednesday at a temple in Ekkamai, and they will last for three days. Sunny's mother is allowed to return home the morning of the cremation after all the prayers have been concluded.

Besides a heart check-up three months from now, the doctor has insisted there isn't much else she needs to do, except take her blood pressure pills and stay as relaxed as she can. With Aunt Oom and Fai both busy with the funeral, it falls to Sunny to have this final conversation with the doctor, handle the hospital finances and bring his mother home.

Sunny hasn't seen his father since their altercation, nor is Father at home when Sunny and his mother return. The place behind the till is taken up by Jack, their neighbour's young son who occasionally does the odd shift in the store.

"P' Sunny, a package arrived for you," says Jack. "It looks like it came from abroad. I put it in your father's office."

Sunny feels his mother's eyes on him as he tries to keep his voice neutral. "From abroad? Okay thanks, Jack, I'll go check it out."

Sunny enters his father's office, with his mother following behind, to discover a thin rectangular package the size of a small TV leaning against his father's desk.

The first thing Sunny notices is the name and address of the sender. It's from Dao. He grabs a letter opener from amongst his father's stationery and cuts open the box. A note falls out. He immediately recognises her flowing handwriting.

Despite everything, I want you to have this.

He flips the paper over, but she hasn't written anything else. He rips open the brown paper to reveal a framed portrait of himself from what feels like a lifetime ago: the Water of Leith is roaring in the background, the trees orange, brown and green like a warm fireplace. He barely recognises the smile on his face, the joy in his eyes. He'd forgotten entirely that this portrait existed.

Sunny remembers what he'd told Dao the first time she'd shown it to him: "I've never seen myself this way before."

Ma moves to stand beside him so she can have a good look at the photograph. "That is stunning," she says with awe. "Who took this?"

He is too overcome with emotion to say much. "A friend," he replies.

"You look…"

He nods. "Free," he says.

//

That evening, Sunny drives the two of them, dressed head to toe in black, to the temple in their old Honda Civic.

Aunt Oom directs Ma to sit right at the front before pulling Sunny aside. "Is your father coming?" she asks urgently.

"I have no idea," Sunny replies.

Aunt Oom's eyes flash towards Ma, who is taking her seat. "She still looks frail," Aunt Oom remarks. "On the one hand, I hope your father has the decency to show up today. But then again, I'm afraid if I see him I might lose my temper and say something that causes a scene at my own mother's funeral."

"You don't have to talk to him, Auntie. I'll do it. I'm planning to, anyway. Like you said I should."

His aunt surveys him carefully. "Do you know what you're going to say?"

Sunny thinks of the portrait from Dao, and nods. "Yes. I think I'm ready."

A small pat on his arm. "Good man," his aunt says. "Now go be with your mother."

//

The pagoda isn't large, but the staircase to the top is steep and crooked. Sunny lets his mother lean on his arm as he guides her up. Right behind them come Aunt Oom and Fai, all of them clutching dried flowers in their hands.

Ma's left hand grips Sunny's arm tightly as her right tosses the flowers atop the coffin, and then again as they make their way back down. Still his father has not come.

The four of them stand in silence and watch as the fire is lit and black smoke billows from the top of the pagoda.

Sunny has known his grandmother his entire life, yet he feels as though he doesn't know her at all. Why is that? Is it his fault, or hers?

Dao would know, he thinks. If they were still talking, she would be able to tell him the answer.

His recent dream about his mother's health scare has turned out to be correct, so maybe there's a chance he'd been wrong after all. Perhaps that dream he'd had before he came to Edinburgh, the one that had been so similar to Dao's...could it still be possible? Maybe their story isn't over yet.

No, he tells himself quickly. This has nothing to do with what he has to do next. He should stay focused on the situation right in front of him.

//

Sunny, Fai and Ma return home after the funeral to find Father's truck parked outside and the light in his office turned on. Fai's eyes grow wide and she throws Sunny a warning look. But a strange sense of calm washes over him, and he tells his mother and sister that they can go upstairs. "I'll go talk to him on my own."

"Sunny, I'm not sure if now's the time," Ma says, alarmed.

"Now's the perfect time, Ma. It has to happen sooner or later."

"Ma, it will be fine," says Fai, taking their mother's hand. "You need your rest. P' Sunny has everything under control."

Sunny gives Fai a grateful look as their mother lets herself be led upstairs.

Sunny stands by himself in front of his father's office. He thinks of the portrait Dao sent him, of the person he sees in that photograph, and then knocks on the door.

"Come in," Father says.

Sunny opens the door to find his father sitting at his desk and going through an accounts book with a bottle of beer beside him. As Father turns around to face him, Sunny sees that his right eye has started to bruise. "I don't remember doing that," Sunny says automatically.

Father studies him for a few moments, and Sunny is expecting reprimands, curses, a lecture. But nothing comes. His father swivels around in his chair and turns back to his task. "There's more beer in the fridge," he says. "Grab a bottle and come join me."

They end up each nursing a bottle of Singha. The television hums softly: a game show or a comic skit, irrelevant background noise. Sunny scrolls through his phone with one eye on the game show as his father finishes up the day's accounts.

Eventually, his father puts away the books and turns to face him. The black eye is even more pronounced up close. His father points to it with his index finger. "Now you have my attention," he says.

Sunny hears the strength in his own voice, as though it belongs to someone else: "Good."

Sunny puts down his beer and addresses his father with a resolve he has never felt before. "From now on, things are going to be different around here," he begins. "This is the last time Ma is ever going to end up in the hospital because of you."

His father looks taken aback. "Because of me?"

"You will not cause her any more stress or illness. Under no circumstances." When his father doesn't react, Sunny continues: "Sir, there's no denying what you've done for this family. You've provided for us, put a roof over our heads and food on our table. Given us an education. But from now on, your...indiscretions will not inconvenience us any more than they already have. I don't care what you do outside this house, or who you spend your time with. All I care about is that you show respect to my mother. You will not leave the house for days on end, mention that woman's name in Ma's presence, or bring her into our house. I will not be signing the Bang Na house over to her. If you must give her a place to live in, give her the condo in Sathorn instead. Grandma's house stays in the family."

Father studies Sunny with an unreadable gaze, his head tilted to the side.

"And if my mother decides to leave you," Sunny says, "you will let her go."

Father's humourless smile is chilling. "You think you're a big man now, talking to your father like this?"

Sunny's gaze flicks to his father's black eye, and with a bravery he didn't know he had, he replies, "Oh, yes, sir, I do." His smile is terrible and frightening to match his father's. "*I'm* the one who's been taking care of Ma and Fai, *I'm* the man who hasn't brought dirt into our house, and *I'm* the one who has the respect of our entire family. You're no longer the man of the house."

Sunny takes immense pleasure in seeing surprise then anger flitting across his father's face in quick succession.

Father brings his hands together, fingers interlocking. "And tell me, why would I just agree to this?"

"Because I will be giving you what you want."

"Which is?"

"Me," says Sunny. "Home. I will abandon this Scotland plan, come home for good and learn to take over the store properly. This business you've worked so hard for will stay in the family. Like you've always wanted."

His father stares at him for a long while. Sunny forces himself to maintain eye contact. He thinks of his mother, his sister, his aunt.

Then his father lets out a bark of laughter, the thunder in his expression transforming to smug satisfaction. "Alright. Deal."

Father extends his right hand. Sunny grips it and shakes it briskly. "Deal," he says.

An image of himself and Dao strolling through Dean Village flashes through Sunny's mind, autumn leaves on the ground and tall trees stretching towards a warm blue sky. His throat feels dry.

His father grins. "We'll get started right away," he says.

//

Sunny returns to his room later that night to find the portrait Dao had sent him on his bed, leaning against the wall. He closes the door behind him and stands there for a moment, looking at it. He stares at his face in the picture, as though trying to unpack the mysteries of a stranger.

He hopes he never forgets the memories they made that day. How he'd felt standing in the cool, fresh air, with the river rushing behind him. Dao's smiles behind the camera.

What was it that she said when she'd first printed out the photo for him? *You are a good person, Sunny. A good person, with a good heart.*

His mother had been right, he thinks. Who'd have thought? He did meet someone in Scotland, like his dream had said, and he has been led back home again by another dream.

Perhaps there are some things that can't be explained, things that will remain beyond his comprehension. Now he sees every one of his dreams as pieces of glass, scattered all around him – a long line of breadcrumbs leading him everywhere and nowhere, all at once. A puzzle, perhaps, for him to solve, or a road for him to lay down to make a path out of the woods. A mission at last.

He takes a deep breath. So what happens now?

Dao

Every time Dao had seen Noon previously had been in passing, and her focus had only ever really been on Sunny.

Now that Dao is looking at the younger girl properly, she notices that Noon is extremely pretty. The same kind of effortless attractiveness that was not too dissimilar from the look of the girls who'd made fun of Dao in secondary school. If Dao had been younger, it would have made her extremely insecure.

Even now, Dao still isn't sure that she's confident enough for this conversation. But she's here, isn't she?

After the last customer of the day has left and Noon has finished closing up the shop, Noon grabs a beer out of a cooler and asks if Dao wants one as well; Dao opts for water. The girls sit next to each other on crates at the back of the store, with Dao sipping on her water and Noon hardly touching her beer.

At first there's an awkward silence as Dao tries to find a way to approach the conversation. But then Noon starts speaking, with an unmistakable defensive edge to her voice: "If you're here looking for P' Sunny, he's back home in Thailand. But you must know that already."

"Yes, I do, he told me. I'm actually here to speak to you."

Noon cracks a sarcastic smile. "Are you here to find out if anything happened between me and P' Sunny?"

Dao feels the blush creeping up her cheeks. "Is it terribly embarrassing if I said yes?"

"No. I would've done the same. Or probably more," Noon admits. "I can be a little crazy when it comes to things like this."

"So…did anything happen?"

Noon frowns. "What did *he* tell you?"

As Dao recounts what Sunny had told her, Noon's expression remains unreadable. Once Dao has finished, Noon drops her gaze and takes a sip of beer.

"Yes, everything he said is true," Noon says quietly, sadly, and takes another sip. Dao waits; she feels as though she is intruding upon something private. "I told him it was my fault, I should've known better," says Noon. "I think, for him, it's always been about you."

Dao doesn't know what to say or feel about Noon's last comment. She thinks of Shane and her heart aches for Noon. Is this how it is? We want someone who doesn't want us back while they, in turn, want someone else who also doesn't want them? Round and round it goes?

"I've told him we shouldn't talk anymore," Dao tells Noon quietly.

Noon laughs. "So what else did he do to mess it up?"

Dao can't help but smile a little, and then, without really meaning to, the entire story spills out – her dreams and the card readings, the confusion and fear, from the day she and Sunny first met until their last conversation on the phone.

After Dao is done speaking, there's a long silence before Noon says: "You're lucky, you know, P' Dao. Things could be so much worse with P' Sunny. I've been with guys who've…" Her voice wavers. "Well, it doesn't matter what they did; it's all in the past. But I try not to resent you for it."

Dao stares at her with disbelief. "Resent me for what?"

"For only experiencing this level of pain, rather than something worse."

Dao breathes in sharply. No one had ever chosen to be with Dao before, so Dao had always thought that someone like Noon – the kind of girl who would never lack for attention or options – had got the better end of the deal.

The pang of envy is similar to Dao's feelings about her own mother, who had never been in love before she met Dao's father. During the height of Dao's heartbreak with Shane, she'd looked at her mother and wondered what it was like for a woman to have the everyday pains and exhaustions of life always sweetened by love. To have never known the longing that comes with loneliness, nor the cost of guarding so much of yourself in order to avoid being broken apart.

"I understand where you're coming from," Dao concedes. She thinks of reaching out for Noon's hand as a gesture of comfort, but she holds back; it feels like overkill. Then she hears herself say: "I can't apologise for who I am or for what I've experienced."

"I know," says Noon, her voice strained. "I really shouldn't be asking you to. But that's why we're here, isn't it?" A crack of laughter. "So that we can tell each other our truths?"

They keep talking well into the night.

It's strange, both of them agree, how complicated everything is when it comes to matters of the heart – whom we love; whether love is in fact a choice or simply your heart pouring out to someone. The intricacies of the hows and the whys and the leagues of ocean we have to cross just to be held in a way that means we are seen; that means we are a little less alone. How sweet it'd be just to have someone to fold your heart into at the end of every ordinary day.

It's such a confounding paradox: how lonely we all are, yet how fearful everyone is of actually being close.

//

A week later, Dao, Simone, Cady and Ella climb Arthur's Seat together for the first time.

The day was forecast to be grey and cloudy. But by the time their bus arrives on the Royal Mile, the sky has brightened and the sun has come out. After just five minutes of walking down the hill to Holyrood Park, they've all taken off their jackets and tied them around their waists. There's an ice cream truck near Holyrood Palace, and they stop there to buy ice cream cones, which they enjoy together as they start their hike.

They take time climbing the hill, chatting all the way and stopping occasionally for short water breaks. During steep climbs, laughter rings out as Cady and Ella – the least athletic members of their group – have to crouch down on the ground and clamber up on their hands and knees. The four of them turn each other's complaints and moans into jokes, jokes into encouragements, and then to exuberant chants until, eventually, they make it to the mountaintop.

Below them, Edinburgh spreads out in every direction. Every landmark Dao has visited – from the castle to the columns of Calton Hill, to the ocean at Newhaven and Portobello beach in the distance – glows in the light of the summer sun. She marvels at how all the places look so close together from this height, as if everything she loves is within touching distance.

After resting for a while at the viewpoint, they make their way back down, choosing a new path that winds through a different side of the mountain. They pass a small patch of daisies and an area with grass growing nearly as high as their knees. Then the path turns stony, sloping down towards a quiet lake nestled between two hills. No one else is around, and they can hear only their own footsteps and the serene sounds of nature.

They squeeze onto a solitary bench by the edge of the lake. Two swans and a family of ducks swim by; the water ripples with their movements and sunlight sparkles off the surface, reflecting the bright blue of the sky.

Still, Dao's thoughts stray to Sunny. She wonders how he is, what he's doing. Is he thinking of her too? She never did have the chance to bring him here.

She links her arm through Cady's, who has already slipped hers around Simone. An uncharacteristic silence descends over the four of them as they sit like that for a moment, taking in the sun, the lake, the tranquil peace. Dao thinks: *I never want to leave.*

Cady breaks the silence by quietly asking that one familiar question: "How are you feeling today, Dao?"

Dao feels a smile touching her lips, gentle like the summer breeze. "Today is a beautiful day," she says.

Everything is well, Dao tells herself. Or at least, everything will be. Whatever comes next, there is now a clearing in the midst of all this forest. Somewhere she can go where the rain cannot touch.

EPILOGUE

One Year Later
Bangkok, Thailand

The gallery – small, cosy, vintage in its decorations – is situated in the Charoen Krung district of Bangkok, an old side of town known for its traditional architecture and proximity to the Chao Phraya river. The exhibition space takes up the entire first floor of a three-storey wooden building, and big, colourful posters adorn the glass doors, announcing works by Thailand's newest up-and-coming photographer.

The exhibition opens in the evening, nearing sunset. There isn't really a ceremony, as such, just a low-key announcement that the photographer herself would be present. Visitors are dressed casually; some show up with congratulatory cards and small bouquets of flowers, and they stroll around the room, admiring the portraits hung on the walls.

It's only a small affair, without much of the gimmickry that would cause it to go viral on social media. But Dao is incredibly proud of it all the same. The photographs on display show the best of her people – the young people of Bangkok, beautiful and ferocious and alive – through her eyes: mingling with friends in Siam Square; taking selfies in cafes; eating in restaurants and at street food stalls; drinking and dancing to a live band in a bar on a night out; waiting in a queue for the Skytrain or motor- cycle taxis. Their faces buried in their phones or in each other's embraces. Breaking into smiles. Cries. Laughter. Colours. Life.

Teoy is the first guest to show up, followed by Dao's other Thai uni friends. Then her parents: her mother wears a green dress for the event, her father sports a neat, collared shirt and a woolly cardigan.

It's the first time Dao's parents have ever seen her in her element like this, and while it's unusual at first, it becomes obvious that they are proud and excited for her. They ask her to take multiple photos of them standing in front of her portraits, and then even more of the three of them together.

The night makes Dao glow inside, a warm glow that chases away all the stress and exhaustion of the past year.

Halfway through the night, she sells her very first portrait: a photograph of young Thai university students protesting at the recent demonstration for democracy, red, white and blue markings for the Thai flag painted on their cheeks.

Sunny shows up towards the end of the night, after Dao's parents and most of her friends have left and there are only a few stragglers left. She spots him the moment he opens the door, a bouquet of sunflowers in his hand.

He smiles.

She stops.

"Hi," he says.

"Hi," she replies, breathless.

Ever since he'd messaged her out of the blue last week mentioning that he'd found out about her exhibition online, she's been wondering what this moment would be like.

Would it be okay if I came? he'd asked. *Totally understand if you don't want me there.*

She had hesitated. But only for a few seconds. Enough time had passed, she'd reasoned. *Yes, sure, it'd be good to see you,* she had replied. Calm. Friendly. *Besides, you owe me a sober exhibition visit.*

He'd laughed and said she was right.

Dao had wondered whether he would keep messaging her after the conversation ended, but he hadn't. And now, here he is, a fantastical creature from what feels like a lifetime ago.

She steps towards him, taking him in.

The past year has matured his face. He has become leaner, has a shorter, neater haircut. Yet just at the slightest glimpse of his movements, she feels like no time has passed at all.

Sunny hands her the flowers; he has remembered that sunflowers are her favourite. "Congratulations," he says, smiling shyly. "This is amazing, Dao. Really amazing. You should be so proud."

She wishes she knew what to do with her hands, her arms; everything feels incredibly awkward. "Oh, well," she says, "I doubt it'll make many waves, but it's a start."

"It definitely is a start." He looks around, eyes shining excitedly.

"Do you want me to show you around?" she asks.

"That's why I'm here," he says.

For the next half an hour, she takes him from portrait to portrait, telling him story after story about the people in the photographs. She's forgotten how easy it is to talk to him.

He asks about her father, her mother. How life is, now that she's living in Bangkok after graduating from Scotland.

"Would you ever move back to the UK?" he asks.

"I still want to," she replies. "There are plans to do that next year. I'm applying for jobs there that will give me a work visa and I have a few interviews lined up. My friend Ella and her parents are opening a gallery in Edinburgh too, so we've had conversations."

"I've always imagined you living there." There is a nostalgic, wistful note to his voice that makes her feel…oh, all sorts of things. "You always seemed very happy there. Like you belonged."

"I suppose I did feel like that," she admits. "You, on the other hand, hated it there."

"Alright, I admit that I much prefer being home. But I wouldn't say I *hated* it there."

"All you did was complain," she teases.

"Hey! I thought this was a safe space!"

They laugh together. He remembers her smile and the sound of her voice, but he has forgotten how it feels to be the recipient of them – to be lit up by her vibrancy and laugh along with her.

She wants to know how his family are doing. He tells her about Fai, who is starting university soon. His mother is healthy, and now even has the time to join an aerobics class; she's planning to visit her sister in Scotland very soon. "And around ten months ago," Sunny says, his voice becoming more serious, "Ma made the decision that she and my father would be living separate lives. For good."

Surprise stops Dao in her tracks. "Sunny, I'm so sorry." She feels like reaching out for his hand, but stops herself from doing so just in time. "Things like this can be so difficult," she tells him. "I wish there was something I could say."

"You don't have to say anything." He shrugs. "It's actually for the best. Fai and I have been urging her to do this ever since she was hospitalised. It needed to happen."

"And your father?"

"He moved out to live in our condo in Sathorn. We see him when he comes in to work in the shop, and sometimes for special occasions. He's doing okay."

Sunny refrains from mentioning that his father is clearly not living on his own. That even though his mother is now much happier, there are still times when a sad, faraway look appears in her eyes. That she still goes to fortune tellers to ask for readings about his father, and tells her friends details about her latest dream on the phone when she thinks her children can't hear.

Dao asks: "And what about you?"

The tour comes to an end. They are standing next to the last portrait, which is of a group of young girls running barefoot, laughing, through the fountain in front of the Siam Paragon Mall.

"I'm working at the shop full-time now," Sunny tells Dao, hands in his pockets. "My father is planning to retire within the next two years. When he does, I'll be taking over and running the business on my own."

"Oh." Dao sounds even more surprised by this news than she had when he mentioned his parents' separation. She studies his expression. "And you're okay with that? You're happy?"

He gives a half-smile. "You're right, it's not what I had imagined for myself, but…" – he shrugs – "…it's not too bad. It helps me take care of Ma and Fai, and keeps my father off our backs. It's good money, and I've even started to enjoy the management side of it. It keeps the business in the family. Maybe one day I'll get the chance to do something different, but right now…it's not been bad at all."

Dao returns his smile. "Who'd have thought? A year ago, you'd have fought tooth and nail against this."

"Right?" He laughs. "It's funny. Sometimes what you think you want is not what you actually need at all."

"Well, I'm happy for you," she says, and she finds, to her surprise, that she means it.

"Thank you, Dao, I'm happy for you too." Sunny's expression turns sombre. He doesn't take his eyes off hers as he says: "I also want to say thank you for that portrait you sent me. It really encouraged me to keep going when times were tough. I would've messaged you then, but we'd agreed not to be in contact so I wasn't sure if I should."

It becomes difficult for Dao to hold his gaze then. She has always remembered what he looks like, but she'd forgotten how it feels to be in his presence – the cadence of his voice, his energy, every rise and fall of his expressions.

"I know you've always liked that photograph," she says, stumbling over her words. "And I liked it too, so I thought…well, I thought it should be with you. It feels right that it is."

"And I want to apologise."

"Oh, Sunny, what for?"

"For everything." He shuffles his feet, and decides to press on, despite his apparent awkwardness. "The last time we talked I don't think I articulated things very well. I had a lot going on with my parents and I was…lonely, and scared, and I just…I didn't want to lose you. I'm sorry for what happened with Noon. For being distant. I really don't know what I was doing. This past year I've thought of you so many times, and I want to thank you for everything you did for me. It meant a lot to me."

She's afraid that her eyes might well up, so she turns away, fixing her gaze on the portrait of the girls in the fountain instead. "I'm sorry too."

"For what? You have nothing to apologise for."

Dao smiles sadly. "Oh, trust me, Sunny, I do." The first thing that comes to mind is the card reading she did with Ella about their relationship, after she'd promised him she was going to put all her superstitions behind her. But there were so many other things she was sorry for, too.

"I spent so many years of my life believing my dreams meant something," Dao says, "that the course my life would take had already been written. But what happened with us…maybe those dreams were all just in my head, you know? My own fears. Simone says it's my own need to establish some semblance of control. But whatever they were, it wasn't fair on you. I shouldn't have tried to force you to become someone I wanted you to be. That wasn't right, and it wasn't loving."

For a second, it's hard for Sunny to speak. He mutters: "I really appreciate you saying that."

Dao notices an openness in Sunny's expression that she's never seen before: a wall, willingly taken down. "Do you still dream?" he asks curiously.

"Not as often anymore," Dao whispers. "At least, not the same kind of dreams."

"Well, I used to dream, too," Sunny confesses, and her eyes grow wide with shock. "Dreams like yours, like my mother's. But I was too afraid to tell you about them because I thought if I did, I'd be giving the dreams more control over our story than they already had. But now...I don't feel so afraid anymore."

Dao's mind is whirling with a hundred questions, but all she asks is: "Why not?"

"Because I've learned that no matter what happens, I'm the one with the power to choose." He smiles. "But I'd still like to tell you about my dreams now, and listen properly when you tell me about yours. If you'll let me."

Dao sees Edinburgh in her mind's eye: the colours of the leaves in autumn; the clear beauty of the rivers and streams; the castle high on top of that hill. The cool air, whispering through her hair. She'll be back there soon. Even the thought of it makes her happier than she can possibly put into words.

And here he will be: home. An ocean away, like he has always been.

For the first time since knowing him, the knowledge no longer devastates her.

She extends her hand to him. "Friends?"

His touch is firm and familiar, and there is warmth from the depths of his eyes. "Friends."

Light breaks in through the curtains as sleep slowly loses its grip.

A new day begins to stir outside. Faraway sounds of footsteps, traffic, construction and conversations flutter in through the walls in tiny rumblings and murmurs.

Soft yet certain, the dream has left an imprint on her chest, like a lover's hand coaxing you out of slumber.

A familiar emotion seizes hold of her, and her eyes fly open.

She wakes to the thrilling dread of morning.

Acknowledgements

This novel has been much harder to write than my first, and so much of it was written during some of the darkest times in my life. I have immense gratitude for:

My parents and my brother Paul – I would be nowhere without your unfailing love and support.

My literary agent Liza DeBlock – your steady encouragement that "It will be fine!" kept me going through the worst of the Second Book Syndrome. Special thanks to **Kiya Evans and Catriona Fida** for reading earlier drafts and providing feedback. To my film agent **Tara Timinsky** for always expressing an interest in seeing this book come to life.

My editors Juliet Mabey, Polly Hatfield and the team at Oneworld – I could not have got over the line without your valuable insight, kindness and dedication to publishing authentic stories. Thank you again for giving a writer from Thailand a shot.

Edinburgh and Bangkok – for the magic, the foundation, the heart. Special thanks to my readers and supporters in Thailand who have shown up for me and my writing.

My closest writer friends, especially Elvin – I value

your constant support as we navigate this crazy industry together more than I can say.

My Edinburgh '19–'20 girls Melis, Annie and Sienna – your sisterhood changed my life and our time in Scotland will be something I carry with me forever. I hope the friendships in this book reflect our bonds and how much they mean to me.

My inner circle in Bangkok – you know who you are. My bloodline. So much of the love in this book is for, and because of, you.

My Sunnys, Shanes and Jamies – I hope you can forgive me for the fact that "part of you pours out of me in these lines from time to time". Wherever you are, despite it all, I hope you know that my heart will always hold a tender place for you.

The one I journal to – for my purpose and my lifelines; every needed reminder of who I am.

© Pongsatien Ngaoprasert

Pim Wangtechawat is a Thai-Chinese writer from Bangkok with a Masters in Creative Writing from Edinburgh Napier University. Her short stories, poems and articles have been published in various magazines and journals such as the *Mekong Review*, the *Nikkei Asian Review* and *Yes Poetry*. Her first novel, *The Moon Represents My Heart*, was published by Magpie in 2023.